RANDOM
HOUSE

LARGE
PRINT

Gingerbread

Gingerbread

HELEN OYEYEMI

R A N D O M   H O U S E
LARGE PRINT

Published in the United States of America by Random House Large Print in association with Riverhead Books, an imprint of Penguin Random House LLC, New York.

Cover design by Helen Yentus
Cover art: (bird) Carrion crow, English School, 20th century / Private Collection / © Look and Learn / Bridgeman Images; (orange) Unattributed illustration / Mary Evans Picture Library

The Library of Congress has established a Cataloging-in-Publication record for this title.

ISBN: 978-1-9848-8289-9

www.penguinrandomhouse.com/large-print-format-books

FIRST LARGE PRINT EDITION

Printed in the United States of America

10 9 8 7 6 5 4 3 2 1

This Large Print edition published in accord with the standards of the N.A.V.H.

FOR ELLA

Þe forme to þe fynisment foldez ful selden
(The beginning and the end accord hardly ever)

Sir Gawain and the Green Knight,
Passus II, Line 9

1

HARRIET LEE'S GINGERBREAD IS NOT COMFORT
food. There's no nostalgia baked into it, no hear-
kening back to innocent indulgences and jolly
times at nursery. It is not humble, nor is it dusty
in the crumb.

If Harriet is courting you or is worried that
you hate her, she'll hand you a battered biscuit
tin full of gingerbread, and then she'll back away,
nodding and smiling and asking that you return
the tin whenever convenient. She doesn't say she

hopes you'll enjoy it; you will enjoy it. You may think you don't like gingerbread. Well . . . just try this. If you live low-carb, she can make it with almond or coconut flour, and if you can't have gluten, she'll use buckwheat or millet flour, no problem.

A gingerbread addict once told Harriet that eating her gingerbread is like eating revenge. "It's like noshing on the actual and anatomical heart of somebody who scarred your beloved and thought they'd got away with it," the gingerbread addict said. "**That** heart, ground to ash and shot through with darts of heat, salt, spice, and sulfurous syrup, as if honey was measured out, set ablaze, and trickled through the dough along with the liquefied spoon. You are phenomenal. You've ruined my life forever. Thank you."

"Thank **you**," said Harriet.

She makes two kinds—the kind your teeth snap into shards and the kind your teeth sink into. Both are dark and heavy and look like they'll give you a stomachache. So what? Food turns into a mess as soon as you chew it anyway. She sometimes tells people that she learned how to make the gingerbread by watching her mother and that the recipe is a family recipe. This is true, but it's also edited for wholesomeness. Harriet's mother,

Margot, is no fan of gingerbread. She stood alone over her mixing bowl and stirred with the clenched fist of a pugilist.

Bambi-eyed Harriet Araminta Lee seems so different from the gingerbread she makes. If she has an aura, it's pastel-colored. She's thirty-four years old, is always slightly overdressed, and wears hosiery gloves when pulling on her tights so as not to snag them. She has a slight Druhástranian accent that she downplays so as not to get exoticized, and she doesn't like her smile. To be precise, she doesn't like the way her smile photographs as forced. So smiling's out. But she doesn't think she can sustain a sober look without seeming unfriendly, so she frequently switches between two expressions—one she thinks of as Alert and the other she thinks of as Accommodating, though she's the only one who can tell the difference. Since her name is far from uncommon, she's encountered other Harriet Lees, Harriet Leighs, and Harriet Lis. Taken in aggregate, Harriet Leigh/Li/Lee is a hard nut, a pushover, thin-skinned and refreshingly forthright, a hedonist and a disciplinarian. She's met Harriet Lee who is a post office clerk by day and a stand-up comedian at night, and she's met Harriet Li the practicing psychoanalyst. She's met Harriet Lee the Essex princess, Harriet Leigh the naval officer, and Harriet Li the sales assistant so rude that you make a note of her name so as to be able to tell the manager about her. The only thing our Harriet really feels she brings to the Harriet Li/Leigh/Lee brand is a categorical sincerity. Her gingerbread keeps and keeps. It outlasts all daintier gifts. Flowers wilt and shed mottled petals, mold blooms greenish-white on chocolate truffles, and Harriet's gingerbread hunkers down in its tin, no more attractive than the day it arrived, but no more repellent either.

The gingerbread recipe came down through Harriet's father's side of the family. It was devised by a person who became Harriet Lee's great-great-great-grandmother by saving Harriet's great-great-great-grandfather's life. In their time there was a clemency clause for those about to be publicly executed. Before he made you climb up onto the beam, the hangman took one shot at matchmaking on your behalf. **Will any take this dross to wed?** or whatever it was they said in those days. Marriage was purgatorial, purifying. All it took was for one member of the crowd to come forward and say that they would handle your rehabilitation. This was rare, but it did happen. And then the two of you were married at once so neither party could think better of it later.

Many viewed public executions in moral terms, or in quasi-cosmic terms, as a gesture toward some sort of equilibrium. Others approached them as spectacle, but due to the clemency clause, public executions occupied a space in Harriet's great-great-great-grandmother's life not dissimilar to the blind dating and speed dating of today. Plenty of opportunity for a realist who has some idea of what she's looking for. At the past five executions Great-Great-Great-Grandma's gut had told her no. But this time, situated as close to the scaffold as she could get, she found herself standing next to somebody sobbing into a deluxe handkerchief, and she thought it was interesting that the woman kept dabbing her face even though not a tear fell. Great-Great-Great-Grandma also found it interesting that the woman kept making hand signals to the man about to be executed, signals the man returned with authentic tears. The ragged reprobate and the lady in silk. And as his list of offenses was read out, it seemed to her that, while brutality had been a near-unavoidable by-product, the motivation was money. Great-Great-Great-Grandma eyed the lady in silk, who was listening with downcast eyes and her handkerchief held up to conceal what must surely be a smile. Great-Great-Great-Grandma took another look at the ragged reprobate and bade him a silent farewell. She thought it something of a mercy for the gullible to die young, as being too often mistaken breaks the spirit.

But then, asked for his last words, Great-Great-Great-Grandfather said he'd do it all again. His voice was so shaky he had to repeat himself a few times before anybody understood what he was saying. Could this man be any more terrible at lying? Great-Great-Great-Grandma put in her bid for him.

Family lore has it that they entertained each other very well, the pragmatist and the man who was almost too gullible to live. One had more patience, and the other had more resolve, and they were about even when it came to daring, so their love established possibilities and impossibilities without keeping score. They settled on caretaking a farm, raised grain crops for the farm's owner, and lived very much at the mercy of a climate that would exhibit dazzling beneficence for three or four years in a row and then suddenly take back all its gifts, parching and flooding and freezing the land or reaching through the soil with a gray hand that strangled growth at the root. The abundance of a good harvest overwhelmed the family with glee and trepidation—it put a bone-cracking temporal pressure on them, like raking in gold that rots. As for the lean years . . . Harriet's great-great-greats shunned both prayer and provocation. They had talked it over, and nature struck them as an entity that was either cruel or mad. Not caring to attempt communication with it, they merely sought not to offend it. They kept having more children, so there were always about fifteen, including the ones on their way in or on their way out. The gingerbread recipe is one of the lean-year recipes, and it stands out because the lean-year recipes are all about minimizing waste and making that which is indigestible just about edible. None of it tastes good save the gingerbread, which is exactly as delicious as it has to be. Blighted rye was the family's food of last resort, and the jeopardy in using it was so great that it made Great-Great-Great-Grandma really think about how to take the edge off. Out came the precious ingredients, the warmth of cinnamon, nutmeg, cloves, and ginger, the best saved for last. After this gingerbread you might sweat, swell, and suffer, shed limbs. Often that didn't happen—often the strenuous sifting of the grain expelled just enough ergot to make this an ordinary meal as opposed to a last meal.

But just in case, just in case, gingerbread made the difference between choking down risk and swallowing it gladly.

That temporary subtraction of fear still gives Harriet's mother goose bumps. It is a veiling of alternatives, a way of making sure you don't reject the choice Mother's made for you. No matter what, you will not starve. She has a hunch that over the years, usage of this recipe has always fallen on the shadow side of things. In her own time, Margot Lee replaced the roulette rye flour with flour from wheat blighted by weather and worm. Nothing that would make anybody sick, just inferior grain that couldn't be sold in the usual way. And Margot never did sell the gingerbread, though it brought her useful things through barter. Information, goodwill, and yes, on at least one occasion, compliance. Gingerbread was all she had to offer in exchange for these things, and all she had to spare.

When Harriet looks through the recipe, she sees the pragmatist and the ideologue joining hands and smiling tiredly at each other. Her version is baked with all organic ingredients, in a West London kitchen awhir with modern appliances. Everything has changed except the gingerbread, which is both trick and treat. This wouldn't worry

Emerson, with his "All things have two handles." Though he does add: "Beware of the wrong one." Harriet can never quite tell which handle she offers her own gingerbread by. She's had even less clarity since her daughter, Perdita, who was born at the end of a week in November when the trees called heads or tails and let their leaves spin like red pennies as they fell. Perdita loves gingerbread and used to plead so sadly and sweetly for more. This after having already polished off a whole tin and in spite of her grandmother telling her, "That's enough for you, Fatty Pigsticks." The nickname wasn't very funny in the first place, and over a period of months it fell out of use as Perdita grew gaunt and feeble.

When Margot observed that the gingerbread was "doing something" to Perdita, Harriet said it couldn't be the gingerbread; it could be any of a number of foods Perdita ate. Some weeks later, when it was no longer possible to deny that gingerbread was all Perdita ate, Harriet said there must be a tapeworm involved and tried various concoctions and home remedies. Margot elected not to sit through a performance of Death by Gingerbread; the soul-cravings of a six-year-old didn't move her in the slightest. She sought medical opinion, obtained a diagnosis, and made it clear that if Harriet ever fed Perdita gluten again, she'd do her for child abuse. Now Perdita only eats gingerbread in her dreams, as the rye version is the only one for her. She'll probably always be a little bit underweight, and her hair remains gray. It turned that color when she was sick, so now it matches Harriet's and Margot's. Pearl-pale hair and bark-brown skin. From a distance Margot, Harriet, and Perdita Lee look like three grannies. Then you get closer and see their unlined faces.

Looking back, Harriet is still aghast that

**Perdita kept asking for gingerbread.
She, Harriet, kept making more.**

Perdita went from asking for more to demanding more, even as her bowels stretched and scrunched up, even as iron was leached from her blood.

Harriet kept making more.

Margot has already filed away this episode under a combination of fairly prosaic categories: masochism, celiac disease, and a maniacally obliging mother. But Margot only thinks that that's how things work with Perdita because Perdita is usually quite ordinary around her. Margot wasn't there the time Perdita's dolls started complaining about a story she was reading aloud to them. The dolls asked Perdita how she'd like it if somebody read them the same story seven nights in a row. They asked Perdita if she was trying to drive them crazy. They shouted through their nostrils, like Susie Greene in **Curb Your Enthusiasm**. Harriet looked up from the essays she'd been marking, let out a startled laugh, and looked over at Perdita, who grinned the jack-o'-lantern grin her mother loves so well. Co-conspiracy began.

That was ten years ago. Perdita is now almost seventeen, and careful with her words, she speaks them as if setting each sentence in print. She may begin to express delight, or to denounce somebody or other, before stopping mid-sentence, looking around in a slightly dazed way, and finishing with: "Huh . . . it doesn't matter anymore . . ." Harriet has never met anyone quite as preoccupied with ephemerality as her daughter is. She wouldn't change Perdita, but there is peril in these diversions. Harriet watches Perdita in the crush at the school gates and intuits that Perdita is neither liked nor disliked by her classmates; she is merely disregarded. Harriet has heard Perdita ask a question and seen the answer directed at somebody else without a skipped beat, as if the question came from the other girl. Perdita doesn't seem to mind this or to sense that she is in danger of losing her right to corporeality. On the contrary, she purposefully deflects attention. When someone accidentally speaks to her, she just shakes her head. If they still won't take the hint, she'll add, "No, I'm not here," in a gentle way rather than a snippy one.

A couple of years ago, Perdita auditioned for her school talent show. She spent weeks arranging the notes of G-Dragon's "Black" for optimal flute-playing. Harriet looked up an English translation of the lyrics. The first words were "The color of my heart is black . . ."

Undaunted by her failure to qualify for the preliminary round of the talent show, Perdita performed the piece for Harriet and Margot one midsummer night, a velvet-clad Titania swaying between lit candelabras. She needed a little percussion, which her mother provided by rapping her knuckles against the tabletop, but otherwise Perdita's was a minimalist rendition of the original, as much silence as it was song. The notes had this aural flash to them . . . it was like glimpsing a swan through reeds. It made no impact when placed alongside the rambunctious charms of her classmates' capoeira routines, comedic rap battles, and inexplicably moving impersonations of Ariana

Grande impersonating Céline Dion. But when Perdita played her cover song for Margot and Harriet, they called for an encore. Which was, of course, completely out of the question.

Perdita considers Harriet's effort to take part in her surroundings excessive. Whenever they pass people happily taking selfies in front of some landmark and Harriet steps in to take an additional picture, Perdita says, "We talked about this." Harriet stops people she sees struggling with surplus shopping, and she tapes the handles of their carrier bags together with washi tape so they won't lose anything. Perdita calls upon her mother to repent, and Harriet repenteth not. She points out that tryhards rarely get enough traction to make a significant nuisance of themselves. For instance: Perdita's school has a PPA, a Parental Power Association instead of a Parent Teacher Association, and, determined to take her own place in this pantheon, Harriet filled nine tins with gingerbread, wrapped rainbow-colored ribbon around each tin, and attached notecards with the names of each PPA member. Every single one of the PPA members left the tins on, under, or behind their chairs without even opening them, leaving Harriet to wonder whether she had caused offense by misspelling names or misidentifying people—she could have been more diligent. She'd been a bit tired when she wrote the notecards, her head full of the GCSE coursework she'd sat up all night correcting. Even so, effort was not the issue. When she told her mother about it, Margot said: "This is sounding exactly like the time you kept saying, 'It can't be the gingerbread,' when it **was** the gingerbread. It really, really was."

Gioia Fischer, head of the PPA, wears no scent and no makeup apart from a touch of berry-red lipstick; her chestnut-colored hair bounces from scalp to shoulder, and she exudes well-being with an aggression that's difficult to deflect; before you know it, her health is arm-wrestling yours. Her living room is a sort of delirium of blue and white, like fighting your way through clouds on a mountain peak. Harriet arrived half an hour early for the meeting, and all the other PPA members were already there in their heartbreakingly casual clothing; catwalk casual, really. They traded gossip and witticisms and current affairs commentary, and Harriet stared and listened. They talked about Felix Nguyen's parenting blog, which seemed to be all about raising twin boys in adherence to a family tradition of "supreme banter" (**SO FUNNY, FELIX . . . almost wet myself. And if I had, I'd have sent you the dry-**

cleaning bill, mate). Harriet looked up the blog on her phone—access password-protected, yes, of course it was. And as these beautiful people talked, they politely discarded the tins of gingerbread that had been forced on them out of the blue. Gioia ran through a list of items and repairs the PPA intended to make contributions toward. Harriet can't remember if she made any fundraising suggestions or not. She does remember picking up her gingerbread and making another attempt to force it on one of the more approachable PPA members. The biscuit tin fell into the void between Harriet's outstretched arms and Abigail's folded ones, and gingerbread tiles spilled out, tessellating with an air of intelligent design. There was so much of it, and it all fitted together so fastidiously . . . it was spreading, and it had to be stopped. Houses are houses and biscuits are biscuits and people are people, and we all know nothing good comes of relaxing boundaries such as these. This is the only reason Harriet can think of for the mass trampling. Gioia bellowed, "Er, excuse me," a couple of times, then gave up when she saw the damage had been done. Harriet spent the rest of the PPA meeting on her knees, dustpan and brush in hand as she chased clumps of sand-colored powder into corners and under tables.

Harriet thought they must be famous, the other parents. She found their faces familiar, and they were either indifferent or accustomed to being gawked at. Days later, walking through the lobby of Perdita's school, she stopped before the wall with all the photos of previous prefects on it, and there they were, every single member of the PPA laughing together in a twenty-one-year-old photo. Gioia Marchesi (now Gioia Fischer), Emil Szep, Abigail Klein, Hyorin Nam, Gemma Jones (now Gemma Ahmad), Felix Nguyen, Noah Finlay, Alesha Thomas (now Alesha Matsumoto), Mariama Guled Ismail. Then, as now, each was an appealing example of a physical type, utterly at ease with his or her genes and with one another. Collectively they were an embodiment of Cool Britannia before the concept had even had a name. And this set of parents certainly is one body—it's impossible to speak to any of them individually. Group communication or deafening silence . . . your choice. Harriet can see why the other parents don't bother with the PPA. Harriet has asked about her fellow PPA members' kids, has seen the offspring around, has not stalked them, not exactly . . . they're Perdita's classmates. There are eleven of them in all, including two sets of twins, one identical and one fraternal, every base covered. And they're shaping up nicely to be members of another impenetrable in-crowd. So Harriet maintains her point, which is that joining isn't a question of effort or overextension thereof. You miss your chance to join several generations before birth.

Still . . . does Harriet want in? Fuck yes. Imagine the sense of invulnerability! What must it be like to clock that someone's staring at you and feel no concern? She wants to know how it feels to be absolutely sure that you haven't done anything wrong. She's not intimidated either—she doesn't believe for a second that these people aren't tryhards just like her. They're tryhards who succeed, that's all. Their striving is never past tense; it's merely concealed. Harriet's close reading of body language at the PPA meetings tells her that Abigail and Mariama are exes, the kind who can't work out why they aren't still together and send their current partners into spirals of paranoia whenever they meet up. Emil and Hyorin are not amused by the way that Noah pervs on Gemma, but they let it go because, against all odds, Gemma likes it. Alesha backs up everything Felix says out of fear, while Felix backs up everything Alesha says out of fondness. This could be down to a couple of specific incidents, or they could've been misreading each other for years. Harriet sees all this and more, and she supposes these factors could be used by a newcomer to destabilize the group. But Harriet would never do that! Well, she might, actually, for their own good. Much can be improved through reorganization.

Harriet and Perdita live in five affordable rooms of a house that has monumental staircases and no lift, which is where the affordability comes in. Each step is so large that climbing the staircases takes more than just walking up; it's also necessary to spring, scramble, and wriggle. This upsets delivery people and is more exercise than Margot Lee likes, but she has a soft spot for houses that look sensible until you get inside. There's lion-print wallpaper to look at on every floor. When visiting her kid and grandkid, Margot brings a book and sits down to read a little at each of her rest stops on the second, third, and sixth floors. Then, one more flight up and she arrives at Harriet and Perdita's front door, swaps her outdoor shoes for a pair of slippers, and is admitted to their cheerfully warped matchstick box of a home, where a velvet forest stands between the rooms and their casement windows. Margot made these curtains herself, embroidering them with vine-like patterns that seem to lengthen in the mornings and retract at night. Above those, silver satin parasols have been turned inside out to take the place of chandeliers—light bulbs dangle from their spokes. On the kitchen wall there's a black-and-white photo of a gingerbread man in an antique frame, a jumble-sale find from a decade earlier. The photo has an outdoor setting; the gingerbread man is posed so it looks like he's ambling through foliage with his gingerbread knapsack, off to see the world. Once, when Perdita was little, she took the photo into school and told everyone the man pictured was her father. She sounded so much in earnest that nobody knew what to say. Perdita's teacher got tears in her eyes telling Harriet about it and flinched when Harriet laughed.

On an evening when Perdita's away on a school trip, Harriet sits in front of her computer eating sample squares of lavender shortbread and practicing her favorite form of procrastination: writing highly positive reviews of her eBay, Etsy, and Amazon purchases. Five stars for everybody. She didn't finish one of the books she just gave five stars to. She just liked the author photo. Five stars for the portrait photographer, then. She's been doing this ever since some of her students told her they do this with one-star reviews. Opposing random negativity with random positivity—that's the main thing. She sips some bitter melon tea; the shortbread is just a little too sweet. When she's run out of synonyms for the word "fabulous," she visualizes a message from Gioia. **Hi, it's Gioia. Just broke my Lenten fast with your gingerbread, and all I can say is wizzy wow. We need this to be part of the fundraising bazaar. Not want, need. I won't take no for an answer. How much can you make? Also, do you want to go bowling with us?**

OK, maybe not bowling, but an invitation to something.

In the absence of that message, Harriet drafts an email to the entire PPA, to Gioia, Felix, Emil, Abigail, Hyorin, Gemma, Mariama, Alesha, Noah. It is both rant and unanswerable questionnaire. **WHAT ARE YOU ALL SO AFRAID OF?** Harriet types. **Why won't you try the gingerbread? Are you looking down on me because you think all I have is a handful of flour?**

But Harriet has this friend . . . well, she doesn't know if Gretel's still her friend; she isn't sure where Gretel is and doesn't know what Gretel is doing right now, but sometimes she receives an opinion from Gretel, an opinion just as clear as if Gretel's phoned her up and said the words herself. Harriet likes the thought of occasionally bursting in on Gretel's thoughts too, advising on all sorts of situations she couldn't possibly be aware of. This time her psychic projection of Gretel calmly and coolly looks over the email Harriet's about to send. **Send it if you want**, the projection says. **They won't reply. It is all pork in different sauces.**

Psychic-projection Gretel has been doing this a lot lately. Giving apathetic counsel. It's as if she knows Harriet doesn't pay her as much heed as she used to.

A word of advice, Gretel: You're losing authority. Shouldn't you put in an actual appearance instead of just talking?

Chop chop—now's the time. What do you mean, why now . . .

. . . there's never been a better time than the present. As you know, as you know.

Harriet's lights flicker, and she hears feet on the long flight of stairs between the sixth and the seventh floors. Skip, step, hop, skip, step, hop, and quick exhalations, **hfff hfff hfff**. But otherwise a dauntless ascent. Long, long strides.

Harriet listens with nothing in her mind but ?!?!

Skip, step, hop, Gretel. Skip, step, hop, Gretel. Skip, step, hope and hope and hope—

This is part and parcel of living at the top of seven steep staircases. Princess-in-a-tower syndrome sets in. You expect momentous visitors, since those are the only kind who would take the time and trouble to seek you out. Visitations from fate or from one you long to behold. But Harriet might do well to bar the door. If the climb from first to seventh floors isn't a big deal for Gretel Kercheval, that could be because the longest climb was the one that brought her to the first floor. The silver lights flicker again, and the stitched vines grow across the windows, grow toward one another. The vines do that sometimes, become a bridge with one tread of its deck missing. Twenty years. Gretel might be dour at first, mostly because of the bother of having to inform her grievances they must part ways. She never was able to surrender a feeling without a review of its peaks and low points.

Harriet stands by the front door with a corner of a shortbread square poking out of her mouth like a stylized tongue. She doesn't remember standing up and walking across the flat: she was in her chair, and now she's at the door, that's all. She listens as two feet settle on the top step. The puffing stops.

She covers both eyes with her hands for an instant before looking through the peephole. No

Gretel. But she'd come close. There must have been something Harriet could've done on her end. She should have gone to meet her guest halfway, and she would have, if she wasn't wearing slippers and a baggy T-shirt that reads FRIED IN BUTTER. Nothing remarkable has ever happened to anybody while they were wearing a T-shirt that reads FRIED IN BUTTER. Harriet opens the door, and it is just her, the smell of her downstairs neighbor's potato pancakes, and tawny lions embossed onto navy blue wallpaper. Each one hails her solemnly, with upheld paws. The lions seem sorry that Gretel isn't here. The square of shortbread falls into her palm. Gretel would have leaned forward and drawn it into her own mouth with her greeting kiss—soft lips, sharp teeth. And then she would have said: "More."

Harriet deletes her draft message to the PPA and texts Perdita instead: **How's Canterbury? Everything OK?** Perdita sends her a thumbs-up emoji.

Harriet:

- makes dinner for one and plans the lesson for the class she's teaching the following day: Spotlight on Lady Macbeth, she's calling it. "Out, out, damned spotlight," the class will not say.

- responds to her mother's flustered inquiry about what to do if you've accidentally "superliked" someone on Tinder and then discovered that the accidental superlike has superliked you too (also accidentally?).
- checks that her bag is filled with the essentials she'll need for the next morning, including the gingerbread with which she bribes a librarian in the Wellcome Library reading room to keep watch over her window seat of choice.
- googles Druhástrana, but there's nothing new. The top result is the Wikipedia page, like it always is.

Druhástrana (druhástranae) is the name of an alleged nation state of indeterminable geographic location. Very little verifiable information concerning Druhástrana is available, as there have been several prominent cases of stateless people claiming Druhástranian citizenship under a form of poetic license, and other, yet more unfortunate cases in which claims to Druhástranian citizenship or ancestry have

been proven to result from false memories or flawed cognitive information.

Even when credible witnesses have described flying over or sailing past an island that could be identified as Druhástrana, there is conflicting data as to whether the island is currently inhabited and further conflict as to who or what the island may be inhabited by. Reports include "a bear-like species clothed in human fashion," "some form of lizard," and "beings either long dead or not visible to the human eye." To date, Druhástrana has been formally recognized by only three nations. (See: Czech Republic, Slovakia, and Hungary.) Slovakia revoked recognition of Druhástrana without explanation on January 1, 2010, and Hungary followed suit on January 1, 2013.

Several prominent thinkers have proposed reclassifying Druhástrana as a purely notional/mythical land since a) nobody seems to actually come from there or know how to get there and b) literal interpretations of the assertion that Druhástrana exists may be a profound mistranslation of Czech humor.

The article is peppered with footnotes that link to a number of essays available online:

"I Belong to Druhástrana, Republic of
Beauty," by Guadeloupe Moreno,
translated by Drahomíra Maszkeradi
"I Belong to Druhástrana, Republic of
Freedom," by Anele Ndaba
"I Belong to Druhástrana, Republic of
Justice," by Tansy Adams
"I Belong to Druhástrana, a Republic
That Is Judging You All," by Nimrod
Tóth, translated by Drahomíra
Maszkeradi
"Nimrod Tóth Does Indeed Belong
to Druhástrana, a Republic of
Breathtaking Hypocrisy," by Simeon
Vesik, translated by Drahomíra
Maszkeradi

Harriet has lots to tell Gretel too. About
Margot and the Kercheval men: Aristide, Gabriel,
Rémy, and Ambrose, four walls of a charmed
prison. But the Wikipedia entry for Druhástrana
would be the first thing Harriet would show her
friend, followed by a selection of maps and atlases
that almost uniformly substitute Druhástrana's
spot on the globe with unmarked stretches of
ocean. Then she'd show Gretel photographs from
her trip to the one country where Druhástrana

does appear on maps. The average Druhástranian has only ever heard tell of the Czech Republic, so Harriet and Margot Lee took a trip there and had a look around. Cream cakes and amber glass, concentrations of cigarette smoke (a blue-gray mist curled out onto the street every time a pub door opened), grim light pressing down on grass so that whole fields of green stalks lean to one side, rainfall that seemed semi-divine in nature, blurring and brightening the faces of the statues. And then there were those street-corner skirmishes—three times Margot and Harriet had held onto each other so as to stay upright in a sudden wave of starched shirts and petticoats as masked men and women appeared out of nowhere, fought with axes made out of balloons, and then ran away crowing into the night, leaving the fallen where they lay, popped balloons strewn all around like burst lungs. Nobody would explain the skirmishes to Margot and Harriet, so Harriet decided they were reenactments of some key battle of antiquity and Margot decided they were prophecies of a battle to come. By the time they crossed off the last cathedral on their list and stood before an altar contemplating a Virgin Mary garlanded with precious stones and grinning an unnervingly modern grin (the kind of grin one stereotypically attributes to corporate fat cats when they're among close friends), by the time they were standing before that altar, Margot and Harriet didn't know what to make of Czechia and the fact that it's a place that doesn't get called notional or mythical, while Druhástrana does. They'll always appreciate the acknowledgment, though. Having glanced through the literature, it's their understanding that Druhástrana wasn't a favorite with the Czech travelers who somehow found their way there. Most describe it as "nightmarish." But at least they don't dismiss it.

Harriet stands in the doorway of Perdita's bedroom before she goes to bed herself. The room is almost entirely four-poster bed, with a doll at each post, guarding the inner sanctum, where Perdita dances, reads, sleeps, does her homework, watches TV, swigs cold tea from a hip flask, and so on. Harriet likes to look in even when Perdita isn't there, because Perdita's dolls have grown with her, and living with them is like having four bonus daughters. When Perdita's among her dolls, she is part of a clique of willowy teens with exactly the same shade of improbably perfect skin. Perdita calls them Bonnie, Sago, Lollipop, and Prim. Their names match the plants they bear . . . it was Margot and Perdita who removed Bonnie's hands at the wrist and replaced them with a pair of bonsai elm trees with leaves that separate into finger-like bunches. And Margot said to Harriet: "Whenever you begin to find Perdita too odd, just think how odd I find you."

Sago has feathery palm leaves for hair, and Lollipop's golden beehive hairdo is a **Pachystachys lutea** shrub. Prim's open chest cavity is a dormant green right now, but for twelve weeks of the year, pink-and-white primrose petals emerge. The dolls haven't got anything to say about these changes. They had these names before they changed, so maybe they already knew.

2

THE NEXT MORNING INVOLVES AWKWARD phone communications galore. It begins with Samreen Shah—Harriet thought they were supposed to be having lunch together. They hadn't made a date or anything like that, but Samreen has been at the library from Monday to Friday for the past three months, and almost every lunchtime she and Harriet have chewed salad together in the café as they exchange details of their morning's reading. Lunchtime was when Harriet would tell

Samreen what those members of the Salinas family who kept diaries and household accounts got up to in the years between 1300 and 1400 (mostly traveling Western Europe with troubadours and/or dying of the plague), and Samreen would tell Harriet about the feral camels of Australia, their exploits, plight, and eradication. Then they'd return to their desks with fresh energy for the research ahead. But Samreen doesn't come to lunch today, and when Harriet phones her, it transpires that Samreen moved to Manchester with her husband over the weekend. This is also the phone call during which Harriet discovers that Samreen hasn't saved her phone number, forgot Harriet's name very soon after first being told it, and in fact doesn't recall exchanging numbers at all, so it's difficult for Harriet to get Samreen to understand who she's even talking to. Samreen is a bit alarmed that Harriet knows so much about the book she's working on, and as Harriet does the necessary reframing of their acquaintanceship, her memory of their lunchtimes is altered too. Samreen never really looked her in the eyes, never called her by name, and never instigated contact. Harriet was the one who'd sit down at Samreen's table, mistakenly thinking that Samreen had been scanning the room for her. The talking was to pass the time; there was no Harriet-specific content whatsoever.

Harriet takes out her pocket mirror and looks at the face she no longer asks anything of. No use wondering why it doesn't register as distinct; it just doesn't. That's just as it should be: striking types never get left in peace. She widens her mouth around her vowels and reapplies her lipstick at the same time as she wishes Samreen all the best. Samreen wishes Harriet all the best too, and though it should stop there, the conversation somehow continues. Harriet sucks her middle finger so there won't be any lipstick on her teeth, and when the call finally ends, she feels somewhat mangled but also relieved that she at least made herself useful to Samreen, had provided an outlet for the minutiae Samreen needed to blurt out before discarding. This is, however, the sort of thing that makes Harriet afraid to think about her other relationships and how one-sided they may or may not have been. Aristide Kercheval may be Harriet's benefactor, but he's also the only person who has ever been up front with her about using her. Which makes him the only person she feels comfortable using. Her work on the Salinas family annals is a favor to Ari, and a well-paid one. It's been a few months since they last spoke, and

Harriet is about to send Ari an update when her phone lights up with a call from Perdita's school. It's Mrs. Scott, the school secretary, inquiring about Perdita's absence. Harriet knows this drill. She tells Mrs. Scott that Perdita's unwell. **Nothing too serious, I hope . . .** Mrs. Scott hasn't forgotten that the first time Harriet covered for Perdita, she managed to imply that Perdita had contracted meningitis. Harriet calls the GP to book an appointment so that Perdita can be provided with a sick certificate, and then she calls Perdita to ask what happened to giving notice before bunking off school. Perdita doesn't answer, and some questions begin to occur to Harriet. Mrs. Scott hadn't mentioned the history class trip to Canterbury. If the entire class had gone on an overnight trip, why expect Perdita alone to turn up at school as normal the next morning? Come to think of it, why does a school trip from London to Canterbury need to be an overnight trip at all? The school letter had been vague about that, but Harriet had signed the permission slip and handed over cash anyway. She'd prefer not to call Mrs. Scott back unless she really has to, so she calls Alesha Matsumoto, whose son, Fitz, is in Perdita's history class. Alesha's phone rings unanswered. So does Abigail Klein's phone, and Emil Szep's. Then she remembers she has to ask the group to get an answer, and she sends a group text saying she's lost the school letter and asking what time the A level history class are due back from Canterbury.

Abigail replies first: **canterbury when? did they go this morning**

Then Emil: **Why would they go to Canterbury? A bit off-syllabus, no?**

Alesha just sends a question mark.

Harriet texts Perdita: **What's going on?** and signs off with three tangerines, their emoji code for love. It would be three oranges, like in Prokofiev's symphonic suite, but iMessage doesn't offer an orange emoji. She returns to her window-seat project: preparing a comprehensive family chronicle for a descendant who doesn't like reading. "Just the turning points, please," this descendant told Aristide Kercheval, and Harriet has been following that brief for half a year, hacking decades down to paragraphs. The result will be one volume, and ultimately she wants it to read like **Spring and Autumn Annals**. Simple sentences in which maelstroms crystallize: Peter Salinas was born to every advantage and lost them all one by one, and then ninety-nine years later, John and Christina Salinas paid down generations of debt and became creditors. The Salinases in between lay low—perhaps it takes that long to forget certain blows and to gather strength. And all the while the seasons passed, as they do, without telling us anything at all, not even whether they will come again. They only turn their blank faces to us as they go by.

The library closes, and Perdita still hasn't texted back. She's a girl who'll bunk off school because she feels like going for a spa day with her grandma, but Margot is working and says Perdita isn't with her today. It's dawning on Harriet that she should've checked Perdita's whereabouts before lying for her, but it's OK, a lesson learned. She goes on to night school in a classroom at the local college near her house, paces in front of the whiteboard as the slate-colored seats slowly fill up. Harriet's class always starts late and often ends a little before the time stated in the course catalog.

Most of her students arrive from jobs as cleaners and builders and nail technicians, and many will go on to other jobs or go back to work after the class. But for three hours a week Harriet's ten students set aside their fear of falling into verbal traps and give Macbeth a chance, and Jekyll and Hyde, and a selection of Romantic poets. They hadn't passed GCSE English at sixteen, for various reasons: they hadn't been in the country, or they had had other things on their minds at the time, or it had been predicted that they'd fail and they'd done as they were told. Every member of this class is under the impression that they are thick, and every single one of them is the opposite. Passing the GCSE now probably won't improve their job prospects or raise their estimation in the eyes of their family and friends. Betty's shy cunning as she whispered, "Alf thinks I'm at the bingo . . ." When Betty said this, some gaudy joy flew through Harriet, chirping and fluttering like a canary. The mad canary sings not only for Betty but for the whole obstinate bunch. No need to rationalize this endeavor to anybody outside the class. Their curiosity and readiness to sail through storms of meaning makes Thursday Harriet's favorite day of the week, though she does occasionally worry about Shura, who has failed this exam three times, even though she'd studied hard and studied from her son's revision notes.

"Dima gets A's . . . just don't understand how this can be," Shura says with a sigh.

A GCSE exam paper is no place for unorthodox theory. Harriet tells Shura that her gloriously abandoned response to a book she likes, basically that of a living being full of contradictory impulses running off into the night with another living being full of contradictory impulses, is largely incompatible with exam language. Shura zips up her puffa jacket, tucks her chin into the collar, and mutters that glorious abandon is nice, but sometimes in life it's good to be able to answer questions in the language in which they are asked. Shura needs to know she can do that if she chooses to, so she would like to get an A this time. Harriet promises her at least a C as long as she demonstrates passing familiarity with a handful of established terms and concepts. Shura says a C will do. She says that very quickly, as if the prospect will be taken off the table if she isn't prompt with an affirmation of interest. At this point Shura just wants a grade.

Harriet comes home to the smell of gingerbread and has mixed feelings, mostly good ones, about Perdita's sudden taking up of the mantle. The fruit bowl in the kitchen was empty when Harriet left, but now there are three oranges in there, and a note propped up against them. The note may be in Perdita's handwriting, but Harriet isn't certain. It's been a few years since she last had a note from Perdita, and she remembers the note very well, though she's a bit hazy on the specific event the note was a reaction to. That note, in an envelope addressed to **Mother**, had read:

You! You've embarrassed me for the last time. Grandma's going to raise me, so don't ever talk to me or come near me anymore. P.S. Thank you for the food and lodging to date.

Harriet can smile at the memory now, but when she received the note, she cried so much a bystander could've given their hands a good rinse beneath her eyes. She cried so much that Perdita got scared she'd make herself ill and relented, dragging Harriet into her bedroom so she could watch as every item in her suitcase was laboriously unpacked. What about the note before that . . . oh dear. Not as upsetting, but still cause for concern: **On this, the day that Jesus was born, I curse you . . .**

Notes from Perdita make Harriet nervous, three oranges or no three oranges.

She picks up the note with tongs and sets it aside, calls out, "Perdita?" and frowns when there is no answer. She looks around the kitchen, smelling gingerbread but seeing none. The oven's empty, but she sees a hedgehog-shaped silicone mold on the pastry board beside her rolling pin, and there is a bowl by the sink with a little dough still left in it. Ever precise, the girl had made just enough dough for one gingerbread hedgehog with three little dots left over, an ellipsis of dough. Harriet

39

squashes one dot with her finger and tastes it, is proud for a moment. Saline, saccharine, piquant, all proportions correct. But then there is an after-taste that shouldn't be there. This throb in the tongue, as though the flesh is swelling and shrinking around the site of a sting . . . she tries Perdita's phone again.

There's a pause while the call connects, and then she hears the phone nearby. The flat is very quiet just then, so the vibrations are like hail rattling against the windows. Harriet follows the rattling to Perdita's bedroom door, which she's only able to open part of the way—what, what on earth is this, what is she looking at? Oh. A limb— an arm—inflexible—a doll's. It blocks Harriet's view of the bed, and its fingers are closed around Perdita's phone. The arm belongs to the doll named Prim, and Prim's shoulder joint almost shakes itself out of its socket until the ringing stops. Harriet only has to jam her shoulder up against the door one more time before Prim's grip buckles and she falls so that Harriet can step over her. Lollipop and Bonnie are kneeling on the bed on either side of Perdita, Bonnie shielding Perdita's head with her tiny trees, Lollipop's palms open: **We couldn't stop her.** Perdita's skin is cold. Her head lolls to the side, and that side of the mattress is awash with the vomit that's spilled from her mouth. When Harriet lifts her up, her plaits whirl into a knotted gray halo. The girl lies meekly in Harriet's arms as she phones for an ambulance. The paramedics will come too late. There are seven staircases—

Perdita convulses, and convulses again. There is no more vomit, but there is bloodstained excrement. She has a pulse, and then she doesn't have one, and then she does. The convulsions stretch the skin of her throat. It looks as if she's holding a bubble of air in there, or a giant marble. A voice speaks from the throat bubble. Not Perdita's . . . it's the croaking of a toad. Harriet holds her—**Oh, please, please, please.** She opens the front door; her voice carries down the stairwells, and her neighbors station themselves along the banister, their arms held out for her daughter. Perdita croaks and cackles as she's passed from person to person; her journey to the first floor is only a little slower than a fall would've been.

AT THE HOSPITAL MARGOT tells Harriet that, on the whole, it's probably better to have sons.

Daughters are enigmatic minefields of classified information, she says.

Harriet would like to act as if she hasn't heard any of this but can't help blurting out: "Are daughters the only ones who fit that description?"

Margot pats her on the head. "I knew you'd say that."

"But really, I . . . suppose Perdita was a boy . . . wouldn't you be sitting here tutting and telling me about the trouble with sons?"

Margot nods and folds Harriet's hands between her own. Eye to twinkling eye, a look passes between them.

"You knew I'd say that too?"

They keep their fingers linked as they're told that the hospital's still working on identifying exactly what Perdita's imbibed. They've ruled out pills; her symptoms are closer to those exhibited by two mushroom foragers who'd recently been brought in with amatoxin poisoning. Both had survived and made partial recoveries, though one had permanently lost his eyesight and the other . . . Doctor Li avoids Harriet's gaze and repeats that both patients survived and made partial recoveries. Harriet has read her name badge: Doctor Li is not a Harriet but a Meizhen.

There's a terraced square just outside one of

the hospital's exits, and Harriet and Margot take turns leaving Perdita's side in order to walk around and around this square, passing haggard-looking escapees from bedsides bleaker than the one the Lees have left. These bench-sitters are all cried out and are holding a variety of objects—a cigarette, a bottle of Lucozade, a cup of coffee—not really doing anything with them, just looking them over. Each object is held ceremoniously, its function purely symbolic for now. Harriet throws away a wedge of her data allowance on an urgent group Skype chat, turning to the PPA to try to find out if anything has happened at school. She can't assume that their kids don't talk to them. But she's reluctant to say "Perdita" aloud; at a time like this, scant reception of the name could push its bearer off the edge of the world. Harriet's hands shake a lot when she tells the PPA that Perdita's had an accident and Gioia says: "Perdita . . . ?"

"My daughter." Harriet provides a little more context. Nothing too disruptive of Perdita's privacy, but nothing factually incorrect either. Emil very much hopes Harriet's not implying that his twins have been bullying Perdita—he says it just like that: "I very much hope . . ." Mariama suggests contacting Perdita's friends. Gemma asks, in the most roundabout way possible, whether this couldn't be a case of heartbreak. Alesha says she is sorry and waves her hands, fending off the question of what she's sorry for. Abigail asks about Perdita's current condition. Felix says he hopes his twins haven't been bullying anybody either (subtly different from Emil's hope that Harriet isn't **saying** his twins have been bullies) and expresses a resolve to get to the bottom of this if he can. Noah and Hyorin say they'll visit. Harriet welcomes this but will believe it when she sees it.

Perdita lies under white sheets, her eyelids so smooth the sockets could be empty. Sunken cheeks and inflated veins. The ICU is keeping her afloat, but its beeping and whirring is impartial; Perdita is alone here in a way that she was not before, when her dolls and bedposts stood watch. Harriet sits beside her daughter, and Margot sits in a chair by the door. They turn to their phones for information and are tortured by the search results: kids hounded to death by messages that pop up in every inbox they have passwords for so they know they are hated—by one person who hates them very much or by a multitude who only hates them a little at a time. **Yeah, tell your parents all about this. Go crying to Mummy or Daddy. Let's all sit down and have meetings with our guardians and sign contracts promising to be** nice to one another—you'll have to sign too even though you're the victim—let's do all of that and see if anything changes. Margot and Harriet swap phones, read each other's findings, and then close all the tabs so as to keep from having to cry out. The scope of their project was petty: they wanted Perdita to get good marks at school; they wanted her not to cause trouble, not to punish them for being unable to afford the very best of everything for her. Oh, and they also wanted her to smile every now and again. Those boxes were all ticked, so they'd concluded that all was well, or well enough. They dare not be noisy now. Sick and injured people are sleeping in the neighboring rooms, and they shouldn't have to forfeit the rest they need just because these two have only just become aware of the fine print. After a time, Harriet hears herself counting aloud. She's not sure what she's counting. The numbers don't seem to correspond to any external event.

Around midnight Harriet gets a text message from somebody who says Hyorin Nam from the Parental Power Association has sent him, and she goes down to the drab terrace, where a young man with bloodshot eyes and hair longer in the front than it is at the back hands her a cardboard box. The young man is Hyorin's nephew, Toby.

He's a university exchange student. "We just got done folding these for you," he says, pointing at the box. "Me and my aunt and two cousins. There are exactly one thousand."

Harriet opens the box. Row upon row of radiant symmetry: a thousand paper cranes.

Toby says: "My aunt said to tell you it's so you can have a big wish."

Her tears don't appear to make anything awkward for him. He seems to be reasoning that she's doing what she needs to. This is a one-thousand-crane situation. Eventually he says he's got to go and backs away, saying: "No," offended by the sight of her money. She's not trying to pay him for the paper cranes. She just wants to make sure he gets back to Ealing safely. The distinction she draws has no effect on his resistance. "Uber . . . I'll take an Uber."

Harriet likes Toby's accent and its ample slice of Decencyville, Canada. Would it be weird to get his email address for Perdita? Yes. Yes, it would.

Now that there are paper cranes to count, Harriet and Margot do this at Perdita's bedside. The night passes slowly, as it must when your wish is that another's won't come true. Perdita has done her best to unmake herself, but they won't let her. They keep on counting the cranes. The odd numbers bring a raggedy comfort, as close to huggability as numbers get. The horror of the even numbers is all-enveloping. You do have to be so very careful, don't you, what you wish for. Mother and grandmother count paper cranes until they see that the sun has risen.

HARRIET DOESN'T THINK about where Perdita may have got her gingerbread additive until about forty-eight hours later, when she's finished cleaning up Perdita's bedroom and the living room and the strip of floor they walked between the two. She's lined the shamefaced dolls up along the edge of Perdita's bed and has intensified their distress with a lecture on their responsibilities. It's true that Prim, Sago, Bonnie, and Lollipop have not been brought up in the usual way, but they are old enough to know better.

Next Harriet sits down at the kitchen table and peels one of the oranges Perdita left her so she can truthfully tell Margot she's eaten something. She opens Perdita's note.

Don't misunderstand: not dead, just traveling. You know where. You'll be angry, but I have to see it just once! Please trust me and leave me

where I am until I wake up? Three times three times three to the power of three (oranges) . . .

As Harriet reads, Perdita's handwriting distorts and elasticates, cakewalks around the page, mocking. She reads her daughter's mind in this, yes, Perdita's whim and will, but there is another mind alongside it. One capable of deepening the fascinations of a suicidal thought until they bloom and shine, gems and flowers woven around an iron crown. Harriet shakes the note and dried ink flies off like soot. Its particles multiply and settle into the chair across from her, the chair facing the kitchen workstation.

That's where he sat as Perdita made her gingerbread. He reread steps of the recipe aloud at Perdita's request; music played as they talked and laughed. Harriet rolls the blank page into a cudgel, but the soot figure flows out of the room before she can strike. She follows it back to Perdita's room. The dolls recognize the figure—this is where he lay down with her daughter as the gingerbread began to take effect, he lay down with her in a manner that was irresistibly illicit, his attentions somewhere between those of a father and those of a lover. And—**Tell me, dolls, did he sing?**

He did. Badly, but with soul. The dolls let Harriet hear the melody of a lullaby Margot used to sing, one that Harriet has sung to Perdita herself. The soot figure lies with Perdita until she is no longer awake. When he rises, Harriet thrashes him. Soot encircles her, looms over her, blots out her vision, even, but she is swift and frantic and doesn't rest until her blows have driven him back onto the paper, back into the words Perdita wrote.

There's a Kercheval mixed up in this somehow. The elder two, Aristide and Ambrose, she rules out. But their sons . . . Harriet knows Rémy and Gabriel well, and not being able to narrow down this hunch to a single name is a mark of how well she knows them both.

So much for all the strategies that ought to earn a peaceful existence. So much for the complete surrender to being unexceptional. Years ago Rémy Kercheval had asked Harriet if she felt she was someone who had a future. She'd said yes even though she had doubts. Doubts he seemed to share. An expression crossed his face as he heard her answer—she saw curiosity there, and perhaps even sympathy.

3

MARGOT AND HARRIET ARE PERDITA'S ONLY visitors, though Alesha Matsumoto has broken away from the rest of the PPA to write a private email to Harriet: she writes that she spoke to her son Fitz, and he doesn't know anything about Perdita's "accident" or possible causes for it, but according to him, he'd tried to befriend Perdita some time ago. He'd thought things were going well until Perdita had suddenly asked him what he thought he was doing and then said: "Friends . . . ? Thanks, but I can't do anything like that at the moment." Alesha signs off, and then adds a postscript—this son of hers, Fitz, an intellectually fastidious boy who never rushed a choice if he could help it, had just approached his mother mid-email to add something: Perdita's telling Fitz she couldn't see him as a friend had flustered him. It had seemed to Fitz Matsumoto that Perdita Lee was hinting at non-platonic feelings, so he'd told her that if she wanted to be more than friends they should talk about that issue separately— on the following day, for instance (**I honestly don't know who my son takes after**, Alesha writes). Anyway, Perdita's response—or at least the response that Fitz Matsumoto tells his mother he remembers Perdita giving: "More than friends, eh? More than friends . . . You know, my mother once told me that half of the hatred that springs up between people is rooted in this mistaken belief that there's any human relationship more sacred than friendship." And after saying that to Fitz Matsumoto, Perdita Lee checked her watch and hurried off. Alesha Matsumoto of the Parental Power Association adds a further postscript to this message: she never listened to her own mother and often regrets not having done so. Perdita being a girl who actually listens to her mother, Alesha would like to meet her when she's well enough.

Harriet is smiling; it's a certainty: this is a smile. And now she laughs a little bit—it's as if Perdita is comforting her. A girl who listens to her mother: not really. No relationship more sacred than friendship? Harriet's never said any such thing—not to Perdita or to anybody else. A girl who listens to her mother indeed . . . actually, Alesha Matsumoto is only half wrong about that. Harriet has the evidence in her phone—a text message exchange she treasures due to the rarity of Perdita's asking her advice:

Mother

At your service—

Suppose I want to make a statement with a low probability of that statement being questioned

How low a probability?

Just enough to break a chain of other questions

So—something you can say and then just make a quick getaway?

My mother catches on fast

Have you already asked Margot?

Yes, and she gave me some chat about cowardice

OK

Well, any ideas?

Make a statement that you're personally invested in—something that you think is 100% true. But protect the statement from being questioned by claiming that it's someone else's belief and you're just repeating it as a bit of food for thought. Ideally you should say these are the thoughts of someone long dead

Someone long dead and white?

Even better if you pin your own statement on someone long dead and white and male

Minimum 90% of all further questions killed dead?

99%

Got it. Thanks

HYORIN NAM OF THE Parental Power Association sends Harriet a recipe for **danpatjuk**, a red-bean porridge she used to eat every winter solstice. Hyorin writes that it's a good meal to have when the darkness of a night begins to seem as if it's aspiring toward the eternal. Hyorin makes no mention of gluten, but since the main components of the recipe are beans and rice flour, it could be that she somehow knows about Perdita's celiac disease. Of the one thousand paper cranes she sent, Hyorin writes: **Don't be thankful yet.**

These lapses in PPA protocol are especially heartening given that Perdita continues to shun consciousness, and domestic snooping is so hard nowadays. Perdita's phone is passcode-protected and threatens to revert to factory settings if Harriet hazards one more guess. Perdita's laptop does the same. Nobody's rung the phone since Perdita was hospitalized, and the only messages Harriet can see on the lock screen are from her and Margot. This is how Harriet learns that her number's saved in her daughter's contact list under the title "Minister of Health, Education & Welfare." Margot's alias is "Nightlife Czar." Between them, the Nightlife Czar and the Minister of Health, Education & Welfare have smothered this child, prevented the formation of extrafamilial relationships, fostered dangerously odd perspectives in her. You wouldn't catch any of the PPA offspring believing that they could do what Perdita had done and have a great adventure in nightmare country instead of coming to harm.

"Strongly disagree," Margot says, closing Perdita's laptop and confiscating the phone. "All we do is love her."

The Canterbury trail grows fainter by the minute, and Margot sees no point in following it. Of Perdita's note, she says: "I thought this must have happened because she was unhappy. Or that it was the gingerbread . . . I thought there must be something spooky about it after all and it had decided to finish Perdita off. This . . . this is idiotic, but better than—"

"No, it's not. It's not better. And where did she even get the idea that eating gingerbread is some sort of fast track to Druhástrana?"

"What do you mean, where did she get the idea . . . she's on the internet all the time, isn't she? Or are you saying you finally see what I mean about the gingerbread?"

Yeah, yeah, the gingerbread did it. Margot would believe that before she'd allow herself to suspect a Kercheval. And so Margot and Harriet stay by Perdita's side as the soot figure escapes scot-free. Each morning, around the time Perdita would normally wake up, Harriet whispers into her daughter's ear. She tells Perdita the date and time of her birth, and she tells her that what was begun then doesn't end today.

Perdita isn't listening. Perdita dies. She dies in a dream Harriet has, and in that dream, grief sends Harriet staggering from place to ruined place in the form of a flightless crow. If anyone looks at her, she scratches out their eyes with her clawed feet, and if anyone listens to her cries, she rips their ears clean off their heads. Another crow hidden in a cloud told her that this anguish is sort of like a trial by jury—it will run out of steam if there's no witness testimony.

Perdita comes back. She comes back while Harriet is asleep in the chair beside her bed, dreaming that she's died. Harriet's eyes open— that's how it feels, as if somebody has plucked them open—and Perdita is watching her and breathing quietly, her lips pinched together with pain. The girl is, after all, swathed in a fine net of electricity, run through with needles and tubing. Here they both are in the middle of the night, Harriet and Perdita, though Perdita's look shifts from devotion to disinterest the millisecond she realizes Harriet is awake too. This is how Harriet knows her child really has come back. She is the first to smile. Perdita says something, but her words come out so slurred that she stops, surprised at the sounds she's making. She chuckles and shakes her head—**OK, I'll come back to this later**—and when Harriet squeezes her, she squeezes back as best she can. But when Harriet calls out for Margot and a doctor and everybody else, Perdita holds out her hand with a look of urgency. The gesture is abnormally stiff, the fist clenched.

"What is it, Perdita? Does it hurt?"

Perdita grunts and punches the air a few more times until Harriet takes her by the wrist. Then she opens her hand, wincing as she lifts each finger to reveal a wooden ring. She's been holding on to it so tightly it's embossed her skin. Harriet's wits scatter when she sees the ring, but she doesn't know this until she recovers them and the room rolls back in. Perdita's watching her again. She seems to know that Harriet has seen the ring before. It's carved to resemble a stalk of wheat that bends around your finger, the head of the stalk reaching for its heel to complete the circle. Harriet runs her thumb over each kernel, then drops Gretel's ring into her coat pocket and listens to her daughter's baby talk as rapturously as she did the first time around.

PERDITA IS MOVED onto a ward where she's popular because the other patients find her babbling pleasant. Thankfully Perdita's only staying until the hospital makes certain that her liver and kidneys are in good working order. Hopefully she'll come home before her antagonism becomes unmistakable. The kids who've mustered up the courage to spend time with Perdita might take her requests pretty badly if they understood them. Most are the same age as her and are recovering from suicide attempts too. Andrew, the ward host, asks Harriet to stop bringing in gingerbread for them. According to him, the patients lie under the covers nibbling away at it all night. He's all for treats, but his instinct tells him not to indulge this: "It's a bit . . . I don't know, like some sort of ritual. I don't think it's right."

There is a girl on the ward named Tuesday; she wears a beanie jammed over locks dyed deep sea-green. A beanie or a brightly colored beret—Harriet never sees her bareheaded. She seems delicate in the refined sense of the word rather than the frail sense. She doesn't strike Harriet as suicidal, but of course you can never tell, even with the type that tends to get photographed for street-style blogs. This just in: Black Indie Ariel spotted at bus stop.

Tuesday writes poems for Perdita.

(**Of course being is an unnecessary thing,
the kind of mistake I
didn't think I'd find forgiveness for.
You went looking and returned saying:
Whatever,**

it's fine,
it's fine, we can do unnecessary things
They are not inferior.
Continue with impunity
Each day a little more mistaken and
a little more forgiven.)

When Perdita gurgles for her to please go away, Tuesday kisses her cheek and says: "Yeah, you too."

Perdita is happy to babble unintelligibly at first, but over the following days, there are tests and conversations and test conversations that establish the extent to which hovering below a waking state for eight days has been hard on her brain. Perdita can only make her simplest thoughts understandable in speech, and marginally more effective in writing. She can follow what is said to her if she really focuses her attention, but even then one out of every five or so words she hears seems to be a unit of white noise. She needs speech therapy and time. Much more time than the eight days she was under. Perdita scrawls something to the effect of this not being that much of a problem because she didn't really talk to anybody before anyway, but she cannot completely hide her frustration. She's never been more physically expressive. Margot has been weeping a lot now that there's no longer any need to show death her poker face, and while the weeping is under way Perdita administers clumsy hugs and says: "Oh no! Oh no!" Her consternation is made cartoonish by the sheer amount of energy she has to put into conveying it. And the way she revs up when she tries to talk about the ring she brought back with her . . .

Hang on. Brought back with her . . . ?

"Oh," Harriet says aloud to Perdita, "what am I thinking? That you went to Druhástrana, that you went there somehow without leaving this bed . . . even though you **would** have had to leave this bed to get there, Perdita, because as I have been saying all your life, Wikipedia doesn't get to decide which places have actual geographic existence and which don't. But OK, playing along for now, I seem to be thinking that you made it across and that Gretel was there. My Gretel. She saw you. She knew who you were, helped you, maybe. She gave you her ring. And she said—now let me see, what is it I'm wishing she'd said: **Tell Harriet Lee I am still her friend** . . . something like that . . ."

Perdita looks dizzy and signals to Harriet to start all over again and speak much more slowly, so Harriet does. As she repeats herself, Perdita nods with increasing enthusiasm. To the bit about Gretel telling Perdita that she's still Harriet's friend,

Perdita throws both hands up in the air and says, "EHHHHHH!" which is her new placeholder sound for "YES EXACTLY!" The hairs on the back of Harriet's neck give this reply a standing ovation and turn the skin there into fur. The same thing happened when she set down Gretel's wheat-sheaf ring alongside her own matching one; the lid of the jewelry box had jerked and buckled until she took away one of the rings. But in this case, while Harriet would love to have made a preter-naturally accurate guess, it's much more probable that Perdita's hearing different questions from the ones Harriet's been asking her. Dr. Ilesanmi has spoken about this:

Expect a fair amount of disorientation for the first couple of weeks. Perdita may have stable or improved verbal recall for five or six days in a row; you may see meaning and pronunciation lining up more or less as it should, but then a day later she could become discouraged by a small slipup. Keep practicing with her; maintaining confidence is going to make all the difference here.

Harriet doesn't ask all the questions she wants to ask. Instead, she tells Perdita about her death dream. Perdita feels bad about the dream but thinks Harriet might not have had it if only she'd read the note as soon as she'd found it. And now

Perdita wants to know what Harriet-as-crow did afterward—after she'd gouged all the witnesses to her grief. Or did she wake up mid-rampage?

All this is whispered. Harriet's laugh is a whisper as well. "Oh, after I'd gouged all the witnesses I ate a small bowlful of grapes, and I was trying to decide whether I myself count as a witness, and I couldn't decide. I just couldn't. Thank goodness you came back. I'm sure whatever decision I made would've been wrong. Hopefully now you see that it's better if you just live on a long, long time after me, as you should."

Perdita grudgingly agrees, and Harriet takes advantage of this to begin saying what needs to be said about the Kerchevals. Anybody who says you must hurt yourself primarily wishes to see you hurt, regardless of rationale or supposedly beneficial outcome. This is what Harriet tells Perdita.

No response whatsoever. Perdita is ICU Girl again; empty-eyed until Harriet says the dolls have been informed that Perdita's coming home. Then she revives, nods, and smiles.

4

It's stupid, but Harriet puts Gretel's ring on before she goes to sleep at night in her room strewn with paper cranes. Stupid because what will all that do? Ward off a return visit from the soot figure? Harriet's the type who frets all the time, but since she read Perdita's note, she's fretting on overdrive. The flat keeps dwindling around her, doors and walls thinning to mere air. She must not be nervous; she must not jump when the heating stutters or when the dripping of the tap changes tempo. The wheat-sheaf ring and the paper cranes bring relief from all dreaming and prognostication. The soot figure is not coming. It has been and gone, and failed.

In the morning Harriet ties on her favorite apron, the one she's had printed with a sketch of Perdita's. The sketch is in the style of a pavement sign: a woman who looks a little like Harriet is wearing a tall, pointy hard hat and clutching the handle of a wooden spoon as if it's a walking stick. Beneath this image are the words WITCH AT WORK. She puts on music that suits her witchy mood: DJ Luck and MC Neat's "A Little Bit of Luck."

Ta-na-ni ta-na-ni ta-na-ni ta-na-ni ta-na-ni . . .

She washes and strains red beans, boils them down to near-mush, grinds the beans, refers to Hyorin Nam's **danpatjuk** recipe for the next step.

With a little bit of luck, we can make it through the night . . .

Harriet pummels rice dough until she has a bowl full of cloud solid enough to rebuild a castle in the air. Instead of crafting ramparts she portions it out into tiny cannonballs. The bean paste bubbles, and Harriet stirs in the dough so that Perdita comes home to a simmering of her favorite things: sugar, starch, and cinnamon. After this and the paper cranes, Harriet almost dares to call herself a friend of Hyorin Nam's, but she mustn't be hasty; she's made this mistake before, and she should wait for a third sign.

At bedtime, Harriet looks in on Perdita and the dolls. They are gathered close, a rustling bouquet of eyes and leaves, and they haven't gone to sleep yet. They look at her expectantly, so she takes one step into the room, then one more.

There's a question Perdita's been asking ever since she woke up at the hospital: **How did you get here?** The question is for both Harriet and Margot, and Margot misunderstands and thinks Perdita is for some reason fixated on the logistics of their getting to the hospital. Harriet understands Perdita's question perfectly and—shamelessly unsatisfactory mother that she is—has been pretending to share Margot's misunderstanding. Harriet and Margot have the kind of past that makes the present dubious. Talking or thinking about "there" lends "here" a hallucinatory quality that she could frankly do without. Pull the thread too hard and both skeins unravel simultaneously. Still. Each time Harriet raises her hand, she sees the two rings on her middle finger. The unaltered fact of Gretel is promising.

So Harriet clears her throat and asks if Perdita is interested in making a deal. Perdita invites her to state her terms, and once stated, they're rapidly agreed upon. Perdita will tell Harriet how she got to Druhástrana, and Harriet will tell Perdita how she left it. **Nggggg**, Perdita's shaking her head, disputing the order of proceedings. First Harriet will tell Perdita how she left Druhástrana. Only then will Perdita tell Harriet how she got there.

Prim, Sago, Bonnie, and Lollipop move outward to sit with their backs against the bedposts. Their arms fold across their bodies, and their faces are in shadow, four geometric sketches indicating a margin.

Harriet settles down next to Perdita; she is cross-legged, and so is her daughter; she's wearing flannel pajamas, and so is her daughter. "Consider this a bedtime story . . ."

But before Harriet can begin, Sago pipes up. She'd rather go to bed without a story tonight, if that's all right with the others.

It's not all right with the others. Perdita warbles something very stern, and the doll named Lollipop lets it be known that she thinks Sago's a coward. Prim says, "What's this, Sago? We've heard bedtime stories before."

Bonnie says they'd all listen to Sago if they had any sense. What are they going to do if this particular bedtime story has an "it was all a dream" interlude that truthfully refers not just to the tale and its teller but to all those to whom the tale is being told? "Suppose we're not even character characters but figments of another character's imagination . . ."

"I'd be humiliated," Lollipop bursts out. "Humiliated!"

"Well, it's not like we'd just sit back and take it," Prim adds. "We've still got our side of the story. It's like having a return ticket. We can all go there and back together, can't we."

Perdita nods. Sago sighs, then asks Harriet to go ahead.

5

A GIRL GREW UP IN A FIELD. WELL, IN A house, with her family, but the house was surrounded by stalks of wheat as tall as saplings. The girl's earliest memories are framed in breeze-blown green and gold. Ice and moonlight, sunshine and monsoon, the wheat was there, tickling her, tipping ladybirds and other pets into her lap.

Druhástrana's small, but everyone who lives there thinks it's huge. This is due to a couple of types of subjective distance. There's bureaucratic distance, by which I mean there are all sorts of formalities to be completed at each stage of travel. It takes hours, and by the time your credentials are checked for the tenth time (tenth out of seventeen), most people feel like turning around and going home again. The other type of subjective distance has to do with the way the land itself impedes rapid motion. For example, the wheat field I've mentioned was hazardously lush terrain. Whether you crossed it on foot or by tractor, wheat was all you saw ahead of you and all you saw behind.

But there were landmarks. The first was in the center of the North Sector, where the Cooper family lived. It was a wooden clog the size of a caravel, a relic from the days of giants. The Coopers were convinced the shoe belonged to a giant Cinderella, and they gave the youngest among them the task of keeping it polished in case someone came back for it.

The second key demarcation was between non-farmland and the beginning of the South Sector, where the Cook family lived. Here you met a jack-in-the-box with a pegged-on smile and eyes that popped out on springs and bounced every which way. His wind-up handle was broken, but that didn't stop him jumping out and squawking **HA HA HA** just as you were trying to tiptoe past carrying breakable goods. Maybe he was solar-powered. Someone always pushed his eyes back into his head and closed him into his box once he'd had his fun. The Cooks had lost count of the number of times they'd moved him, only to find that he'd returned to his preferred spot overnight. Mr. Jack-in-the-Box would never become an intuitive meeting point like the Giant's Clog, but the farmstead people would veer off course without him.

The third landmark was a broken loom on an iron stand, austere in its rust. Frills of hemlock (or cow parsley?) grew through and around its rolls and beams, trying in vain to mend the shattered frame, or heightening the display of the damage. That one was in the East Sector, where the Lees lived: it was the landmark closest to the girl's cottage. It was said that three sisters had quarrelled there. She who couldn't stop laughing at the Coopers' Giant Cinderella theory was sad to think that harmony could go so long unrestored. She'd wound measuring tape around one of the legs of the loom stand and placed a pair of scissors on its lowest shelf, so that if by some chance the weaver, the measurer, and the cutter reconvened there, they'd see that somebody else had hoped for this too.

The fourth landmark was a dry well known as Gretel's Well. It marked the end of the West Sector, where the Parker family lived, and the beginning of non-farmland. The mouth of the well was paved with jade-colored tiles, and past kneeling-reach, the darkness within was utter. If you dropped a stone in there, you had to listen intently for up to ten minutes before you heard it hit the bottom. This could mean that the well was exceedingly deep, or it could mean that some acquisitive creature lived in the well and thoroughly contemplated each stone it caught before deciding it wouldn't do and letting it go. There was no tale that anybody knew of concerning this well. The name attached to it both suggested and withheld a story, and thus was invention forbidden. Children asked parents, younger siblings asked older siblings, and all were told: **No story.**

There were many smaller landmarks, but the girl I'm talking about still sees the big four sometimes, when she closes her eyes. She was often sent on errands to fetch tools, pass messages, and deliver neatly wrapped parcels of the gingerbread her mother made, so she traveled with a foldup stool that she stood on to see above wheat level. When her feet touched the ground again, the girl felt a gentle pull on the soles of her feet. The wheat drew a curtain around her and promised she'd be a beauty beyond compare by the time she was unveiled. When that didn't work, it promised her boundless wisdom. All she had to do was place her feet here, and here, where the soil was softest . . .

The girl never fell for that. She walked faster. She'd seen some plant-vertebrate combinations in the clearings, glassy gazing dormice and owls that earth had risen up around; the ground was growing them, and they looked uncomfortable, as if they'd been stretched and stuffed with straw. There was a leaf that people chewed for relief from pain, and the girl brought this leaf to the plant-vertebrate combinations when she had time; it seemed to make things a bit better for them. The extreme bitterness of the mercy leaf acts as built-in portion control, so she planted bushes of the leaf all around the captives and left them to it. She was busy running the farm alongside her father and mother. They tended the seedbeds and harvested the wheat, threshed it by hand and funneled it into sacks, then started again from the beginning. Once the wheat was threshed and in sacks, it was collected by the truckload. That was when money was handed over, but evidently not enough, as the girl and her parents were hungry almost all the time. So were the families who lived nearby and worked alongside them. Their farmstead was always behind; they'd been shown ominous regional comparison charts that highlighted this fact. The girl's mother—her name was Margot—did what she could to get more work out of everybody; she made gingerbread for her husband and for anyone else who asked for it; there was a great deal of mercy leaf in the gingerbread, so it helped. They worked on saints' days even though it was a sin.

The unrelenting work and the malnutrition hooped their spines; the girl would have walked along stooped over if her mother hadn't kept whacking her every time she displayed bad posture. Margot was the only person she knew who held life to a higher standard than that available. She'd seen the rest of the country and admitted that it was mostly farms in the rural areas and sprawling factories on the outskirts of small, pristine cities. The speed requirement in the factories made risk of injury equal to that of farming, so when asked how factory work would be better than farm work, all Margot could come up with was, **Fewer maggots?** It was assumed that Margot had come from factory stock, that she was accustomed to being famished and exhausted, and her assertions that things could be otherwise were mere daydreams. She would've set her co-farmers right if they'd asked her, but nobody did, so only her husband and daughter were aware she'd been born into a wealthy family that had got rich off the barely solvent. That's what was behind her demands to know why they toiled and toiled without profit; she knew a racket when she saw it.

Getting disowned had been something of an inevitability for Margot Leveque—her cousins took bets on the cause, and the one who bet "proposing marriage to a pauper" raked it in. Margot was ashamed of her father's squalid opportunism, and even if she hadn't had romantic notions about growing her own food, she'd still have fallen for her husband's good looks, rough courtesy, and self-reliance. She felt like an ant that had somehow lassoed a mountain. Simple Simon Lee. She forsook her mansion for the fields he oversaw and soon learned that the farm was his captor and hers, unreliable units of manpower that they were. The wheat was weighed upon collection, and the rate they were paid was sharply cut if the grain weighed any less than the previous time. Week after week of throwing every single grain that could be scraped up onto that scale, and week after week they fell short. By the time Harriet was born, Margot hated Simon's guts. Margot's father, Zahir Leveque, had foreseen it: **So you asked him to marry you? And he said yes? Hilarious. You're going to want to go back in time and do whatever else it takes to fix**

that. Don't be silly; I'm not going to do anything to either of you! You'll reach that point all by yourself. Margot had told him he didn't actually know her that well, but it turned out he did.

Simon Lee remained keen on Margot, who was equal parts propriety and slightly frightening candor. Simon's bride was rural-pageant-winner pretty—fresh-faced, with a trim figure—but good luck getting her to sign on as a role model. Simon found her spectacular, and she had time for everybody but him. He picked wild flowers for her. He ran her baths and insisted she take half his food rations, rose earlier to begin Margot's share of the work so she could sleep longer. Such was his care before, during, and long after Margot Lee's pregnancy, and still she hated him so much she could only look at him out of the corners of her eyes. This was a state of affairs that their daughter could hardly have guessed at if she hadn't been right there in the middle of it all. The closest Harriet can get to comprehending it is this: the circumstances of the farmstead families were dictated by a person, a theoretical person, a corporate letterhead, really. Whatever the thing or person was, it had never met them and most likely didn't know their names or what they looked like. The Lees, Cooks, Coopers, and Parkers farmed in exchange for places where they could live together in between attempts to meet this theoretical person's ever-varying requirements, requirements that went beyond the fantastic and left the realms of reality altogether. The theoretical person may have noticed that they were human, but if it had, that was of no importance. There's no way you can treat people like this without earning hatred, so the least this theoretical person could do was accept the hatred that was due. But no, the farms' owner(s) remained in the subjective distance and the Simple Simons took the blame instead. That, too, was made part of their work. The dodge was magnificent in its totality.

"Oh," says the doll named Prim. She's lying flat on her stomach now; she rests her elbows on Harriet's crossed knees for a moment. "I wouldn't feel too bad about it, Mother-of-Perdita. Didn't you say the mercy leaf could only be taken in small doses when eaten raw? I think it's safe to assume Simple Simon was being extra nice so Margot would make him more mercy-leaf gingerbread. She probably sensed the change in motive and was hating that more than she was hating him."

"Hmmm . . . thank you, Prim," Harriet says. They're speaking very slowly, so that Perdita can understand. "A change in motive. I hadn't considered it in that light. I think it was a mixture. He was definitely addicted. Definitely. At his most desperate he got . . . ah, he just troubled us. He'd emote. Pathos, wrath. It wasn't acting. Acting isn't coercive in that way, doesn't probe or test your response, doesn't cost you anything if you don't believe it. This was more like lying, but with affect instead of words. There were these cascades of emotion we had to respond to at once, and it all looked and sounded like the end of his world and ours, until you caught this icy strategy in the way he fine-tuned his tone, working out what pitch to speak at. And it all fell apart once the objective had been reached. He'd stop mid-sob and stuff the gingerbread in. He wasn't the only one. The things some of the Coopers tried! Margot overlooked most of that, but Dad . . . I was there . . . she'd wipe her hands after touching anything he'd touched. He'd look at me to see if I'd seen, and I'd run over and try to distract him. Arm wrestling, or 'Guess What's in My Pocket?'—usually nothing. Or if it was hot, I'd fan him with the straw fan. Otherwise I'd play hairdresser and style him until he looked a fright. He'd always let me, and then he'd style my hair too, and we'd go out and put on a sunset fashion show for the crickets and the cicadas. I swear they went quiet when we started parading up and down. I'm saying that whatever else was fake, the kindness and the wanting us to stay together wasn't. I don't know why you need to know that, but you do . . ."

"You were on Margot's side, though," says Prim.

"Was I?!"

"Unquestionably. All you're demonstrating is that you know it was wrong to take sides, or that you feel bad for not taking his side."

Perdita scrambles across the bed, grabs a notepad and pen, and writes at length. Her hieroglyphs are passed around for analysis, but nobody can read them.

Harriet says: "I think it was more like what Sago was saying about being a figment of someone else's imagination. I thought I was part of her story and not part of his, and there didn't seem to be anything I could do about it."

Perdita jabs a finger at the notepad as if to say, **That's what I wrote.** She has firsthand experience of this, having asked who her father is to no avail.

But Prim says: "Come off it—you liked Margot best. You can't fool dolls, you know. Anyway, I probably won't interrupt anymore."

"**Probably**," says Lollipop.

By the age of fourteen, Harriet Lee had become presentable enough to pin a few hopes on. Margot wrote a letter to Zahir Leveque. It was an "I know you've disowned me, but you might be interested to hear that I have a son" letter. Margot was an only child, and her father was indeed interested to hear that she'd had a son. He'd long been preoccupied with the question of an heir and was tormented by the notion of some unworthy person getting their hands on his money after his death. Zahir Leveque was the founder of a numbers game with cash prizes beyond most Druhástranians' wildest dreams and rules nobody understood. You laid a wager not just on winning numbers but on a winning number of numbers. There could be three numbers, or there could be five, or seven. There were a few other numbers games in operation, but Zahir Leveque's appealed to hard-working, law-abiding, but none-theless impoverished stoics. Whether they won or not, the outcome of this game confirmed what they'd already suspected: The finer things in life aren't earned by working around the clock and doing everything you can to uphold the law. We're given to understand that such activities ought to be enough to do the trick, but they're not. You've got to be lucky too. Really, really lucky. This lesson was all the numbers-game stoics ever got from their ticket purchases; the winner was always a company employee who returned 90 percent of the cash prize the day after being publicly awarded it. The only Druhástranian numbers game that operated with integrity was the one that hardly anyone played because the tickets cost twice as much as the ones for Zahir Leveque's game. Plus newspapers and the other numbers-game magnates had decided to single out the honest game as the one that was rigged. This "rigged" game was fun to play, though—since the media wouldn't run the winning numbers, the company had to use alternative methods to announce them; this meant that players had to seek out clues all around them. Any string of nine numbers written on a wall or a pavement could correspond to the ticket you were carrying around that week. From time to time the company hired a jet to write the numbers in the sky, so on Thursday, winning-number day, ticket holders always looked up at frequent intervals so as not to miss anything. The majority of players who won that "rigged" prize never found out that they had. Other players were winners for five minutes, twenty, however long it took to run or take the bus to the nearest claims office, where they'd find out they were two weeks too late or that the number that matched the ticket was somebody's phone number and nothing to do with the prize at all. Yet the memory of that cartwheeling elation tended to permanently beglitter the players' outlook. They took other chances. Those who dialed the phone numbers they'd thought were winning sequences found commiseration on the other end, or a work lead for a jobless friend of theirs, or some pressing dilemma the caller could only resolve by drawing on an almost forgotten ability of theirs . . . things like that. The players are so few and far apart that they seldom meet, but when they do, they ask each other who or what is really behind the "rigged" numbers game. Even the official winners don't believe redistribution of cash is the game's true purpose.

We're sparing a lot more thought for the "rigged" game than Zahir Leveque did. He'd played it once, won big, and immediately disengaged from anything that didn't help his money grow. This made him so rich he couldn't believe how rich he was. He kept calling his bank and listening to the balances for all his accounts with a dreamy look on his face. Now if only he could share the joys of financial apotheosis with someone truly appreciative, someone who'd build on his accomplishments. Policymaking without popular mandate or even public awareness—that gave Z. L. a buzz, as did the certainty that any complaints made against him to the police would be mislaid, and that journalists might yap as much as they pleased but his name would never be mentioned in an unfavorable context in any law court in the country. His other favorite perk was the way the president rushed to return his calls if she missed them. All this would go to waste unless an appropriate heir could be found. He'd visited a lot of psychics back when he was just another lottery player, and most of their predictions clashed, but they'd all told him his lucky number was 1. This subliminally influenced his abandonment of any endeavor that wasn't immediately embraced as a success. Belief that his fortune was guided by the number 1 was also a source, perhaps **the** source, of Zahir Leveque's sneaking suspicion that all he did would die with him.

Mr. Leveque sent train fare and told Margot to bring her son over to the mansion so he could have a look. Margot assumed that her father would excuse her lie once grandfatherly feelings kicked in. Grandfatherly feelings didn't kick in. Harriet Lee looked up, Zahir Leveque looked down, and Z. L. saw no heir. Harriet curtsied. An amusingly zealous greeting, a cross between a curtsy and a bow, really—he'd never seen anybody curtsy so that their forehead touched the ground. But that was how the girl curtsied, and then she prattled on topics her mother must have coached her on. She asked him if he had hobbies.

No. Do you?

She recoiled. **Me? N-no . . .**

Zahir Leveque didn't like his daughter because she'd told him to his face that she'd give away half his fortune. His daughter's daughter was another matter: she'd get rid of it all. It wasn't that Harriet Lee would fritter away the Leveque fortune; he'd almost have preferred that. He didn't detect an above-average level of generosity in the girl, but she'd squander his wealth all the same. The trouble was she did not calculate. She did not calculate! Her stomach made the most extraordinary noises when she saw the afternoon tea he'd had laid out. Scones and buns, tarts and hot buttered toast. She didn't eat any of it. Nor did she drink the water; she only pretended to. He let her pantomime feast go on for a bit before asking her what was going on. **Not hungry?**

She said apologetically, **It's because I don't like you.**

He was displeased. Fourteen is too old not to have some inkling of diplomacy. But she really did seem to wish she felt differently.

Well, my girl—do you think you're going to like everybody you share a meal with? There are

a lot of good things you won't get to try if you go on this way.

Zahir handed Harriet a plateful of sweet pastries with a magnanimous flourish. She passed them on to her mother, her gaze lingering mournfully on the flakiest puff. But all she said was: **Yes, I suppose you're right.**

To say that Harriet didn't calculate wasn't quite correct—she did. But there was some sort of bonfire in her brain. Her calculations were tossed onto the flames within seconds of being made, and this must be what lit those enormous eyes of hers. The pair were sent back to the wheat fields, where Simon had discovered that Margot hadn't packed for a short visit to the city. Margot had packed as if leaving forever, and she would have done, without a word of regret or explanation. This marked the beginning of Simon's own disillusionment with his hardship-averse wife.

"There's something you left out just now," Sago says fearfully. "You can't go thinking of things and then leaving them out—I don't like it! This is why I didn't want to hear a bedtime story, this is why . . ." The rest is muffled, as Prim has inched over to her and covered her mouth.

"Mind telling us what it was you were thinking of?" Bonnie asks, leaf-fingers swirling over Sago's back. She's drawing perfect circles that spin Sago into stillness.

"I was only thinking," says Harriet, "of something that Margot doesn't know that I know. I had to use the WC . . . don't know why, when I didn't drink anything there . . . anyway, I heard them talking on the landing below. Granddad must've decided that somebody who'd only give away half his fortune was better than nothing. He asked Margot to stay. He told her she could remarry and have another go at bringing someone worthwhile into the world; I gathered from that that if she agreed, I'd be sent back to the farm on my own. Margot didn't even pause. Granddad made his suggestion, and she said—"

Harriet's sentence goes unfinished long enough for Perdita to cover a page of her notepad with question marks.

"Sorry, I was just wondering whether or not to come up with something that sounds like a Margotism so that you would feel you've understood something about her. Something that helps you conclude that relationships are more important to her than money."

"But?" asks Prim.

"But . . . Z. L. wouldn't have bothered saying what he did if the odds hadn't been in favor of her taking him up on it. Money actually is a priority for my mother . . . you'll see later on . . ."

"So the truth is?" asks Sago.

The truth is that when Zahir Leveque suggested Margot stay and Harriet go, Margot simply said: **Bye then.** Unfortunately it was impossible to leave immediately, as Harriet hadn't yet come back downstairs. So Margot made a little conversation.

By the way, where's Mum? I wanted to see her.

She's in prison.

Prison?!

Yes, for tax evasion, the greedy little minx.

That's just the way things turn out for you if you ask the likes of Zahir Leveque for a divorce. The mother hadn't mentioned her change of address in her letters, and the daughter never looked at postmarks. The divorce was going ahead, though. Mrs. Leveque had told Margot that much. Margot talked about the weather for a while; then a new question occurred to her.

Who's in charge of the farm I live on?

Zahir told his daughter the name of the theoretical person named on the farmstead company letterhead.

No. You know what I mean. The owner.

It was funny Margot had brought this up, as the

owner was actually a relative of sorts . . . **There's this distant cousin of your mother's . . . three times removed, or something like that . . .**

And that cousin owns the farm?

No, his wife does. Clio Kercheval.

Home was seventeen long credential checks and a short train ride away. It was good that they'd brought such massive trunks along, because all the seats on the train were full. Harriet looked out at factory after fenced factory. The fences were low, so it didn't seem as if the factory owners were that bothered about people escaping.

Mother, what do they make in the factories?

Almost anything you can think of.

Margot asked Harriet to write down the names of everybody who worked alongside them at the farm—she said she wanted to think about them all, and she was sure Harriet would remember. She'd felt guilty for having put Harriet through the ordeal of learning to read and then not providing adequate reading material. There was Zola, and there were farmers' almanacs, and that was it. Harriet took to both; they were actually respectable options as far as variety was concerned. This is why, as an adult, she drives Perdita up the wall with her constitutional inability to discuss fiction without making reference to **Les**

Rougon-Macquart. Worse still, poetry, plays, and nonfiction never escape comparison to the farmers' almanacs. Harriet read more voraciously than Simon and Margot ever had. They discouraged this; she'd be so bored once she ran out of texts that were new to her. She surprised them with the discovery that once an avid reader runs out of books, she reads people. Harriet read everybody she met, and when she met them again, she reread them.

Harriet was none too impressed by Margot's appraisal of her, having seen and heard plenty of parental overstatement on the farmstead. Still, not wanting to disappoint her mother, Harriet listed farmstead names. Some of them were made up, just for fun, and when she'd finished Margot crossed out all the made-up names, then read the list again.

You haven't forgotten anybody; they're all there.

Harriet was greatly relieved by this, though she couldn't have said why. But back at the farm, as they passed the cottages where the Cook family lived, the jack-in-the-box sprang out for the first time in ages, his peeling skull pummelling the air: **HA HA HA, HA HA HA**. And later that night Harriet's list was in Simon's hands, accusing him and keeping him from sleep.

Margot had told him she'd come back because she had nowhere else to go. There was the cottage and there was the mansion and no place in between. He answered: **But I thought we . . . I thought we could . . .**

As he spoke, her mouth moved too, only barely suppressing mimicry. **I thought we, I thought we could.** With each generation the Lees grew poorer and more dutiful. So did their co-farmers, the Parkers, the Coopers, and the Cooks. They didn't know how to change anything. They only knew how to continue.

So we'll come to nothing, Simon said. Not to Harriet, who stood before him, but to the list of names, of which Harriet's was only one.

Or—not quite nothing—a few additions to somebody's wardrobe, or a Catherine wheel window in some mansion a few miles from here. That was the true end their acts pertained to, the result of everything they thought they did for each other's sake. Each breath they drew condoned this end. On the upside, his part in it wouldn't go on for very much longer. Like his parents and their parents, there was little likelihood of living past the age of fifty. That's how he'd found the nerve to marry Margot even though it seemed likely they'd make each other terribly unhappy sooner rather than later.

Simon said: **Come here, Harriet Leveque.**

That wasn't her name. Also, the look in his eyes suggested it wouldn't be a good name for her to suddenly answer to. He lunged at her, and she sidestepped. Lunge, sidestep, lunge, sidestep, but she didn't run; she had to stay—it was this Harriet Leveque who had to leave them. Finally, he seemed to grow drowsy or to awake—he rubbed his eyes: **Harriet, I'm sorry, I . . .** and he walked toward the closed door of the bedroom he shared with Margot, his steps very slow—it didn't seem as if he wanted to go in, but he was waiting for a better idea to occur to him. He placed a hand on the doorknob but didn't turn it. Margot might very well have locked him out, and it looked to Harriet as if he was afraid of that. Simon Lee held the doorknob for another moment, held it gingerly, as if it would break in his hand, and then he left the cottage. Harriet followed him through the fields with a flashlight and blankets; he was clearing space with his hands and feet, squinting up at the crescent moon and thinking about where the sun would be when it rose. He was looking for a good place to lie down, and not necessarily just for the night, a good place to just lie down with no thought of standing up again. When Harriet saw that her father had curled up on the ground with fronds of mercy leaf flattened beneath him, she waited until she heard him snore before creeping over with three blankets, which he accepted wordlessly, without looking at her. And yet he asked her not to go. He kept telling her he couldn't sleep, and it worried her very much that he choked out those words even as he slept. So she had no choice but to watch him until morning, when the two of them were surrounded by combine harvesters chugging along with only a slight modification to their preordained paths. Then Harriet Lee returned to her mother, who'd just completed a particularly large batch of gingerbread by way of neighborly apology for any nocturnal disturbance.

GINGERBREAD BAKED TO THE Lee recipe takes at least three days to really come into its own. Once that had happened, Harriet went from cottage to cottage doling out gingerbread. Only the very young and the very old were at home, looking after one another. Harriet heard someone say that Simon should've married Gwen Cook instead of

Margot. This was muttered when Harriet's back
was turned, so she didn't see who said it, and when
she looked over her shoulder, there was no one
there. Whoever it was, they were probably right.
Gwen Cook was a gentle and capable woman who
mainly handled grain storage, and it was hard
to imagine her stirring up an atmosphere as foul
as the one that festered in the Lee home at that
time. Harriet's parents kept trying to kill each
other. You couldn't tell from listening to what they
said, but they were tearing each other limb from
limb. They snarled at each other and smiled at
Harriet, snarled and then smiled . . . she shud-
dered to think of it and sought out silver linings.
Let's see: there was the gingerbread, and the ease
it brought. But she didn't even feel she could argue
that there wouldn't be any gingerbread if her
mother hadn't come to the farmstead. The recipe
had been right there in Simon's cottage when
Margot arrived. Gwen Cook (or any other alternative bride) could get just as good results from
it as Margot did. Gwen and Simon's daughter
or son would've delivered gingerbread exactly as
Harriet did, obediently refraining from tasting it
as Harriet did. They'd be a Lee, after all.

She had one more cottage to visit: Maggie
Parker's, in the far west. Then she'd join the other

kids of working age: Thibault, Titus, and Dottie Cooper (Dottie flew into rages if you called her Turandot); the Cook cousins, Erzurum (Zu for short), Elsa, Atif, and Nathan; and Maggie Parker's grandsons, Raphael and Jiaolong, the latter of whom really did look like a dragon, especially about the eyebrows.

Harriet passed an array of plant-vertebrate combinations. There were two new ones, droopy-eared rabbits. She watered them with the watering can she left out for rainfall. She passed a cabbage patch and a carrot patch, cottages, cottages, a miniature crop circle. Sparrows have such an appetite for grain that she was supposed to chase away any sparrows she saw, but she asked them what the crop circle depicted. **What's that you say? I really don't want to know? So you sparrows are just going to eat all you want and not even spy for anybody . . . ?**

Harriet passed a bucketful of muddy boots and a winnowing fan she picked up as a bargaining chip for when its owner, probably Nathan or Thibault, realized he'd lost it. She passed a willow-cane carriage sans horses (a lesser landmark), Gretel's Well, more plant-vertebrate combinations, almost there . . .

The sun set. The wheat field had done it again, stolen the afternoon. Harriet had already missed the threshing-floor sweep. Maggie Parker was the hospitable type, and her family had bred homing pigeons for just under a century, though the pigeons' homing ability seemed to lessen by the generation. That or the Parkers' talent for training them. The three Maggie herself had raised were a washout—it had been four years since Maggie had accepted a challenge from a pigeon breeder on the neighboring farmstead and released her birds in the capital city. As yet none of the Parker pigeons had returned to their nests, so the other pigeon breeder won by default, and Maggie was probably the only Parker not to view this incident as the unmentionable end to a grand legacy. By the time Harriet had drunk half a jumbo pot of tea and heard some tales from the annals of Parker's Pigeon Post, they'd be well into nighttime. But it wasn't just that. The darker it got, the sharper Harriet's senses grew, and the sharper Harriet's senses grew, the better the gingerbread smelled. Rich, sweet embers, nourishment of djinns and other fire-eaters. Harriet in the waning light, with only the wheat and the crickets and the cicadas to see. Maggie always tried to make

Harriet take a piece away with her, so there was no substantive distinction between taking one now and taking it at Maggie's bidding.

Just a piece? Harriet could eat the entire packet and go without recrimination for a while. Maggie wasn't expecting her this evening. She usually sent thank-you notes, but even the most scrupulous forget to send notes sometimes. (Zahir Leveque would've appreciated these calculations of Harriet's. Not to the extent that he'd reconsider her potential as a grandchild, but enough to make him wonder from time to time whether he'd written her off too quickly.) Margot had told Harriet to leave the gingerbread alone, though, and Harriet always did what her mother said. They had an agreement.

Harriet, do you like responsibility?

Me? N-no . . .

Thought not. I was the same when I was your age.

What did you do about it?

Tried to get other people to take responsibility for me.

And did they?

No. But I will for you, if you'd like.

Yes, please.

OK. I'll take responsibility for anything

you do on my say-so. But if you go against me, Harriet Lee—if you do something I expressly told you not to do—you have to handle the rest all by yourself. Do you understand?

Harriet's soul quaked. **I understand.**

Good.

(Is it really OK to talk to one's juniors like that? Looking back on it all, the this or thatness of Druhástrana aside, both Harriet's parents are a bit . . .

Perdita and the dolls unanimously concur: "Yeah, say no more.")

Goodbye to unconditional obedience; Harriet looked around for somewhere to sit as she savored the dawn of a new era. She fished her flashlight out of her bag and doubled back on her steps, all the way to the yawning mouth of Gretel's Well. Waxed paper rustled as she sat down, placed the packet of gingerbread on her lap, and pulled at the ribbon. Then:

Harriet! Harriet Lee!

Voices bawled her name from all four sectors. Torchlight and tractor beams danced across the fields, eager to expose a girl who'd hoped to rebel against her mother. She raised a hand against them, shielding her eyes, and with her other hand she dropped the gingerbread into the well.

A few things happened after that, and one of them was that the well murmured with delight. Not the well—Harriet almost fell in after the gingerbread—not the well itself. Someone within the well. The readjustment was no better than the initial impression.

The person inside the well said: **What?! I LOVE gingerbread. How did you know?**

Atif Cook and Jiaolong Parker were coming for Harriet. She heard them stomping and whooping. Dottie Cooper was only quiet because she was filling her lungs for another yell. And the person inside the well raised her head. It seemed there were footholds, or she was standing on something. The girl brandished the packet of gingerbread as if it was a newly won trophy.

This is super. I was just getting hungry. Hi, I'm Gretel. And you are . . . ?

Harriet didn't say a word.

The girl laughed uneasily. **Some sort of fairy godmother in training? Don't understand Druhástranian?**

Harriet still couldn't speak.

Oh, said the girl. **Right. I just popped out of this well and . . . right.**

She asked if Harriet was going to get into a flap. Harriet quickly turned her torch on and off. She saw that the girl was no more than three years older than her, if that. She saw that the girl was of similar build and skin color to her, but she didn't wear her hair in the dreadlocks typical to black peasants in Druhástrana. This girl's hair was gathered up into a bun of modest size. No freshly baked bun could look softer or be more of an impeccable sphere. Must be a city girl: Margot Lee had worn her hair like this until farmstead life had forced her to give up. Harriet flicked the flashlight on and off again to check a couple of more details: she coveted the girl's ever so slightly turned-up nose. And the girl had two pupils in each eye; that's why her eyes looked like bottomless lakes in the torchlight.

I'm not going to get into a flap, Harriet said. This fell under the remit of eventualities she had to deal with by herself if she went against Margot. She had expected to be able to taste the gingerbread first, so she did have to ask herself whether this wasn't a bit unjust . . .

HARRIET LEEEEEEEEEEEEE!

Harriet snatched the packet of gingerbread back from the girl's hand and stuffed it into the bottom of her bag.

The girl grabbed her wrist. **Better give that back! What kind of person . . .**

Yes, let's talk about different kinds of people. Why don't we start with the kind of person who lives in a well, Harriet hissed.

Gretel said she liked a good riddle but would rather have her gingerbread back. **You want me to pay something, don't you? But I haven't got any money on me at the moment.**

Shhhh!

I'll pay later. I honestly, honestly will. You have my word.

There were echoes in the well backing up everything the girl said, but Harriet meant to have her gingerbread even if she had to battle demons for it. Gretel made one last attempt to snatch Harriet's bag, then disappeared from direct view just as Nat Cooper, Jiaolong's father, appeared.

Harriet Lee, you've a visitor at home and your mother wants you.

Is that all? Who is it?

Some Mrs. Moneybags. Funny thing, though . . . she's got all these sweaty men in suits combing the fields. Asked if I could help them with anything and got told, "No you can't." That where you've been all afternoon? Digging up buried treasure?

6

DOTTIE COOPER AND JIAOLONG PARKER RAN ahead shouting, **Found her, found her**, and Atif Cook held her hand as they walked home. Handsome, ironical Atif, who only ever looked at Harriet when he received extrasensory notification of her being about to fall over or spurt milk from her nose.

Atif, Harriet said. **Why are you holding my hand?**

He didn't really answer her question. He said

she smelled really good. Maybe he thought that was an answer. He seemed to be in a receptive mood, so she tried to place a "hypothetical" Gretel's Well scenario before him. What characteristics could one anticipate in a being that lived in a well?

Atif wasn't interested. **There's no story about Gretel's Well. Now if this was about the Giant's Clog, or Mr. Jack-in-the-Box, or even about Marco, Chris, and Francisca Drake—you know, Maggie Parker's pigeons . . . we think those birds are still alive somewhere. It was such a simple route, and they were so carefully trained that there are really only two things that could've stopped them coming home to roost years ago.**

Having put in some time searching for Maggie's pigeons among the farmstead's plant-vertebrate combinations, Harriet gave in: **Two options . . . are we including Maggie's envious kidnap theory?**

No, we're not—nobody buys that. The first possibility is that they got captured by the military and have been turned into war pigeons.

Oh, come on.

It has been known to happen. The second possibility is extraterrestrial interference . . . you smell really, really good. Did I already say that?

Atif lifted her hand and gnashed his teeth,

playacting that he was eating her up. Harriet shook him off and ran indoors.

CLIO KERCHEVAL DIDN'T LOOK like a Mrs. Moneybags to Harriet, but she was sitting bare-foot on the sitting-room floor when Harriet came in, so perhaps it had been her shoes that gave her away. She drew Harriet into her arms and said, **How beautiful, how beautiful, she does you both proud.** Both Margot and Simon looked immensely relieved that Clio thought so. What if she hadn't approved; would they have kicked Harriet out?

Clio repeatedly declared admiration for Simon, who had been starved of it so long he hadn't the faintest idea how to cope with this surfeit and began a detailed discourse on co-farmers of his who were much better than him. Nat Cooper could work for longer without a break; Vasily Parker never took a day off; Paul Cook's mustache was indisputably superior. Margot offered Clio more gingerbread. Clio was pleased to accept, and then it was Margot's turn to be told how wonder-ful she was. Was Margot absolutely **sure** the wheat wasn't food-grade . . . it tasted so very like . . . Clio talked breathlessly and fast, so that nobody could interrupt her even if they wanted to. You could only receive her sentiments, all of which were warm and cozy. Clio was the same kind of perky-pretty as Harriet's mother, her hair in a bob that flipped out around her dangly earrings, and all this was incongruous with the fact that she was the owner of the farmstead. She was the theoretical person who limited at least four families' ability to thrive. Harriet spent most of the evening waiting for Simon and Margot to gang up on Clio or to pursue the appeals they and their co-farmers had made in their many letters to her, beseeching letters many pages long. They could also have asked Clio how many farms she owned. Simon or Margot didn't do any of those things. They told Clio she could sleep in Harriet's room, no bother, it was so late, and she was a cousin, after all. Clio and Margot talked about people Margot used to know. Everybody was doing well.

Harriet, aren't you having any of this?

Harriet ate a piece of gingerbread and tingled all over. It was a square meal and a good night's sleep and a long, blood-spattered howl at the moon rolled into one. She took another piece, and another, avoiding her mother's laser stare.

We must try to save some for Gretel, Clio said,

snatching one more piece before they all vanished. **My daughter, you know. You'll meet her once she's found.**

She ran away? Harriet asked, trying her very best not to look like someone who'd already met the missing girl.

Oh no. Not really. I wouldn't put it like that. She's just hard to keep up with. But you'll meet her very soon. I just know she'll love you. You're a lovable lamb.

Clio Kercheval bore no real physical resemblance to the girl in Gretel's Well, but she talked like her. Bright, innocuous, and a little too deliberate to be truly naive. That's how a woman might distract you from observing her level of experience and how a girl might distract you from observing her lack of it. Harriet thought of Gretel burrowed at the bottom of a cold, deep well, hungry and alone, her begging mistaken for bargaining.

At about two in the morning, when everyone in the cottage was asleep, Harriet crept out and made her way down to the well, proceeding with caution because of the men in suits she'd heard about. She saw a few of them inspecting footprints in the grass around the rusted loom and others delving into grain bins, which made her cross—that grain was now unsellable and would all have to go into gingerbread. Clio had said that her people knew what they were doing and Gretel would be found before morning, but there they were still looking for her. Harriet wasn't convinced the suited search party wanted to find the girl. They were disgruntled insomniacs who created disorder to spite others for sleeping.

Gretel wasn't hiding anymore. She sat with her back against the well's mouth, fingering the buttons of a thick jacket she hadn't been wearing when Harriet had first seen her.

You're the girl who came with something to eat?

Obviously.

OK, but so far you just turn up and shine a torch in my face. How am I supposed to know what you look like . . .

Harriet handed her torch to Gretel, who swung the light around for a couple of seconds and then handed the torch back without comment. She only shook her head a little before sticking a hand into the pocket of her dress and producing a square of paper, which she tore in half and held out. **This for the gingerbread.**

Is it money? There were numbers printed on it.

Half a lottery ticket. The prize is enough

wealth for two lifetimes, so if we win, you only need half.

And you need the other half, Gretel Kercheval? Gretel was too forward. Harriet had to push back, make her acknowledge that they were unacquainted.

Gretel would not acknowledge this. She rubbed the side of her nose. **So worried about the other half . . . seems like sharing's hard for you.**

She held out Harriet's half of the lottery ticket until she took it. She ate all the gingerbread and licked the crumbs out of the packet. As with Clio, the gingerbread didn't seem to transport her—she just liked the taste. She was thirsty, so she drank from the watering can Harriet brought her.

Why's this well called Gretel's Well?

They say . . .

They say . . . ?

They say there's no story here.

Ha! But there is.

Gretel took Harriet's torch again and shone it into the well. As usual the light didn't touch the bottom, so Harriet couldn't see anything. Gretel had to tell her: **Some girl died here.**

That's sad, Harriet said. **How long ago, do you think?**

A couple of hours ago, Gretel said.

Harriet laughed politely, but Gretel sighed and said: **No, seriously.**

Where one girl had sat with her back against the well's mouth there were now two, Harriet Lee and a murderous sprite with two pupils in each eye. Harriet regretted having left the cottage that night.

Gretel said: **Thinking about it now, that girl might have had an idea that she'd get a reward if she brought me to my mother. If that's what she thought, she was right. Mum loves giving rewards. But the girl was too rough. I'd almost left this farmstead and crossed over into the next, and then SWOOSH. I didn't know what was going on.**

So you . . . so you . . . did whatever you did and then dumped her in the well?

Yeah.

Gretel. I don't know what to say.

The body in the well was Dottie's, or Elsa's, or Zu's. They had lost Dottie and the mad, gory eloquence of the nosebleeds she had when most impassioned. Or one of their leaders was gone: Elsa, with her nascent showmanship and daredevil scythe-spinning. Zu and her tendency to draw them all together: **What do we think, lads?** If you were unwell or in some kind of disgrace with the other kids, Erzurum Cook would bring you a small restorative or a reset token. She'd say it was from everyone, and you knew Zu had talked them around.

She really scared me—Gretel demonstrated the grab. Harriet screamed.

How could she just suddenly grab you like that?

I'll tell them what I did in the morning, Gretel said, and Harriet said, **I'll tell them you were scared.**

They clung to each other. Did the death penalty apply to them?

If neither of us says anything, she won't be found, Harriet ventured, in a very small voice so the sound of her disloyalty to Elsa or Zu or Dottie wouldn't carry.

She'll be found all right, Gretel said. **There'll be a smell.**

We could cover the well mouth.

Too suspicious.

Is that her jacket you're wearing?

Yeah . . .

GRETEL.

She doesn't need it anymore.

A bit of an expert on needs, was Gretel. Harriet only needed half of a lottery prize; dead girls didn't

111

need warm jackets. Harriet didn't recognize the jacket; something in her still hoped that the well was empty and Gretel had just been exercising her strange sense of humor.

We could . . . move her. Harriet said it, since it didn't seem Gretel was ever going to. **We could hide her.**

Gretel looked as if she was having regrets too. Regrets that she'd confessed. **Thanks, but let's leave everything as it is for now.**

Are there footholds?

Ledges . . . you can go up and down them like a ladder. But you can't just—

Helpful Harriet knew where to find rope and rushed it over from the Parker family's barn. Time was of the essence. All Gretel had to do was pull on the rope when she felt a weight at the end of it. Harriet would follow the weight up and hold her . . . **it** . . . when Gretel was tired.

Harriet, Gretel said. **I don't make jokes. There's a body down there. And once you come close to it, you'll know you can't move it or hide it. You're going to get upset.**

By the time Harriet lost sight of Gretel's livid face, her end of the rope had already slipped out of her hand. **See you at the bottom.** She stopped looking up and concentrated on the torch that spilled light at her feet. Just enough for her to get to the next ledge, and the next, provided she didn't misjudge distance. Some of the ledges were sticky, and some crumbled beneath one heel so she had to slot her fingers into the earthy gaps in the brickwork of the wall while her foot sought out a new outcrop. The temperature decreased as she descended. She lost feeling in her fingers and toes and kept casting her torchlight back onto ledges she'd just left, checking that she hadn't left any behind (fingers, toes). She reached out to touch the rope that ran down alongside her, praying that Gretel wouldn't drop it. She couldn't hear anything from the world above, but she heard a hectic pitter-patter around her, marathons hurtled through as only many-legged can. And she heard Dottie below, calling out: **Who's there? Don't—don't—**

Turandot Cooper. Dottie. Relief made her careless. She missed a foothold, pedaled air, and caught her torch before it followed the rope. **It's me. I'll be there in a minute. It's all right, Dottie.**

The remainder of her descent took longer than the minute she'd promised, but they kept calling out to each other:

You came for me, Harriet, you came for me.

You're OK, Dottie? Are you hurt anywhere?

Didn't think anybody would come—because there's no story—

Somebody told me there was. Are you hurt anywhere?

Dunno—everything's sort of jumping and down. Harriet, there's a bad girl up there.

Dottie's form swam into view, and Harriet stepped down onto a springy amalgam of moss and sneakily discarded mattress. **Careful**, Dottie said, and the floor swelled and knocked Harriet's feet out from under her; it was no floor, but a bed of slugs and soft-shelled organisms shiny with filth. She crawled the rest of the way, and Dottie flung both arms around her neck. So her arms were all right. There was a nasty cut on the side of her head and her left leg was sprained, if not outright broken. Harriet rummaged for their end of the rope and tied it around Dottie's waist. Slow work for numb fingers, but she got the knots corset-tight, chattering away so as to obscure the fact that they were depending on the girl who'd sent Dottie down here to haul her up again. It was so cold that they blew steam as they spoke, anonymizing each other's features. Harriet jerked the rope. **Oi**, she screamed, careful not to use any names. **Oi, you—start pulling!** She didn't have much hope of being heard. Dottie had already shouted herself hoarse. And Gretel hadn't actually agreed to anything.

Then Dottie went **hyuuuurgh** as she flew up five or six ledges above Harriet's head, higher, and higher still, each elevation a feat of bad-tempered strength. Harriet climbed up after her, singing. Her torchlight battery died halfway up, and she sang louder.

7

DOTTIE WAS TOLD SHE COULDN'T JUST LURK around in the night grabbing people, and Gretel was told off for . . . Clio didn't even know where to begin at first, but once she warmed to the theme, she managed to come up with a catalog of Gretel's "simply **bloodcurdling**" character defects. Both Dottie and Gretel resented the criticism and transmitted malice in each other's direction when their parents weren't looking:

You'll wish you left me down there.

You'll wish you'd stayed down there.

At the end of her diatribe, Clio cried: **Oh, Gretel! Has Mama been too cross with you? It's only because I do so love you and we are among strangers who don't know what an angel you are really! Gretel, don't cry . . .**

I'm not crying, Gretel said. She really wasn't. At all.

Margot and Simon looked Gretel over as Clio expounded on the girl's sensitive nature, opposing every point she'd just made in her rant of two minutes ago. Then Margot tucked her arm around Harriet and said, **Hmmm.**

Dottie had been bashed on the head so hard she'd lost her sense of smell. Gretel was informed of this and felt remorse when Clio reminded her that sense of smell and ability to discern and distinguish flavor are linked. Yes, Gretel felt remorse, but she didn't say so. She would only say, **Oh well.** She'd pulled Dottie up, hadn't she? What more did everybody want from her? Also the expensive doctor Clio sent for was of the opinion that Dottie's sensory impairment was temporary, if of indefinite duration.

Gretel's double pupils were evenly spaced, so it was possible to be disturbed by them without knowing quite what you were getting disturbed

by. The effect was clearer than the cause: you felt
your sight blurring when you made eye contact
with her, and most interpreted this is as a prelude
to some act of spectral thuggery. The kids stared
at Gretel's clothes and the way she hopped and
skipped all over the place; all that spare energy.
There was a lot of bad feeling toward Clio and
her daughter, especially when it got out that Clio
owned the place. Clio had to act fast to nix the
growing possibility of a strike. It was the parents
she wanted onside; she'd noticed that on the
farmstead the childless went along with what
the parents decided. Past a certain age, childless
adults reverted to child status, and their co-
farmers patronized them and didn't really care
what they thought. Clio would've been treated
in a very similar way (only with more external
deference) had she not had Gretel in tow. But
since she was a mother, the farmstead parents accepted all the assumed character credentials that
entailed and heard Clio out as she proposed turning the Lee family gingerbread into a commercial
concern. That was the reason she'd paid a visit
to this farm, notable among the many farms she
owned only for its consistent underperformance.
As for how Clio had sensed an opportunity—that
was thanks to Margot Lee, this distant cousin by

marriage, who'd drawn on what she'd gleaned from their familial acquaintance and written directly to Clio urging her to think of the children. Margot had circled the names of all the children on that list made in Harriet's wonky handwriting, before putting it in the mail. This was how you got Clio's attention: she only really revered the callow. Youth was a state of utmost truthfulness and grace, and its ambassadors should be indulged, venerated as household deities, even. As for the ex-children, including Clio herself—well, it was a pity, but it couldn't be helped. And there were still ways to receive the blessings of youth. In fact, gingerbread was an ideal vehicle for returning its consumers to a certain moment in their lives, a time before right and wrong. And the key selling point would be that the gingerbread was produced by 100 percent genuine farmstead girls, raised among the very wheat that went into it.

Clio patted three scowling heads—Zu's, Dottie's, and Harriet's—and one smiling head—Elsa's. **Just let me borrow these four for a while and I'll make you all rich.**

Rich? Margot Lee asked a question about potential export sales that was intelligible only to her and Clio, an encrypted warning not to exaggerate. Time and time again Clio's audience had been refused the little they'd asked for; their confidence couldn't be secured with assurances of excess.

I meant there are prospects here for you, and for the girls. Stable ones that will grow more profitable in time. What you get out of it will really depend on what you put in.

Annie Cooper said: **Jiaolong and Nathan should go too. They're good cooks—**

I'm afraid it wouldn't work as well. There's something unhygienic about boys. Not once you get to know them as individuals, of course—no no no. Purely in terms of image. It's the sort of thing that decreases the appeal of an edible product.

Nathan and Jiaolong were annoyed to hear her talk like this. They weren't boys; they were fifteen-year-old men, and if this woman wasn't able to see that, then they couldn't be bothered with her. Zu put her arms around as many of her peers as she could gather—the fourteen- and fifteen-year-old adults and the fourteen- and fifteen-year-old kids alike. **What do we think, lads? Are girls yummier?**

The Coopers and half of the Cook delegation agreed to the plan. Zu Cook and Harriet Lee were to wait three months, long enough for Dottie Cooper to have recovered from being thrown down that well. Then the three girls would join

Clio Kercheval in the city and take the biscuit world by storm. But Elsa . . . Elsa wasn't allowed to go, even though she was the only one of them who was chic in dungarees and therefore seemed most suited to a city sojourn. Zu would willingly have swapped places with her cousin, but for both the parental decision was final. Elsa pleaded her case with all she had (the most memorable of the scenarios she enacted had farmstead life grinding to a halt as frustrated teenaged men fought over her, the only girl left), and this only reinforced her parents' conviction that they were too fond of her tomfoolery to let her go just yet.

As expected, Margot said. **I mean, look at who her mother is.**

Elsa's mother was Gwen Cook, the woman whom someone (Harriet still didn't know who) had suggested was a better match for Harriet's father than Harriet's mother was. Gwen's objection was guileless, maybe as guileless as Gwen herself.

Isn't it factory work that Kercheval woman's talking about? Our Elsa's not cut out for that.

HARRIET AND ZU convened in Dottie's bedroom to play nurse, fluffing the patient's pillow and tying

122

garlands of dried comfrey leaves around the plaster cast on her leg. Dottie had a little bouquet of sweet peas and mint leaves that her younger brother had picked for her, and she sniffed at it hopefully as all three agreed on Zu's summation that they'd help meals stretch further on the farmstead just by not being around. And it was daft not to jump at a chance to send money home.

Is Gretel definitely not here? Dottie asked, for the fifth or sixth time.

Seeming like someone in love, Harriet sang, but Dottie said: **There should be more songs about needing to know where someone is so you can take it easy and not have to keep thinking about your kicking leg being out of action. You're sure she's visiting another farmstead? I feel like she's right here, hiding again. Or she's around a corner plotting something. Don't you feel like she's listening in right now?**

THE NEXT MORNING HARRIET found Gretel standing outside the Lee cottage and surveying the clouds. **It's Thursday,** she said. She took out her half of the lottery ticket, and Harriet produced the other half. They held the two pieces together and hunted rogue numbers in the vicinity of Giant's Clog, Mr. Jack-in-the-Box (who did not emerge), and the rusted loom. The measuring tape wrapped around the loom stand had fallen down and looped in a skew-whiff sequence, but the numbers didn't match the ones they had.

As they went about, Gretel spied more numbers than Harriet did. Harriet wondered if it was because she was seeing things four ways, and she asked about that. Gretel said she didn't know what Harriet was talking about, so back at Gretel's Well Harriet rubbed a tile clean with the corner of her jumper and bade Gretel take a look at her own eyes.

Huh, said Gretel. **Four pupils. But there were only two last time I looked.**

She said her eyes hadn't been like that before she went down the well . . . "her" well.

Maybe I was completely different before. I'm not going in again, so I guess we'll never know.

Dottie and Harriet had gone farther in than Gretel had and they hadn't changed. Harriet put this to her point blank.

Oh, la, Gretel said. **So you didn't change. Is that anything to brag about? Three girls went down a well: two were made of gingerbread and one was—not . . .**

Made of gingerbread . . . this was insulting. And yet. And yet Harriet had heard Gretel's musings over consecutive platefuls of gingerbread: **Is there anything that this foodstuff lacks . . . is there any other food that so completely nourishes body and soul, any food more absolute in its embrace of the life-force of its eater . . . ?** Gretel Kercheval would defend the virtue of well-made gingerbread before any gourmet tribunal. So all right, insult wasn't really what Harriet had just taken from those words. It was more chagrin at being lumped in with Dottie. This was a wholly new chagrin, as being lumped in with Dottie and the other farmstead kids had been something she'd welcomed up until then. The newness of her chagrin may or may not have mirrored Gretel's upon hearing Harriet partition the three of them on the basis of cellular stability. They stood on opposite sides of the well, sad and angry, trying to decide whether to patch things up or whether this was just the way things were and therefore there was nothing to patch up.

What were you doing down there, anyway?

Point of view, said Gretel.

What?

I thought there might be a point of view down

there. Most of the time I just go here and there
without one. So.

Jiaolong, Nathan, and Atif walked past with
threshing forks over their shoulders. Harriet and
Gretel put away their lottery ticket halves,
and the Threshing Fork Three greeted Harriet.
Gretel they snubbed. It seemed to them that she'd
come to take the girls away. She'd tried to do it one
by one beginning with Dottie but had got caught
at first attempt, so then there was this drawing of
some bonkers distinction between the boys and
the girls, and now all the girls were going to go
and live with Gretel. They were sure Elsa would
end up going too. If the girls came back, if they did,
they'd come back awful, in lace shirts and satin
overalls and boots that fastened with gemstones.

The Threshing Fork Three walked on, and
Harriet and Gretel watched them go. There were
numbers shaved into the tangled hair on the backs
of their heads. Nathan, Thibault, and Atif were
never able to determine at what place, time, and
by whose hand those numbers were shaved, but
there were nine. Three numbers per head. Harriet
and Gretel got out their lottery ticket halves again.
They hadn't won. They hadn't won, but the shock
bulletin sent tremors of mirth through them. The
Threshing Fork Three heard snuffling and looked

back—what was Gretel up to . . . weeping croco-
dile tears, perchance? She and Harriet were rolling
around on the grass, crying with laughter. Harriet
already seemed to be a bit of a lost cause, but the
Threshing Fork Three had known her all her
life and were reluctant to give up on her. Nathan
went back, handed Harriet a threshing fork, and
reminded her that she wasn't a Miss Moneybags;
she was only a sidekick.

Gretel got up and demanded a threshing fork
too. The Threshing Fork Five got down to work
and had their share of the wheat ready for winnowing faster than ever before. There was even
time for a game of carrot-patch tag before Gretel
was bundled into a limousine, torn clothes and
all, leaving the other four draped around motley
items of farm machinery wheezing through what
felt very much like perforations in their breathing
apparatus. They'd kept up with her and it had felt
easy while they were keeping up. While they kept
up they were all child, fast and light, testing the
stretch and reach and pull of their forms and finding laughably little resistance. Falling so much as a
millimeter behind Gretel brought them up against
joint and bone and sinew.

8

HARRIET DIDN'T SLEEP WELL IN THE CITY. The dormitory was too hot. She sat up in bed and looked down the row of gently snoring girls, punched herself in the side of her head, and whispered: **What did you think this was going to be like, idiot? Did you think you'd have free time to tumble around Druhá City searching for lucky numbers with Gretel Kercheval?**

Back at the farmstead Gwen Cook had suspected the girls were getting roped into factory work, and it turned out they had been, but the nature of it was more diffuse than they'd imagined. Clio had collected thirty-three farmstead girls age fifteen and under, all of whom had a guileless look that complemented the simple goodness of the folk delicacy they mixed, baked, shoveled out of ovens, and boxed with handwritten labels. On weekends she kitted them out in dresses, petticoats, bonnets, and aprons and scattered them around what Harriet described in letters to Margot as an authenticity theme park. The house Harriet, Dottie, Zu, and the other Gingerbread Girls slept and worked in was cinnamon-colored and had a sugar-dusted effect to its roof and windowsills. The girls were too gaunt to be the legitimate inhabitants of a house like that, so Clio met with nutritionists, came up with a potion that guaranteed vigor, and had the girls eat seven meals a day. Seven bowls of vitamin- and mineral-enriched gruel that couldn't really be differentiated from hogfeed. The gruel ensured that the girls came across as the epitome of plump-cheeked country childhood in photos and in the documentaries and TV adverts. Their eyes and teeth sparkled, their skin was smooth, and their pigtails were extra-bushy. The gruel that took care of all this had a stomach-turning odor of rotten eggs and roasted rubber. There was envy toward Dottie, who supped her gruel with a tranquility of sorts. Her sense of smell hadn't yet returned. **Did that eerie brat do me a favor? I think she did . . .**

You had to finish the whole bowl. There was water to wash it down, and the mixture was so claggy you had to have a lot of that. If you rebelled, a matron came and brought you a new letter from some member of your family who was either bursting with loving pride in their miraculous breadwinner or anxiously awaiting your next pay packet or both. About three weeks in, Harriet and a few of the others twigged that Clio had a forger in her employ and the letters were faked. Harriet stopped writing home. The temperate wisdom of the replies she was receiving from "Margot" rang a lot of alarm bells for her even though the handwriting was an impeccable match. She could only assume that Margot was receiving reassuring missives from "Harriet" too. A lot of the girls didn't mind this: they found this mother Clio Kercheval had assigned to them was much better at cheering them on than their actual mothers were. The fake mother took more pride in them.

So none of the Gingerbread Girls were forced to do anything. Not forced, no, nobody could say that . . . it was more that there were frauds they helped perpetrate against themselves, hoaxes they somewhat willingly became beholden to. If being manipulated like that did your head in too much, you could run away, like Gretel did, but unlike Gretel, you wouldn't be welcomed back. Bearing this in mind the Gingerbread Girls stayed on and were sorted into different teams each weekend.

Team 1 was on in the afternoons, hosting tea parties on the third floor. Tasks: pouring tea, handing round gingerbread, giggling a lot, and conveying country sayings they'd memorized from a book. The book was almost certainly a parody, but Clio lost her temper when asked about it. **Things said with a pure heart are pure!**

There was a warren of kitchens on the second floor, and in the evenings Team 1 donned daisy-patterned hairnets and piped pink icing onto gingerbread figurines. They leaned so close to the gingerbread that this was where they'd have been in danger of depleting stock if it hadn't been for the perennial nausea induced by all the gruel they ate. Zu became an art-nouveau icing artist, blending her yearning for the forbidden into every embellishment. Gingerbread compasses were her speciality.

Team 2 played "Pass the Parcel," "Please, Mother, May I," or "What's the Time, Mr. Wolf?"

in the garden with other kids who were biding their time until their parents took them home. Team 2 always found it impossible to convince the visiting kids that they weren't robots.

Team 3 spent the afternoons concocting gingerbread lore in the library on the fourth floor. **Gifts of the Four Wise Men: Gold, Frankincense, Myrrh + Gingerbread . . .** In the evenings they hosted Breadcrumb Balls. They had no problem with the singing and choreographed dancing with Hansel dolls; after weeks of practice they had those bits down to a tee. But the bit where they had to skip around the grown-ups' chairs with their skirts shimmying wasn't easily done without flashing underwear. Some of the grown-ups didn't like that bit either, but a greater number had a good old stare. Might as well; they were allowed. With a "look but don't touch" rule, everybody knew where they stood. You could ask some of the older girls to jump higher and most obliged, looking convincingly abashed at their naughtiness. This wasn't done for tips—they didn't receive any—it was done out of determination to give their all to the gingerbread experience. The less idealistic Gingerbread Girls were free to refuse, but the worst they could say was "Fudge off," as Clio had a zero-tolerance policy toward swearing.

Another option for Breadcrumb Ball attendees was taking turns dressing in gray shock-haired wigs and ankle-length black gowns and chasing the girls around growling, "Give-me-Hansel-give-me-Hansel." **Stop it**, Zu said, the first time that happened. **Just . . . stop, OK? You can have him. Here.**

At the end the grown-ups would ask if that had been fun. They wanted to show that they were high-spirited and spontaneous, perhaps even a teensy bit unsafe to be with. They'd had what they remembered as carefree childhoods and wanted a reprise, or they'd had unhappy childhoods and wanted another chance. **Yes, we had fun, we are bona fide children and we think you're great, please come again soon.** That was the only permissible response. If you gave any other, you were sent home to be a drain on resources again: that was the biggest threat Clio had up her sleeve.

The girls' commitment to endorsing adults aged them a bit, but they were fine with it as long as they got to stay where they were. Failing to hack a cushy job as a professional child impersonator . . . that was a defeat too terrible for the girls to contemplate.

Besides, the cash cauldron was boiling over. City dwellers paid less tax than farmstead people, but they were subject to a Compulsory Purchase Law, which made sure all the overpriced farm and factory goods were sold. You could get a waiver if you bought Druhástranian Experiences like visiting the Gingerbread Girls instead. Some of the visitors asked, "Can't we have a sleepover with the girls? Can't you offer a package that involves staying here awhile?" and every other night a gang of bankers got drunk and tried to break in, smearing their faces against the windows and reciting the names of their first loves. Harriet held out her hands to them, and a matron cuffed her around the head: **Exactly what are you seeking to encourage right now?**

At their morning assemblies Clio told them they should feel flattered that people wanted to be with them. If you were a Gingerbread Girl, people found shelter in your company. At least, they did until you were sixteen and became an ex-child. Then you were to take on the role of a blue-and-white-uniformed matron and stay in the background.

Harriet wasn't homesick like Zu was, and she wasn't happy to be there like Dottie was.

Mrs. Kercheval.

Yes?

How's Gretel?

Gretel? Bless you. She's fine. Keeps bringing home new friends, all sorts, honestly . . .
her friends are my friends, but I do spend a lot
of time combing her for lice. Take for instance
this picturesque old man she brought home on
Saturday. Silk tie, bowler hat, and holes in the
soles of his shoes so big he kept stepping through
them and having to yank the shoe up after him
step by step. Of course as soon as she saw this
man Gretel couldn't think of anything she'd
rather do than spend the whole day helping him
search along the roadside for a bean. Yes, somebody had given Gretel's new friend a bean, and
that somebody had said: This bean will serve you
well. But Gretel's friend didn't want the bean . . .
I suppose it does put you in a mood when you
want someone to stay with you and get fobbed
off with a bean and a mysterious recommenda-
tion instead. He didn't want the bean, so he
went up the tallest building he could find and
he threw away the bean. Apparently he had
second thoughts and tried to catch it even as
it was falling, but it was gone. Almost immediately after that he started to have suspicions
that his bean wasn't like any other bean after all.
He went to all the supermarkets looking at the
dried beans they had. He looked at pictures of

beans in encyclopedias. MY bean's an altogether different shape and color . . . I thought it was just a nothing bean, but it isn't, it's a bean of influence and I want it back! I should never have let it go. Whatever possessed me, **he said.** It was just such a sullen, shriveled little lump . . . I should have given it loving care . . . all that is living thrives on loving care . . . **On and on about that bean. Gretel brought him home for dinner and he sat there going,** bean bean bean, **and I said I thought he should track down the person who gave him the bean and ask for another one—a good excuse to reopen a conversation, at least—and he said,** Oh do you think that would work, **and was just becoming a tad more sensible when Gretel stepped up to the dinner table with a little button box. She had some buttons in there and he was all** yes yes, very nice, thank you for showing me these buttons, **but she also had his bean! He was beside himself. He'd been searching for years. She found it as she was just going about here and there, as she does, and she'd recognized his description so she brought him home while she checked. I must admit it did look like the sort of bean you should keep close by.**

Has he planted it, the bean? Will he?

Not he. It's a scoundrel's bean, for people

who know they'll be leaving an unbearable gap behind them and have the cheek to try to fill it in in advance. "Here's a bean that'll serve you well," my foot. He'll keep it until he needs to use it the way it was used on him . . .

Oh no, that's not it at all. The person who gave him the bean has been waiting for him to plant it . . .

Well, you would say that, wouldn't you, darling, with your background? Planting as a solution for everything. I'd try to find out for you, but with Gretel it's another weekend, another searcher . . .

Dottie had made two new friends, Rosolio and Cinnabar: when they got bored during afternoon tea they'd pick a guest they felt they could nudge out of his or her right mind—a man or woman of straitlaced appearance, a black-coffee drinker with too much discipline to reach for anything sweet. Dottie, Rosolio, and Cinnabar selected that person and locked eyes on them as they nibbled away at their gingerbread men. Systematic dismemberment was necessary, as Dottie preferred the head, Rosolio the legs, and Cinnabar the torso. They fed one another accordingly, pecking crumbs out of one another's hands like fiendish hatchlings, never for a moment taking their eyes off their target. **We don't know what we're doing . . . or perhaps we do, a little . . . anyway, it's to please you.** This was how they made a tea party guest theirs. **Back again?** the other girls asked joyfully, as the captive fumbled toward the chair with the best view. Elsa Cook would've been amazed by this: she operated on the principle that spectators only grew attached to you if they saw you put in direct danger. But also, who would've thought Dottie of the Vesuvian nosebleeds had coquetry in her too?

Zu pushed the product itself and nothing else. Her no-frills desperation had its own efficacy—like the Little Matchstick Girl, but with gingerbread. She kept getting her pay docked for being below the ideal weight for her height. She couldn't keep the gruel down, so every meal was a catch-up meal for her. Two bowls at a time. Spooning up the gruel took too long; Zu just tipped back her head and slopped the gruel straight in.

Harriet could stomach any mess, but she was Margot-sick. The symptoms were various and sometimes debilitating; tearfulness, being intensely critical of people for not laughing the way Margot did or hugging her the way Margot did or interrupting people mid-story in order to predict what they were going to say next with a fifty-fifty success rate the way Margot did. There was also a lot of desultory raising and dropping of the arms, as if seeking a hold, as if the whole lopsided world was just a badly hung picture frame she could tilt back into balance. She missed Simon and Elsa and her favorites among the farmstead boys too, but they could all manage without her. Still, Harriet had been counting the contents of the pay packets she'd held on to ever since she'd realized Margot's letters weren't from Margot. Six months in, Harriet and Zu were already a quarter of the way toward the amount they wanted to make before retiring. Nobody at the farmstead would recognize them at first. They could pretend to be tourists, city mademoiselles who suddenly made it rain with gifts and letters from Dottie. They would make a down payment on the farmstead: land owned by kids was an idea that would probably appeal to Clio.

The heat of the dormitory was a desert heat, so mirages kept Harriet awake. She shook off her blanket, and it clung to her leg for a moment, an itchy briar coiled around the skin there. She prodded the blanket with a sweaty toe and it fell to the floor. Three other girls already lay naked with their arms and legs splayed, not sleeping but staring up into the surveillance cameras above, challenging the matrons, security guards, and anybody else to get off on this. Zu had a theory that what they felt was some emanation of their combined body temperature and nestling in might be the only way to endure it. Harriet got out of bed. She walked out of the dormitory and up the boiled-sweets bedecked staircase, briefly returning for a cardigan when the chill hit her outside the dormitory door. This was their house, and they were free to roam it, watched all the time but not interacted with by ex-children unless they strayed into the no-no territory of being about to come to harm. Trying to leave the premises brought guards out so fast they seemed like holographic projections. Harriet checked the tearooms one by one on the off-chance that some gingerbread had been left out, but she knew how thoroughly the premises were purged of the stuff as soon as the guests left. Clio had told them over and over again about how when she was a girl a school friend of hers had given her a gingerbread mansion as a keepsake and how beautiful the little mansion had been until some cockroaches moved in and ate it from the inside out.

The Topkapi tearoom was Harriet's favorite; she lifted the lids of the boxes stacked up between the table legs and stroked the pistachio-colored porcelain. All the cups and saucers were square, like pieces of Turkish delight. The teapots were too; there was one on the tabletop with tea still in it, since cockroaches didn't go for tea. Harriet drew open the gold-tasseled curtains, sipped her cold tea, and looked out over a city the girls only went out into whilst being ferried to and from the factory. Druhá City was as shiny and as loud as a rhinestone-studded rattle. And it was a Thursday, so Gretel would be out playing the numbers game under the night sky.

9

MARGOT HAD GIVEN HARRIET FIVE CITY commandments.

1. Make sure you eat enough.
2. Avoid getting sick; let people with colds fend for themselves.
3. Turn in no more and no less than a proper day's work.
4. Don't like Clio more than you like me.
5. See some sights if humanly possible.

The fifth command proved the trickiest to implement. One afternoon Harriet went into Clio Kercheval's office without knocking. Clio clicked her computer screensaver on in case Harriet came around the desk, and then she folded her hands together.

What can I do for you, er—Dottie.

Harriet shook her head.

Sorry, what can I do for you, Rosolio? Lyud . . . no? Camille? Child. What can I do for you, child?

Harriet petitioned Clio for a group trip to the city.

To the city? Clio patted her knee until Harriet inferred that she was supposed to come and sit on it. Harriet shook her head again. **I'm fourteen**, she said.

Well. What do you want to see in the city, fourteen-year-old?

Historical monuments? Or we could go to the zoo?

Listen, child—there's no need for you to see the city. The city would corrupt you.

Harriet had another go. **School, then. School would improve us.**

School is a greater corrupter than any city.

I'm really doing the best I can for you—in loco parentis, you know.

Oh, said Harriet. I think I'll go home, then.

You want to go home? Clio was thunderstruck. The most recent opinion poll had returned the results that going home was the last thing the girls wanted. What was going on here? Was Margot Leveque's kid negotiating? Clio may not have been able to remember the child's name, but she was one of the more convincing Gingerbread Girls, and her absence would induce no small loss of revenue. Harriet opened the office door. Clio jumped up and closed it again.

Don't be like that. I'll order textbooks, she said. Books from Gretel's curriculum. You can study from them, be your own teacher. And you can teach the others, if you'd like. You can all be home educated. What do you think? Is it a good compromise?

Harriet accepted. In the dormitory she gathered the girls around and told them she'd got Clio's permission to turn the Buckingham tearoom into a classroom for a couple of hours before they were due to head to the factory. They could gather around the tabletop held up by nutcracker soldiers and follow the National Curriculum with seed-pearl crowns set upon their studious heads. Nothing is impossible for royalty. The plan was unanimously agreed upon, but rousing the Gingerbread Girls the morning after the textbooks arrived was a different story. Harriet got called names and was told she'd better watch her back . . . so she let the sleepers sleep and relied on textbooks to help her transport other textbooks. They made good doorstops. She put down her notepad last. At four in the morning in the Buckingham tearoom, Harriet put on the crown that hung off the back of her wooden throne, stuck her hand into the pocket of her dressing gown in search of a pen, and found thirty-two folded notes. All were variations on **Go Harriet! Get that knowledge!** and **Sorry I'm so lazy ❤ ❤ ❤** and **Please forget what we said this morning . . . when it comes to solid-gold boffins we have no one but you.** Her friends knew themselves and had written these the night before.

The history textbooks were the ones Harriet had been most interested in, but the only ones available were all about the histories of other countries that had greater global relevance and the suspiciously bravura role Druhástrana had played in their fortunes. Humble Druhástrana, friend to all nations, forgotten by all in its own time of need (but when had that been?). All aggression against Druhástrana was unjust and ultimately unsuccessful; there beneath the national emblem (three black griffins with their backs turned atop a gray mountain) on the flag was the motto: **Never wounded, never wrong.** The referendum had been the only way to definitively withdraw from the so-called brotherhood of nations; let them see, yes, they'd all see how well they'd get on without all the contributions Druhástrana had made toward world peace . . . Harriet bent the textbook in half at the page she was reading and banged it against the tabletop, trying to shake some of the opinionation out of it. She was oppressed by this opinionation; each sentence threatened to turn her into a cynic by the time she reached the end of it. She turned to another textbook, on the history of England, and got on with that one a bit better, especially the bit of Druhástranian history the author had managed to slip in as an aside on referendums. The author asserted that the need for Druhástrana's Great Referendum (the one that had divorced it from all formal international relations and most informal ones too) had been brought about by a general taking of umbrage against all the foreigners who kept coming in and trying to propagate distracting inequalities, stuff about physical appearance and who people should and should not fancy and places of prayer that were better than others, or notions that the best people don't pray at all . . . Druhástranians didn't need any of that. What Druhástranians wanted was to keep things simple and concentrate on upholding financial inequality. Even that inequality could have been ironed out if the populace really wanted it, but singularity, the possibility of singularity, was something that the voting majority found impossible to sacrifice. **Ask any Druhástranian man or woman and he or she will admit this truth—** (Harriet did not admit this truth, but then she was neither man nor woman; she'd have to ask Margot sometime)—**the truth that he or she can find the strength to live out a lifetime under the most dire privations as long as there's a chance, however irrational, that he or she could someday stumble upon some abundance that's accompanied by the right to keep it all for himself. Or herself. Thus did Druhástrana turn away from the world, like those three black griffins we see on our flag, and if only we could see what lies before those griffins! What is it they've been watching over all these years? What could have kept them from turning to face us?**

After this the textbook author returned to a discussion of the Magna Carta and stuck to that, so Harriet dropped history and turned to maths and science and a handful of languages, English foremost. Clio tested her, neglecting to mention that the test papers were past exam papers for each subject. The difficulty was meant to be demoralizing, but Margot Leveque's kid got motivated by it instead. She stopped talking about going home and followed the applicable rules and guidelines with gusto. Harriet's logic was malleable regarding anything that wasn't a matter of the heart, and even when she was conscious of having been led into fallacy, it pleased her to reassemble her thoughts to order. It was the only way she could be sure they wouldn't go to waste.

Two things happened—one pleasant and one unpleasant.

The unpleasant thing: a busload of rail-thin farmstead girls came to the Gingerbread House for a visit. Clio wanted them to see how happy and nurtured and well clothed they'd be. The parents were wowed, but the farmstead girls were stone-faced. They gazed upon the Gingerbread Girls as you would some badly made counterfeit you'd bought at the same price as the original. The Gingerbread Girls trotted through all their farmstead reminiscences and led the visitors to the photo wall replete with images of them as they'd been when they'd first arrived. **Yes, that's really us! Ha ha, no—no replacements!** The farmstead girls paid no attention to the photos. They only had eyes, such cold and confrontational eyes, for the three-dimensional Gingerbread Girls standing right in front of them. And as soon as the grown-ups had wandered away to watch a slideshow presentation, the farmstead girls closed in. **What are your names?** said Dottie Cooper's crew. They were still trying to get a convivial atmosphere going. **Ours are—**

Shut up. The Gingerbread Girls were held down, their pigtails knelt on until they stopped struggling. Then the farmstead girls pinched them, pulled flesh and fat away from their arms and thighs and stomachs, and flicked it back into place. For a long while they didn't speak, just stuck their hands right inside the Gingerbread Girls' clothes and pinched them hard. Harriet looked up through the web of skeletal hands and into the eyes of one of the girls who was pinching her, trying to see if the girl was giving vent to anger or fulfilling curiosity or enjoying this in any other way, but those eyes told her nothing. The only thing Harriet would later be able to liken the pinching to was a beauty treatment given by a masseuse who was at the end of her shift and had already checked out mentally. Another girl placed her foot on Harriet's cheek and rolled her head back and forth in the mud. She seemed to be doing this so Harriet couldn't maintain eye contact. **Laugh**, the girl said. **Let the grown-ups know we're getting on.**

But they can see we're not getting on. There are security cameras, Harriet said, pointing. **There, there, there, there, there, and there.**

The farmstead girls waved at the cameras one by one, waved cheerfully, with both hands. **Laugh, I said.** Flaky-nailed fingers slid up the legholes of Harriet's knickers, into the armholes of her vest. Pinch, pinch, pinch. And Harriet laughed until she hit the happy note that released her head from football duty. One by one, the Gingerbread Girls giggled for dear life. The farmstead girls would probably have gone on administering pain by the thimbleful until the grown-ups were ready to see what they'd wrought, but Dottie's nose erupted, and it was their turn to be harrowed and perplexed, most of all by the fact that she kept up her squeaky laugh throughout. They fled.

After the farmstead group left, some cameramen arrived to film a documentary on Clio and the Gingerbread Girl Power phenomenon. Dottie missed out on TV stardom, laid up in the infirmary as she was, and her friend's "Violation of the Gingerbread Man" game just wasn't the same without her. The director of the documentary seemed to be under the impression that the Gingerbread Girls were a charity organization, that they had been rescued from neglect. How to explain that Clio had rescued them from her own neglect of their parents? And anyway they weren't confident that their current situation was a truly protected one. Their countryside counterparts came to chasten them for accepting treats, probed their bodies, and it all just ran along as part of the security-camera feed. Clio had seen what happened and said, "Agricultural peoples, you know," and "Child's play mirrors such powerful traditions . . ." The pinching reminded her of a fertility rite she'd seen abroad. The matrons and the older Gingerbread Girls no longer feigned comprehension as Clio ruminated aloud; they'd found that she liked a look of puzzlement better.

Abroad. Clio would always say "abroad" without naming a specific country; she'd never been anywhere. Interestingly (to Harriet), Clio Kercheval wasn't trying to fool anybody when she said things like this. She made no secret of being overbearing and having her eye on the money. In spite of everything—and there was a lot—Harriet did not dislike this woman, who was open about her requirements that the girls be healthy, good to one another, kind to those who sought their approval, and fond of her at all times. Clio was no liar, at least not in the sense in which Montaigne presents the act of lying as that of gainsaying the testimony of one's own knowledge. On the contrary, Clio never held back from full avowal of what she knew. But there was a problem with the information she was acting on—very little of it was true. Being neither mad nor sane, Clio Kercheval was just going to keep juggling her priorities at the same time as saying things like, "Oh, you girls were like celebrants in a fertility rite I saw abroad," and she was going to drive all her charges around the bend without the slightest blip in her own peace of mind. The director of the documentary had had cameras on Clio and Harriet as they talked without microphones, and being a connoisseur of the violent facial twitch, he got his sound team to mic them up and asked Harriet if she had anything to say to fans of the Gingerbread Girls. Harriet put her hands on her hips and fitted a smile over her teeth like a gum shield. And what did she say? She wouldn't watch the footage back even if you paid her, but it was something along these lines:

Come and see us! Look, but don't touch.

We'll always be here. We'll never grow up, and we're forever grateful that you picked us.

Please don't use that, Clio asked the cameramen, director, and everybody else on set. I mean . . . an unschooled country child coming out with these phrases in English . . . our patrons won't know what to think, they'll have fears we haven't been honest with them . . .

Harriet had spoken so fast that few non-native English speakers would've been able to understand what she'd said, but nobody on set asked her for a translation. A cameraman played Harriet's outburst back for Clio: **But doesn't it look wonderful? She's like a little fallen angel speaking in tongues!** Harriet did a long-distance money count, adding up the banknotes stuffed between the mattress she slept on and the bedframe. Wouldn't she regret it if she left without adding to them? She thought she'd regret reining herself in more. She clapped her hands and slapped her knees, turned toward Clio and then away, a derelict soul in a pink-and-white petticoat. The cameras kept rolling.

Look but don't touch. Look but DON'T TOUCH. Don't touch, don't touch.

The words were scuttling out of her mouth quicker than she could crunch down on them. One handclap per syllable. Remember, Clio, remember decay, remember that cockroaches ate your lovely gingerbread mansion, clicking their mandibles as they gnawed away the floor beneath them. She ran at Clio with her head down, but Clio made no retreat, and when Harriet thought to discomfit the woman by other means and wrapped her arms around her waist, Clio didn't recoil. She rested her chin on the top of Harriet's head.

If only Gretel was this affectionate, and this fond of studying the English language! Yes, let's cuddle, overtired little girl. You've had a long day. All your days are long. Don't film this, please. Yes, sorry, I do understand we're going to run into difficulties if I keep . . . can they have their dinner first and start again in an hour?

Up in the dormitory Zu and Rosolio made garters the girls could wear beneath their petticoats. **Let them come, let them come from the farms and try to pinch us again,** Rosolio raged as she sewed. **Who the fuck did they think they were dealing with? From now on we're all carrying gingerbread shivs, OK?**

You said it, Ros.

That's how it's got to be.

Zu's was the only voice of semi-dissent, and she

spoke without dropping a stitch: **Violence isn't the answer, but I'll make the shivs pretty at least.**

THOSE WHO REMEMBER that I said an unpleasant event was accompanied by a pleasant event might be thinking that the pleasant event had some sort of symbiotic link to the unpleasant event and that this is why it's worth entertaining foolish hopes even in the midst of having a bad experience that then gets retold to you as a good one. There are several fine verses concerning Hope, including two that tend to come to mind whenever I hear the word. Both are the work of poets named Emily who were alive around the same time, so you can't even say that one was channeling an Age of Pessimism. In one poem, hope is a wild, stubborn thing with feathers that darts into the lyric to be caressed on the understanding that nobody will try to tame it. In the other poem, hope is clammy and clinging and plays toxic mind games: **Like a false guard, false watch keeping / Still, in strife, she whispered peace / She would sing while I was weeping / If I listened, she would cease.** When you endure some poison in the hope that it'll give rise to its own antidote, on what terms does that hope come to you . . . ?

Anyway, in this particular case, the unpleasant event and the pleasant event had hardly anything to do with each other, so the jury's out. Harriet got the wrong idea at first too. She was summoned to Clio's office later on the very evening of the pinching incident, and, thinking that she was about to be banished, she only went downstairs after she'd stuffed all her pay packets into the pockets of the quaint patchwork coat that was part of a Gingerbread Girl's outdoor uniform. She remembered to knock, and Clio called, "Come in." The proprietor of the Gingerbread House was shrugging herself into her own coat—a fur one.

So you're Harriet? I mean—that's your name?
Yes.
I should've known. Well, let's go.
Go where?
Home with me, to dinner. Gretel said she wouldn't leave me alone if I forgot this time.

So HARRIET saw some sights after all, albeit through the rose-tinted windows of Clio's limousine. She saw the gates of the zoo and the gates of the science museum, the gates of the presidential palace, the gates of the national opera house, and the gates of the national art gallery and sculpture park. She saw all the notable church, mosque, temple, and synagogue gates too. Gates and gates and treetops rising out of the courtyards within. The traffic jams gave her ample time to take it all in. There was a riverside walk famed for its breathtaking beauty that had a gateway too, with mosaics depicting the path in each season. Druhástranian gates reward close inspection. Their designs are usually so intricate that they serve as sparkling microcosms of what you'd see if you went in, which most people didn't because they had shopping to do and also there are too many uncontrollable variables at play when engaging with cultural artifacts. Casual walkers were far outnumbered by the maintenance teams who cleaned every inch of pavement and glass in sight and made sure the gates looked their best.

And there was Gretel, walking out of one of these gates and along the pavement with six friends, all in school uniform. Two of the friends were aristocratic-looking boys. One was chubby and debonair, the only schoolboy Harriet saw who wore a cravat in place of a school tie, and the other was svelte, with a steely glint in his eyes that might make you think twice about challenging him to a duel. So these were the types of boys Gretel had something to say to. The farmstead boys hadn't got a peep out of her, though she had smiled at the ten-year-olds a couple of times. The girls Gretel was with had tracksuit bottoms on under their skirts and sported a variation on that trendy city hairstyle—two puffs on the tops of their heads rather than one. Those whose hair didn't have natural puff must have been using some sort of filler. The limousine idled along at about the same pace as the group was walking. Clio and Harriet watched quietly—they watched and waited—when would she notice them? It took some time—she was engrossed in conversation, after all, one hand tucked into the blazer pocket of a bespectacled girl who looked as if she was named Enid. Gretel's other hand was tucked into her young dandy's coat pocket until she bent to pick up a huge sycamore leaf that was so freshly fallen it hadn't yet been cleared away. This was then presented to the svelte boy as a gift. He accepted it but threw it over the next gate they came to, and nobody was more amused than he was when the leaf flew back and plastered itself across his forehead. Harriet shrank down in her seat in case she could be seen from the outside. In this lot's presence her already somewhat timid claim to Gretel's friendship would vanish altogether. Her money was tearing the lining of her coat pockets; that's how heavy the rolls of notes were. But they couldn't even begin to buy her the charisma she'd need to face Gretel's companions. She felt Clio's deeply comparative gaze on her and braced herself for unfavorable remarks. But Clio only said: **She's spotted us**, and there was Gretel on the street corner, waving goodbye to her friends and flagging down her mother's limousine as if it was a taxi. She climbed in beside Harriet and placed half a lottery ticket in her hand. **Since it'll be Thursday tomorrow**, she said.

Clio, Marcus, and Gretel Kercheval's home was an inversion of the garishness to be found over at the gingerbread house. There was hardly any furniture, no pictures on display, and no lamps overhead. Strings of tiny lights ran along the bare floors and down the gray walls, and fado played from camouflaged speakers. This was all because of Marcus. It wasn't just that he preferred open, low-lit spaces; he and Clio were funneling all their spare money into various ventures of his and inventions he was developing prototypes for. He was extremely good-looking, but the real factor that allowed him to boss Clio about was being in his early forties while Clio was in her early fifties. He made dinner, interrupting his chopping and stirring to argue on the telephone about dates and deadlines and fines, and even then he still found time to ask Harriet all about herself and compose a droll little jingle with the key words she and Gretel told him. He played the chords on his guitar, and when he sang along, he made Harriet sound like . . . a really good idea that was more likely to fall through than it was to succeed, but nothing ventured nothing gained, so on to the next one . . . ?

Harriet just put her head down and ate. Marcus's cooking was so much tastier than seven months of gruel that she couldn't talk about or evaluate anything else while the food was in front of her. Clio didn't eat dinner, but she did sit at the table with them, taking pills, sipping bone broth, and reminiscing about delectable foods she'd eaten when she was young and "could afford to eat such things."

Marcus noticed a new addition to the pill menu and picked up the bottle so as to have a closer look at the ingredients. **I hope you don't think any of this is going to turn back time,** he said.

No, these ones are more or less preservative.

Haven't you seen the ads? An after-school deten-tion concept, with a grizzled headmistress type shouting: NOOOOO WHINGING—YOU'VE HAD YOUR FUN AND THIS IS WHAT YOU DESERVE NOW THAT YOU'RE OLD!

That does ring a bell. But how can I be in love with someone who's susceptible to that kind of advertising?

Oh, that's easily answered. Self-sabotage, Marcus, self-sabotage . . .

Harriet and Gretel cleared the table, and Gretel nudged her and said, "Go ahead," then went and made sure neither Marcus nor Clio came into the kitchen before Harriet had finished licking her plate.

Well—what now?

I've been thinking, Gretel, it'd be great to just grow up all of a sudden. I mean, wake up tomorrow and just be grown up.

Why? Gretel looked as if she thought growing up would be an utter fiasco.

Well, I've got a favorite author.

Have you? A Druhástranian? Who?

No . . . Zola . . . Émile Zola . . . and as a grown-up I could do things like—like look up all the people who translated Zola into Druhástranian and take them out for a drink.

You don't have to be grown up to do that, Gretel said. We can probably do it tonight.

Can we?!

Yes, of course. Well, not all Zola's Druhástranian translators, but one of the best ones, anyway. This guy Oskar Procházka. He taught my dad at university.

They paged through Marcus Kercheval's book of contacts after he and Clio had gone to bed, and Gretel dialed Oskar Procházka's phone number.

Hi, Professor Procházka, are you busy tonight? We're two great admirers of yours, and we'd like to buy you a drink or two and thank you for translating Zola into Druhástranian. Is it OK if the drinks are nonalcoholic? We're underage.

Harriet heard the professor saying he was in recovery, so meeting for nonalcoholic drinks was perfect.

Super, Gretel said, already unbuttoning her pajama top and looking around for something else to put on. Can you meet us at the Jedovna Café in an hour? Thanks so much! Ha ha, what do you mean you don't care if this is a trick . . . my dad was a student of yours and speaks very highly of you . . . Marcus Kercheval . . . yes . . . see you soon. Please wrap up warm; it's cold out.

As she spoke, she undid Harriet's pigtails and

held up an oversized white shirt against her. Harriet retied her pigtails, did up her bonnet, and said, **You wear that yourself.** So Gretel did, with tight jeans, floral-patterned bovver boots, a long black cloak, and a heap of woolen scarves. They went out of the residential complex arm in arm, Little Miss Muffet and a scarf model. They walked past Clio's limousine, which should've been parked underground, so they went back and looked in at the window; Clio's limousine driver was asleep on the front seat. Gretel banged on the window and said, **What are you still doing here?**

Clio had told the chauffeur he couldn't go home because Gretel would most likely be up to something after dark. He thanked them for waking him up. He would have got the sack if he'd lost track of them.

So . . . where am I taking you?

Professor Procházka was already waiting in a booth near the back of the Jedovna Café when they arrived. He was short and bald and wiry and had shed his outer layers of clothing to reveal a very comfortable-looking pair of flannel pajamas. He spotted his fans at once and waved them over. He was drinking Harriet's favorite, cold tea . . . not iced tea, but hot tea that had cooled. They liked him so much. They liked the way he talked when he talked, and they liked his quiet when he was quiet. He was a little sad, weary perhaps, distracted by some problem he wasn't sure mere time and industry could solve. He said Harriet and Gretel were doing him good just by sitting opposite him, and Gretel said he was easily pleased.

He rubbed his beard. **None of my students seem to think so.**

Harriet asked him if he thought Zola was a misanthropist. He said, Oh—er—a misanthrope? **I can see how it seems like that. To me his stories are like bandits that aren't interested in anything you'd willingly flaunt but demand you furnish them with all that's hypocritical and cowardly and self-satisfied in you. You deny being in possession of such trash, of course—why would you admit such things to a stranger? Wouldn't the strange brigand rather have this lovely diamond necklace instead? But it would've been better to own up, to just own up to it all, because the next thing a Zola story does is frisk you and hit you ten times for each flaw you denied being in possession of. It's oddly . . . I don't know the word for it. Someone who searches you for the things that secretly make you miserable and then forcibly takes them from you, at least for a while—there is a bit of misanthropy in that, in the searching. And yet . . .**

165

He also told them that there was another writer who was probably going to have a similar effect on them if they hadn't read him yet . . . they hadn't, so they wrote down that writer's name: Honoré de Balzac. Then he said he had to get back to work. Harriet tried to stall him; he hadn't drunk that much tea and had declined dinner, and she wanted to spend a lot of money on him. But they were the last customers left in the café, and all the chairs had been put up on the tables around them—a man with a mop was waiting to tackle the floor beneath their own table as soon as they got up.

I'm buying, Harriet said.

The professor demurred, but Gretel told him: **We did say it was our treat . . .**

Harriet went to the till, pulled a fistful of notes out of her pocket, and put them in the cashier's hand. The cashier was nonplussed; it was either much too much or . . . she added more notes to the pile, just to be on the safe side.

The cashier handed the notes back to her with exaggerated politeness. **That was . . . entertaining, miss, but I'd appreciate it if you paid with actual money now.**

This isn't money?

The cashier gave her an incredulous look. Harriet went back to the table where Gretel and the professor and the man with the mop were waiting, and the professor asked what was wrong. She showed him her money and told him what the cashier had said. Professor Procházka flattened the notes on the tabletop before him and then turned them over, smoothed them again, counted them. He asked her how many more she had, and she emptied out her pockets. The way he and Gretel looked at each other and at the note-covered tabletop . . . that gave her a very bad feeling.

It isn't money?

They were searching for words. Harriet muttered that she hadn't seen money up close before, so.

Harriet Lee, Professor Procházka said. **I can see you've collected all this carefully, and that suggests you've been doing all you can to earn it, so these . . . items are valuable in that sense. But it's not money, no.**

What to do, Gretel murmured. **I didn't bring any out. And we were supposed to treat you!**

I don't—what is it, then, if it isn't money?

The professor showed Harriet a banknote that bore a passing resemblance to the ones she had and said he'd go and pay with that, and it was his pleasure entirely, really, it was.

This is what Harriet would have liked to hear

Gretel say: **You mustn't worry; we'll go to Clio together and straighten everything out.**

This is what Gretel actually said: **Seems like there's nothing to be done about you.**

What? What do you mean by that?

Do you remember when I offered you half a lottery ticket and you asked: Is it money? After that you go away, hoard these worthless bits of paper, and ask: Isn't it money . . . ?

You're saying getting tricked is my own fault, for doubting when I should believe, and believing when I should doubt . . . ?

That's not what I'm saying.

You are. You're telling me I'm stupid.

Oh, stop it. Gretel's expression was a soundless fireworks display, the sort you see when someone's trying very hard not to laugh or cry.

Professor Procházka had slipped away without saying goodbye, so they left too. Back in Gretel's bedroom they watched a TV show about a woman who had an interesting job, a nice house, a great many high-heeled shoes, and a seven-year personal memory limit. This woman absolutely couldn't do without a proper past, so in each episode of the TV show she dived into Druhá City's criminal underworld and stabbed hoodlums with her stiletto heels, demanding to be told things that would lead her to her lost memories. This was counterproductive; most of the hoodlums just said any old thing in order to buy the time to get away from her, and she had to beat a lot of other people and compare statements to uncover some sort of truth. Harriet and Gretel were unsure about the show for the duration of the first two episodes. Each second of screen time was designed to advance the plot, even the coded way people greeted each other or talked about the habits, diets, and personalities of their household pets, so you couldn't relax at all or you'd get left behind. But by episode 3, they couldn't stop watching. They were propelled by a strong premonition that when the woman finally managed to retrieve her true memories they would disappoint her, and she'd wonder why she hadn't just kept living peacefully with her fabulous shoes and her girlfriend, who only had eyes for her. This expectation was probably one the writers of the TV show (and elements of the Druhástranian government) preferred viewers to hold, undermining the urge to clamor for systemic change as it did.

Gretel's floor rug was a woven map of the world—its threads glinted bronze and blue and emerald-green, and the two girls bridged oceans with their bodies. Harriet asked: **What about Clio, Gretel? You say there's nothing to be done** about me, but is there anything to be done about your mother? For instance, can't you get her to actually pay us?

By the way . . . Gretel lifted up one of Harriet's pigtails and pointed at the bruise on the left side of her neck. **What's this?** Her eyes narrowed. **Is it a love bite? Are there more?**

Swindlers are the ones who need to be different, not the swindled, Harriet continued.

Have you been letting people bite you for . . . those bits of paper Clio gave you? That's unexpected.

Shut up. Some girls came and . . . pinched us. Zu, Dottie, me, and all the others. It wasn't a question of letting it happen; they just did it.

Harriet, I don't—

I don't really want to talk about it.

Later, both kneeling and both undressed so that it was fair, they looked at the bruises together. Harriet tried to cover the sore places on her breasts but moved her hands away.

We're going to start carrying gingerbread shivs, Harriet said.

Gretel said she didn't think that was a proportionate response.

You're sounding like Zu. She said violence isn't the answer.

No, it is the answer. The shivs aren't enough.

Gretel looked down at her rug, muttered that the world that lay at their feet lacked detail and pulled an atlas from her desk drawer. Maps of 196 countries including Taiwan and excluding Druhástrana.

Now then, Gretel said. **Let's do this before I forget. Where shall we meet once you've grown up?**

Anywhere but here . . . hang on. Aren't we going to do that together?

Gretel looked up from examining Budapest street names through a magnifying glass. **Hmmm? Do what together?**

Grow up.

Oh no, said Gretel. **All that happens when you grow up is that your ethics get completely compromised and you do extremely dodgy things you never imagined doing, apparently for the sake of others. Plus, growing up isn't in my job description.**

You've got a job? What is it?

Changeling.

Changeling as in nonhuman replacement for a human child?

Changeling as in changeling. We've had bad press.

Right. What are your duties, then?

Mainly we assist people who've changed their minds in a way that means their lives have to be different too.

Harriet tried to hold Gretel's gaze, but the other girl kept looking at the pinch marks instead. Even though she now knew they were malign in nature, they still came across as evidence of jaunty affection, of having been nibbled here and there just a bit, a tiny, tiny bit . . . the pinch marks really bothered Gretel, to a degree that enabled them to play an interrogative role and startle her into disclosure she might not otherwise have made. **We—er—we try to help out with practicalities, next steps, etc. No two workdays are the same . . .**

Is the pay good?

There is none. Usually I need a second or third job to get by, but being Clio's daughter this time around makes things a bit easier in some respects.

No pay? Really none at all?

I'm not saying I don't have serious talks with myself sometimes. I'm not saying there aren't moments when I say to myself: This is a mug's game . . . let's just hand in that resignation letter, you and me, let's give two lives' notice and leave all this behind. **But.** "Whát I dó is me: For that I came," Gretel said. That's from a poem I read once, and that's really all there is to it.

So . . . am I a client?

No. You're very . . . I trusted you at once, so you're a friend. Even changelings need people they can place confidence in.

But not people to grow up with.

Like I said, that's your job. You'll get your real wages this time, but there's an underlying issue here. I'm not sure how to put this . . . it's about value systems . . .

Try putting it in terms of gingerbread.

Oh, then it's simple. About that gingerbread of yours: What do you want in exchange for it? Look at your little face . . . had you really told yourself you intend to give the stuff away for free? If that were the case, would you really be this upset about the fake money? Right. So think. What's the minimum you can accept in exchange for your gingerbread? And what about the maximum? Better to set honest prices if you want to make an honest profit, don't you think . . . ?

After a pause, during which Harriet thought to herself that this was the sort of thing that would take decades to work out, Gretel said: **Best get**

going then, hadn't you, and Harriet jumped, then pretended she'd only been sneezing. Gretel laughed and held up her atlas.

But first: Where shall we meet once you've grown up? Stick three pins in so we have two backups.

They sounded out the names of foreign towns and cities. Consonants clattered and vowels unwound like parchment scrolls—every word they mispronounced sounded good to them. In the end it was the vividly tinted photographs that helped them refine their short list. Harriet flipped through the atlas backward and there they were—three photos in which the same two women recurred. One city scene, one spa-town snapshot, and the third was neither city nor countryside—two semi-smooth surfaces met and cast multilayered light. Harriet considered that light and said: **Wasn't this taken on a beach? Sand and sea?** Gretel said it could be a beach, but there was a castle nearby . . . she definitely saw the type of mildewed shadow cast by a castle. At first the two women were barely distinct from the scenery, just two blurry figures holding on to each other. Gretel's magnifying glass revealed that twice they were looking in the same direction and the third time one was looking down and the other was looking off to the side. Harriet pointed out that the one on the left was slightly in the lead. **I think she's guiding the old biddy on the right. It must be me and you.**

Gretel looked up the place names and stuck three pins into her map.

Was Clio unnerved by the scene that greeted her when she opened Gretel's bedroom door? Two girls fast asleep and as naked as the day they were born, sharing pages of a map book as a pillow while a blaring TV screen tracked the progress of a woman beating her way through an identity parade armed with nothing but a pair of scarlet stilettoes . . .

She probably stayed calm. She certainly managed to do so when Gretel and Harriet confronted her about the counterfeit money. Clio looked at the stacks of paper, looked at Harriet, put her hands up in the air, and said: **Whoops!**

Margot Lee has made Harriet recount that moment tens of times, and each time she's assured Harriet that if Clio had done that in Margot's presence no power in the heavens or upon the earth would have been able to save Clio Kercheval from getting strangled to death.

But of course I was going to pay you, silly. It's just that as a mother I know how careless

children are with money, so I issued these slips as
tokens you can exchange for your actual wages.
There's a note about it in the contract your parents signed . . . oh, you didn't see it? Well, it'll all
be there in writing when you go home and check
with them.

Harriet hadn't the faintest doubt that even if
this clause hadn't originally featured in the contract Margot and Simon had signed, they'd find
it there when they looked. There was nothing
Clio Kercheval couldn't switch around if she had a
mind to. Clio would stop at nothing to make sure
the girls weren't upset. Or, at any rate, not upset
with Clio.

I would certainly have paid you before you
left. Darling, you must have been thinking
such terrible things! I'm glad you came straight
to me . . .

Well, the truth is, Harriet ought to report
you, Mum, Gretel said, in much the same tone of
voice as someone at a bus stop might say, "I see the
bus is late again today."

But she won't. Will you, Harriet? It's all
cleared up now. Besides, each of these representative vouchers I gave you—

Representative vouchers. So many switches
were suddenly being pulled that it was hard to

know what money actually was in and of itself. It seemed you got hold of some and then people told you what it was on that particular day. It was also hard to know whether money was like this because of Clio or whether Clio was like this because of money.

Each of these representative vouchers I gave you corresponds to ten English pounds, Clio continued. **The strongest currency in the world, you know. Much stronger than ours. The exchange rate's so good you've got much more than you thought you had! Isn't that wonderful? No need to thank me . . . you know I'd never cheat you.**

That's the thing, Harriet said. **I don't know that. So I'm not going to work for you anymore, Mrs. Kercheval. I don't want to find out what else you've got in store for me.**

Clio gaped, and her daughter said: **Oh. Not even slightly curious?**

No. I'll take the money—the real money, whatever that may be—and run, thank you.

Gretel handed Harriet a dressing gown and told her mother to bring the full amount in small notes.

Don't count on being allowed back into the Gingerbread House to lead some sort of rebellion, Gretel said, when Clio had gone.

But she won't pay the others.

**Yes, she will. I'll make sure of it. It'll be . . .
nice to see your friend Turandot. Maybe I could
help her out—if I hit her again, it might reset her
sense of smell.**

**I'll thank you in advance for not hitting
Dottie again under any circumstances,** Harriet
said, through nervous laughter. **And I'll write to
you from the farmstead.**

They went for a walk along the misty riverbank. Every now and again there was a parting
in the clouds and sunlight struck the bridge's iron
fin and spliced the surface of the water. The girls
liked that, but more wondrous still—nine divers
surfaced. Nine snorkeled divers, each bearing a
board with a number painted on it.

Thursday, Harriet said. **It's Thursday, Gretel.**

She searched her coat pockets for her half of
their lottery ticket, and Gretel turned out her own
pockets too. The drivers began to disperse, but
they stopped when they heard Gretel's shrill command: **Please wait a minute, just a minute . . .**

Then one by the one the divers approached to
shake hands and join the girls' celebrations. Above
them pedestrians gathered on Dolphin Bridge
to deliver a round of applause. The pedestrians
weren't sure what was happening, but there's no

harm in showing you're glad for people when they're jumping up and down and screaming, WE WON! OH MY GOD, WE WON!

By the time Gretel and Harriet had collected their winnings, there were ten missed calls on Harriet's phone, all from the phone Harriet had sent to Margot. So Harriet phoned back.

How do you feel about England? Harriet's mother said, without preamble.

Hi, Mum. One sec. Harriet held the phone against her chest and consulted Gretel.

(How do I feel about England?

Well, one of our three pins is stuck in England, so . . . good?)

Harriet told Margot she felt good about England. "Good" felt too committed, so she backtracked. **Good-ish. Why?**

Listen, Harriet . . . I've been so fed up with all the intercepted letters that were supposedly from you, but a few weeks ago a real one came. Through the Pigeon Post.

Eh?

Maggie Parker's homing pigeons came to roost . . .

179

What—the geriatric ones everyone decided had been abducted by aliens?

Not everyone . . . just the Cook family. But yes, those pigeons! All three of them. Well cared for . . . positively GLOSSY, actually, each one carrying a carbon copy of the same letter. Couldn't tell you who was more excited—me or Maggie Parker. She was doing high kicks and all kinds of risky moves . . . seriously thought she was going to dislocate a joint. And you should've heard her. They said the Parker talent was dying out, but the Parkers have still got it! Better not talk about the Parkers unless you know! Parker's Pigeon Post, YEAH! Nonstop for eighty-three years! From here to England and back, that's right! She's tapped Jiaolong for next Pigeon Postmaster, and she's teaching him how to raise the next three squabs . . .

Oh Maggie! She used to live so much in the past, didn't she, thinking she was the least impressive of the Parkers . . .

Nobody can ever say that now.

The letter—was it addressed to you?

Sort of. It was in English, and it began: If your daughter's name is Harriet Lee—

Oh Mother, Harriet said, in English. So you can English? I can too!

Margot responded in English, too fast for Harriet to understand, but Harriet still had to show some ability, so she kept up the English: **Lovely!**

Margot switched back to Druhástranian: **Sweetheart, I'm so pleased we can both English.** (Hearing this in Druhástranian, Harriet understood her grammatical error.) **What a pair we are—the daughter's got brains and perseverance, and the mother's got parents who paid for her to go to International School. So when that note came, I wrote back at once. I've had to keep Maggie from spoiling those pigeons, mind. She's so proud of them there's a chance they'll get overfed, and there can't be a Pigeon Post if the messengers can't even carry their own body weight. Anyway, I wrote back, and he replied, and . . .**

He? Who is this pen pal, Mum?

A Kercheval. He must be a distant cousin on my mother's side.

Oh no. Not another one.

Sorry about Clio.

Apology not accepted. Just . . . just be related to better people!

Well, Clio did marry in . . . Let's give the one in England a try.

Family reunion time?

I think not. As far as this Aristide Kercheval is concerned, I'm just the mother of a Gingerbread Girl who tugged his heartstrings through a television screen. He said you spoke in English . . .

Oh no . . . that's right, I did . . . I, er, Englished . . . but how did he see it . . . ?

He's rich, Harriet. His satellite subscription includes every existing TV channel everywhere.

Well, what else did he say?

That you were pitiful.

Oh.

Don't be embarrassed; it paid off. One thing I like about Parker's Pigeon Post is that when using it, you have to come straight to the point. Aristide Kercheval wants to become your sponsor. Sounds fishy, I know, so I'm coming too.

Harriet looked over at Gretel, but Gretel had her head bent over her phone, texting somebody.

So this Kercheval becomes my sponsor. OK. And what do I have to do in return?

He says he has no expectations whatsoever, but I imagine he'd like to see some gratitude. Shouldn't be too hard.

Can you put Dad on the phone?

Harriet's pause here is so tremulous that it puts Perdita and the dolls on alert.

"What's going on—about to make something up, are you?" asks the doll named Sago.

"Deciding whether or not to break a promise," Harriet says.

She looks at her daughter for a while, and Perdita seems to want her to keep the promise, whatever it was. Harriet proceeds accordingly.

Harriet and her father didn't talk for long, but conversation was halting and heavy in tone. They didn't know when, or if, they would see or hear from each other again, and both sides were prepared to hear excuses or to make some. They were ready for vengeful utterances, maybe even a parting curse or two. Instead, one of them—either Harriet or her father—said: **We're very much alike, you know, you and me.**

And the other—either Harriet or her father—said: **I know.**

It's good that you know that.

But it isn't enough—it doesn't help—

I think it could. We're so much alike that when you're happy, I am too. And when you're sad and cross, I am too. This can work at a distance.

So I should be happy if I want you to be happy? This doesn't help either!

If you think about it little by little, over time you might see it another way.

And if you think about it little by little, over time you might not want to remember that this is all you had to say.

Can't we make a deal?

Like what?

If this does turn out to be the last time we hear from each other, don't think of what you remember saying and what you remember me saying. Don't separate things out like that.

And you'll do the same?

Of course.

"Sounds like you've finally found some shame after trying to force your father to be happy even as you abandoned him," says the doll named Lollipop, and the doll named Sago says, "That's a bit harsh . . . actually it sounds to me as if Mother-of-Perdita's just keeping a promise," and the doll named Bonnie says, "Or, how about this, guys: Thinking about it little by little, over time, it now seems to Mother-of-Perdita that almost exactly the same suggestion and rejection and deal would have been made regardless of the order in which father and daughter spoke. She was only saying what he would have said if she hadn't got there first, and vice versa. That's how alike those two really are."

Harriet pulls tissue out of the pocket of her

dressing gown, blows her nose, and says: "Did I mention that we won the lottery, Gretel and me?"

When they went to collect their winnings, the man behind the counter at the claims office handed them two laughably light envelopes. Harriet opened hers, closed it again, and steadied her nerves before showing Gretel the wooden ring inside.

Half a lifetime's wealth, Gretel?

Gretel had slipped the ring onto her finger and had held up her hand, admiring it. A sheaf of wheat carved in such a way that it rippled around the finger.

To Harriet, Gretel said: **Usually the top prize is cash. I'm guessing this happened because it's you.**

Margot was on her way to Druhá City, and, to Harriet's great relief, told her exactly what to do, where to be, and even what she ought to be wearing by the time Margot arrived.

Well then, I'll leave you to it, Gretel said, but Harriet prevailed upon her to help navigate Druhá's numerous boutiques; it transpired that Gretel could see the difference between black and certain shades of navy blue much better than Harriet could. She stayed a little longer, then a little longer still.

At sunset, outside the five-star hotel where Margot had said they should meet, Gretel tried again:

OK, off I go, leaving you to it.

They're not going to let me check in. I'll go in there and they'll look at me and say, "Excuse me, but aren't you just riff raff? Go back."

Whatevs. You look like you could buy and sell this place and everyone in it. Your mum knows her stuff.

Can't you come in with me?

Gretel handed Harriet the bag that held her Gingerbread Girl uniform and patchwork coat.

Another time. I'm already running late thanks to you, so let's just say bye for now . . .

She pointed at the hotel's revolving doors until Harriet went in. And it all went off without a hitch: smiling doormen, smiling porters, smiling receptionist. But what was it Gretel had claimed she was running late for? Harriet stood by her hotel-room window watching Gretel through the magnolia-scented lace curtains for a half hour. Gretel's busy evening seemed to consist of standing out on the pavement trying to work out which of the windows belonged to Harriet's hotel room. Then Harriet sent her a text message: **Infiltration complete.** Upon receipt of that message Gretel walked down the street toward the metro station, not hurrying or anything; plus she had time for five backward glances, so how busy was that girl really . . .

Harriet took a nap, thereby tackling the challenge of waiting for one person whilst trying to keep herself from making an overly needy phone call to another. But Margot still wasn't there by the time Harriet woke up. So the overly needy phone call to Gretel had merely been postponed.

Hi, Gretel said. **I'm at the Gingerbread House with your colleagues.** And she passed the phone from girl to girl. They told Harriet that things were looking up now that Clio was doubling their pay . . . due to inflation, she said. They got Harriet to read out the room-service menu and told her what they'd order if they were her. Rosolio made Harriet run a hot bath—**with LOTS of bubbles. And don't just stand there; get in. This is the thing about boffins; they don't understand the principles of enjoyment . . .**

Dottie tried to make her promise to come back. Zu tried to make her promise not to. Harriet asked them to put Gretel on the line, but when the phone got back to Gretel, the line disconnected before Harriet could tell her off for never doing or saying any of the things a friend ought to do or say. Though of course now Harriet thinks about it, if Gretel hadn't left her at the hotel, she wouldn't have had that chance to talk with the other girls again, to hear their laughter and chatter and to remind them that she thought about them too.

ONCE MARGOT WAS SAFELY in the hotel room with Harriet, she took the identity papers she'd needed to get through the checkpoints between the farmstead and the city, and she took the papers Harriet would have needed to get through the checkpoints between the city and the farmstead, and she tore up both sets of papers and flushed them down the toilet. If they'd had passports they could have traveled as people, but decades after a country's borders close for good, passports tend to be done away with, so—

We're going as cargo.

Sorry, we're going as what?

Harriet. Sweetheart. There's no time.

There never was any time to argue with Margot. And if you said no to her, she was sure to find somebody else who'd say yes. This was chief among Harriet's fears—that her mother would find some accomplice who was more able but less fond. Still . . .

This is too reckless for me, Mum.

OK, Harriet. What should I tell you?

Where's Dad?

Margot told her she was sure she could guess the answer to that. Simon Lee was with Gwen and Elsa Cook, drinking nettle soup. No more gnawing on gingerbread for him . . . he'd come to his senses. If Simon Lee had had his pick of the farmstead, Gwen Cook would probably be his fourth or fifth choice. Gwen, who didn't even have enough imagination to let her daughter leave the farmstead. But Simon was sticking with Gwen out of satisfaction that he was her first choice. And not returning Gwen's ardor now didn't mean he never would. This was all up to Gwen and Simon, and Margot wouldn't have had a word to say about any of it if Gwen's discarded husband hadn't started bothering her, knocking on the cottage door in the evening and asking if they might drink a little nettle soup together, he and Margot. Instead of using words, Margot had shaken a frying pan at the man until he went away.

But if I stay in that place, Paul Cook will end up being your stepdad. Who are all these

people who keep speaking to me when I'm try-ing to work . . . ? They come up to me and say, "Aren't you lonely? You're putting a brave face on, Margot Lee, but you do seem lonely . . . ," or they'll remind me that nobody can match Paul Cook's mustache. Some of these people—Harriet, some of these people have come over from the neighboring farms to talk to me about Paul Cook's mustache. It's as if talking to me about his mustache is an additional job on top of all the other work they have to do . . . one last bout of industry before they go home for the night. Six months from now you'll come home and Paul Cook will be sitting at the kitchen table, drinking piping-hot ditchwater out of a soup bowl, and I'll put my hand on his shoulder and say, "Whatever was I thinking, turning this man away when I was so lonely and he has such a fine mustache?"

That seemed likely. One way or another, the numbers would stabilize so that Harriet and her farmstead friend had one of each parent: mother plus father plus Elsa Cook, mother plus father plus Harriet Lee.

And if I move here . . . well, it may take a while longer. A year. Give me a year in Druhá City and Clio Kercheval won't have a patch on me.

That also seemed likely, and just as uncanny. Was there really no way out?

Sweetheart—can't we just go and live with Aristide Kercheval? If it's good enough for Maggie Parker's pigeons, isn't it good enough for us? Have some of this.

The gingerbread tasted stale, and Harriet thought that was the only catch until the mass in her gullet began to descend. The plunging weight of it—Harriet remembers trying to push her entire hand into her mouth, sticking her fingers down her throat, trying to drag the thing back up, this ever-thickening, slug-like mass. It turned her spinal cord into a bed of nails as it went down. Gasp by gasp.

Don't look at me like that, Harriet, Margot managed to say, as all the breath in her own body condensed and then congealed. **It's really not what you think. See . . . you—soon.**

"This is why I'm dead certain you've been talking to a Kercheval," Harriet tells Perdita and the dolls. Only the Kerchevals know enough about Harriet and Margot's departure from Druhástrana to be able to put a "follow the gingerbread road" spin on it.

Well, the Kerchevals, and the person or persons who must have come to Harriet and Margot's hotel room after they'd blacked out. But perhaps all the removal team knew was that their evening schedule involved arranging two corpses into the yoga-like poses necessary for transportation in steamer trunks. This was done in the shortest time possible before the steamer trunks were dropped off at the nearest naval submarine base. That kind of professional doesn't tend to be bothered about before-and-after scenarios.

A few hours later, when the steamer trunks were opened aboard a boat moored in Whitby Harbour, Margot and Harriet spilled out like "vats of custard." Ari Kercheval opened the trunks himself. He still has nightmares about it. **We thought your bones had melted or something.** Margot said: **Yes, so did we.**

"Do I go on?" asks Harriet.

"YOU DO," says Perdita and three of the dolls.

"I mean, you said Whitby Harbour. So why are we here in London? Why aren't all six of us in Whitby right now . . . you tell us the reasons, and no funny business," the doll named Sago says.

10

HARRIET HEARD SOMEONE SAYING SHHH-HHHHHHHHHHHHHH so loudly and for so long that she felt she should check on the situation. Being unable to, she listened for a few more days and realized it was water falling down rocks. That was outside, beyond several walls. The nearest wall held a door or window that twisted around on itself like an hourglass—this acted as a light delivery service. The sun's rays came and tickled her under the chin, but the waterfall never stopped saying, SHHHHHHHHHHHHHHHHHH, **this is no laughing matter, young lady**, so she stayed straight-faced and giggle-free.

Once she'd ceased being overwhelmed by the sound and feel of still being alive, Harriet was able to understand that there were people around her, talking. Not to her, but about her. The people were speaking in English. They sounded like doctors, and they were talking about her hair. They were saying it had gone gray all at once, as if all the pigment had spontaneously dimmed. They'd thought it was all over when this had happened, but in fact the graying had accompanied the restoration of vital functions and the return, the doctoral voices said, of the patient's ability to lie there pretending not to be listening to them talking about her hair. Since the jig was up, Harriet opened her eyes, looked around at the people clustered around her bed, and dry-heaved on and off for the rest of the day. An old woman wearing what looked like a gray fright wig on the other side of the room did the same, but for longer. Upon closer inspection the old woman turned out to be Margot Lee.

I told you, Harriet . . . I told you everything would be all right . . .

This is your idea of all right, is it, Mum?

Well, have you got a better one?

Harriet couldn't help mourning the loss of her hair color; she hadn't known how much she'd enjoyed having black hair until it was gray. But whenever she felt the hair-color mourning become excessive, she emulated Gretel's calm surprise (if there could be such a thing) upon realizing that she had four pupils instead of two. **Huh, well, it's a change.** And slowly, names were put to the bedside visitors. Both of the doctoral voices belonged to Kerchevals. One voice was Tamar's, and one was Kenzilea's. Tamar Kercheval, MD, was round and soft and had a polished look to her. You could picture Tamar putting in stints as a cover model for medical journals. Her hands were cold, but her gaze was warm. Kenzilea Kercheval, MD, had a Romany's working knowledge of many places in the world that are said not to exist. She was frizzy-haired and deeply agnostic in manner; her silences were an alternative to the skeptical repetition of other people's statements.

Aristide, Harriet's benefactor, was married to Tamar. At rest he might have been a classic silver fox. The wise-looking kind—King Balthazar graying at the temples after all those years of studying the stars. But Ari was never at rest. Everything about him was lean and tense and rectangular; he was tuned into conversational subtext at a frequency that caused him nervous headaches. He took ambiguity as a personal attack. If a summary wasn't concise, he'd shout it down or walk away halfway through. **Are you trying to be clever with me . . . are you trying to be fucking clever with me?** he'd roar.

So you're the one who wants to grow up. That was the first thing Ari said to Harriet. Through gritted teeth, no less. It would've been easy to start off on the wrong foot with him by saying something like "M-me?" but the waterfall was Harriet Lee's best adviser just then (SHHHHHHHHHHHHHHHHHH), so she just looked at Aristide Kercheval without saying anything. This must have put him into a peaceable mood, because after a couple of moments of looking back at her, he fluffed up her pillow, adjusted her blanket, and said, **OK, OK. Welcome.**

Aristide's older brother, Ambrose, walked with the aid of a striped cane that looked like a peppermint stick, spoke without insistence, and gave no hard stares. There was a triplicate softness to the man, as if he were a combination of poet, invalid, and monk. This may have been due to constantly having to soothe people's feelings in Ari's wake . . .

Last of all were two boys; one was sixteen years of age and the other was seventeen. The younger boy was Aristide and Tamar's son. His name was Gabriel, and the other, older boy was Ambrose and Kenzilea's son, Rémy. When Harriet got a proper look at the cousins, she thought, **Seriously? Do they seriously have to look like this?** It was like looking at faces printed on banknotes—no, they were a pair of black pre-Raphaelite muses. Their features had the same sort of almost unacceptable clarity; the sort designed to appear in an idealized shepherd-boy scene, close-shaven curls and all. All each needed was a backdrop of moonlit cloud. Not that it was possible for them to inhabit the same canvas. Gabriel's half-frown belonged to a dreamer who chased errant flocks in his sleep. His version of Endymion's story would end with the young man telling Selene that she's very pretty but he finds her advances inappropriate and has neither the time nor the resources to adequately pursue a romantic relationship. Rémy's half-smile was more knowing, less chaste. This Endymion's rational objections could be overcome. Yes, he was a shepherd and Selene was the moon, but really it all depended on how good they could make each other feel.

("Oooooh, I should get a prize," the doll named Prim announces. "I should get a prize for not asking which one you lost your virginity to, Mother-of-Perdita."

"More like a prize for presumptuousness," says the doll named Lollipop.

The doll named Bonnie has something to add: "While we're at it, let's give Perdita a prize for not asking which one's her father."

"Never-ending spiral of presumption," says Lollipop.)

The younger boy, Gabriel, asked Harriet if there was anything he could get her, and she asked for a piece of paper. He gave her a whole blank notebook, the nicest notebook she'd owned to date, its pages flecked with papyrus pith. Handmade and heartfelt; Harriet wanted everything she did to be like this. Each time she opened the book and saw Gabriel Kercheval's monogrammed initials, there was an instant, the briefest instant, in which it seemed to her that a note from Gretel had been slipped in among her own.

Harriet started out using her notebook for new words but soon switched to keeping a weekly ranking of the members of the Kercheval household. Margot was number one week after week, though the list didn't run in order of liking—Harriet liked most of her housemates about the same. She slept well in that house even though it took her by surprise at first—**Er, when will it be finished?** Margot asked as Ari pulled up in the driveway. It looked like a Brutalist building site, a single block of checkered granite with a number of deep gaps and crenellations that seemed to think they answered the need for windows and doors. The white squares glared . . . perhaps it was a Kercheval rule always to conceal the extent of one's wealth, whether in Druhástrana or abroad. Exteriors aside, the Kerchevals' was a household that made room for them. Its members carried furniture from spot to spot in order to get what Margot called "the vibe" right, and they drew alternate floor plans for Margot and Harriet when they got lost due to certain qualities of the building itself. Ari did most of his work from home and liked to move his office around at the press of a button, so the staircase that ran through the center of the building was the only fixed unit, and all the other rooms slid up and down like beads on an abacus. Harriet would knock on what she thought was Gabriel's bedroom door only to find herself chatting with Margot or Rémy, as Gabriel's room had gone up or down a floor.

Every now and then the adult Kerchevals would

make offhand references to a collective good deed they carried out annually. The less traceable it was in terms of possibility/probability, the more likely they were to take it on. One year it might be the seeding of a long-term investment, and another year it was **a question of stopping something from happening . . . blocking somebody else's move. You'd be surprised how taxing that can be . . .**

From this talk Margot inferred that taking in the Lees was that year's good deed, and also that the annual good deed was meant to be therapeutic for the family conscience. Tamar and Kenzilea were noticeably defensive about practicing medicine in the private sector, and Ari and Ambrose were cagey about the source of their wealth, so it was probably exploitative, true to known Kercheval form. This had no effect on Ari's ranking in Harriet's list of household members.

"Let's have this list, then," says the doll named Prim, and the doll named Sago says: "Oh no, not a list." The doll named Lollipop agrees: "I wasn't going to say anything about this, but lists—you shouldn't do that to people . . ."

The doll named Bonnie wants to hear it and says Lollipop and Sago can just cover their ears if they're so much against cataloging people. She, Bonnie, will listen carefully because it's like a list

of suspects, only rather than being suspects connected to a murder they're suspects connected
to a birth. One of the people Harriet's about to
list might be Perdita's father, and another two
of them might be Perdita's grandparents on the
paternal side. Speaking on her own behalf
the doll named Bonnie would like to know what
kind of people the English Kerchevals wanted the
Lees to think they were and what kind of people
the Lees actually ended up thinking they were.
Furthermore, Perdita has her pen poised over her
notebook and looks ready to take notes, and the doll
named Prim repeats her, "Let's have this list, then,"
adding that she's already decided who she thinks
Perdita's father is (!), but she doesn't mind hearing
about the rest of the household since these people
were good enough to take Mother-of-Perdita in.

"If the list isn't in order of dodginess, how does
it run? In order of how much you liked or disliked
each household member?"

Harriet's list ran in order of readability, and
Margot Lee was number one. The rest of the list
generally went like this:

Mr. Bianchi the cook and Ms. Danilenko the
housekeeper took joint second place. They were
happy when Harriet and Margot stayed out of
their way and unhappy at all other times. But

at a meeting held in Margot's bedroom on their first evening in the house, the Lees decided that signaling their desire to earn their keep was more important than warding off the combined hostility of the cook and the housekeeper. They rolled up the sleeves of their silk pajamas and got down to work. Margot did a lot of late-night cleaning and laundry, and Harriet sneaked into the kitchen in the earliest hours of the morning to bake ginger-bread for everybody, even though Ari and Tamar told her she was free to develop other interests and Mr. Bianchi had plenty of derisive things to say about the fruits of her labor.

If you wanted proper gingerbread, you should have told me. Are we treating this as a rare delicacy best prepared by small hands? Where is the complication in this? Is this pashmak, **I ask you . . . is this patisserie? I can make gingerbread like this with my eyes closed, with my hands tied behind my back; I can make this kind of thing in my sleep!**

If Harriet were ever to accept an award for her gingerbread, her first shout-out would be to Mr. Bianchi. He was such a perfect hater. His denun-ciations of "this basic snack" never stopped him eating it, and for all that he went on and on and on about how easily he could match Harriet's gingerbread, he never let anybody taste the batches he turned out. Gabriel took to studying in the kitchen while Harriet was baking. He'd seen Mr. Bianchi on the prowl with a rolling pin and thought Harriet needed a bodyguard. Margot joined them as additional backup and pored through job listings while waiting for the wash cycle to come to an end, and Rémy joined as a supplementary buffer between Margot and Ms. Danilenko. He was also helping Margot to craft a perfect(ly fictitious) CV for the jobs she wanted but didn't have the experience for yet. Harriet looked around at her sleepy companions, each one insisting that he or she felt wide awake, Gabriel reluctantly posing as this or that former employer in order to field inquiries from American companies that were considering Margot's latest job application across time zones, and she felt she had Mr. Bianchi the angry cook and Mrs. Danilenko the even angrier housekeeper to thank for the 3:00 A.M. kitchen team.

Ari Kercheval was the next most readable. Ari was happy with you as long as you didn't need something it was not in his power to give. Rémy's independence put a great big smile on his uncle's face, though at times it seemed to arise from a determination to neither give nor take that struck Ari as unsuitable for—well, a human being. Margot made Ari happy too: he found her requests moderate. Tamar, Kenzilea, and Harriet made Ari about 78 percent happy . . . he understood them; he mostly understood them. Ambrose and Gabriel were bothersome. They hid things from Ari, and even when he was able to discover what it was they had hidden, there didn't seem to a sane rationale for the hiding. For instance, why did Gabriel hide his perfect school reports? Really it was self-effacement that Ari Kercheval couldn't understand. Besides, there was nothing to be gained from parading the reports around, since the C's Rémy earned without studying got more praise than the A's Gabriel went flat out for.

The problems between Ari and Ambrose and the problems between Ari and Gabriel didn't just stay between them . . . for instance there was the way Rémy couldn't seem to let a day go by without offering his father some token of disrespect. This wasn't something Ari liked to see, and he kept having ineffectual heart-to-hearts with Rémy about it. There were other nasty episodes, like the tearful drunken rages during which Tamar would repeatedly ask Ari if he didn't wish he'd fathered Rémy himself, or the time Tamar consulted inheritance lawyers behind Ari's back about how to proceed in the event of a nephew being made chief beneficiary of a will instead of a biological son. Margot assured Ari he wasn't overreacting to Tamar's level gaze as she'd said: **What if your nervous headaches are an undetected tumor—what then?** As if she was wishing it on him . . . what dangerous place was this stuff coming from, and how could this be the same Tamar who still sent Ari love notes via homing pigeon . . .

So Ari's readability was affected by his wariness. There was rarely a day when he didn't have to prepare for the next trap that was going to be set for him as a father/husband/brother/brother-in-law/ uncle, though not, thankfully, as a benefactor.

Tamar Kercheval was the fourth most readable. Tamar liked to be depended on and didn't have Ari's reservations regarding ability to follow through. When Ari had shown her three captive pigeons he'd just been given by a client and repeated the story the client had told him about their being Druhástranian pigeons, she'd said: **You never know, it could be true**, and had proceeded to bone up on pigeon husbandry. Had Maggie Parker seen the way those pigeons now doted on Tamar, she might've been upset—or she might have claimed Tamar as a Parker. Tamar remained mindful of the doctor-patient bond she'd had with Harriet, but she was slightly unhappy about having an attractive and unemployed woman (i.e., Margot) drifting around the house while she was away. For a while Ms. Danilenko was paid extra to send confidential daytime reports. But the Lees soon discovered that Tamar Kercheval resembled the God of the New Testament in that she was keen on anyone who was keen on her son—the boy had been brought forth for the sake of love and therefore ought to receive plenty of it. For Harriet and Margot, doting on Gabriel was very easily done, so they could count on Tamar for anything. She filled in all their immigration papers herself and had lawyers check them over. And she pressed Harriet to make free use of Parker's Pigeon Post: **Write anything you want . . . I won't read it.**

Harriet wrote in Druhástranian, just in case: **Hi Zu, I'm staying with very nice people in Yorkshire and everything's great except sometimes people try to act as if they don't understand what I'm saying when I think they actually do understand but just think my accent should be more like theirs. Are you well? What about Dottie and Lyudmila and Suzy and Rosolio and Cinnabar and the rest of the GGs? Lots of love, Harriet.**

Zu wrote back: **Hi H, the GGs bought our farm! We're doing well—busy—and it just so happens that we're looking for somebody to come** and read farmers' almanacs to the cows; the job's here for you if you want it. Our accent may not be the world's most melodious, but English accents are annoying too, so if anybody makes fun of the way you talk, just give them one slap in the face with your foot! You have to do that for us. Sending love.

Harriet wrote: **I'm well, and I'm glad you're all well.**

Zu wrote: **We're glad you're well and glad that you're glad we're well.**

They couldn't write down all they wanted to; the pigeons couldn't carry it all.

At least a few of the Gingerbread Girls would've liked to hear about Tamar Kercheval's beauty spot. It was on her nose, just over her left nostril, and it was so vivid it looked drawn on. In the very early days of Ari and Tamar's relationship, Ari told himself the beauty spot was the reason he kept asking Tamar out. He was so irritated by it, so irritated by the affectation of it . . . he couldn't end things without telling her how much it pissed him off, but the occasion for criticism had to arise somewhat naturally. One day she'd forget to draw on the beauty spot, or it would be a little higher up or a little lower down than before, or lighter in color, or it would just have changed in some way, and then he'd pounce. But Ari was never able to catch Tamar out. Somebody must have told this woman she had a cute nose once, and she'd made the beauty spot a crucial step of her makeup routine ever since. Ari didn't see anything wrong with playing up one's best features, but Tamar's nose wasn't that distinctive. There were several far more advantageous locations for a drawn-on beauty spot. Her chin was nicer, as were her cheeks, the corners of her eyes and mouth. What was her nose compared to these? By their seventh date, irritation had become abhorrence, and Ari reached across the dinner table and tried to remove that attention-seeking little dot. He tried with a napkin first, then with a finger and thumb. To no avail, since the beauty spot was a birthmark. After about five minutes, Tamar said: **I think I'm having the crème brûlée. What about you?** She'd been looking down at the menu throughout.

Something else: Harriet's mother was uneasy about Tamar. This came up as a topic during one of Harriet and Margot's late-late-late-night consultations as the two lay side by side in Margot's bed, shuffling and reshuffling the English-vocabulary flashcards they rarely remembered to actually test each other with. Whisper-gossiping in English served roughly the same objective anyway.

Want to see a couple who's madly in love in very different ways that might cause big trouble?

Where do we go to see that? Harriet asked.

Not far—just watch Ari and Tamar for a while. Tamar Kercheval . . . why did I have to meet this woman . . . ?

Mum, you don't like Tamar?

I do, actually. It's more that I don't like meeting her after meeting Clio Kercheval. We three . . .

What about you three?

You still don't see it? Why do you think I forbade you to like Clio more than me? She's just your type, Margot said. And so's Tamar. Tamar's take on being in love, for instance. I've worked her out there. Her "I love you" doesn't mean "If you seem cold toward me for one morning I sleep poorly two nights in a row," nor does it mean "I can no longer imagine a situation in which I choose self-preservation over whatever you need," or even "If you look at anyone else the way you look at me I will almost definitely want to kill you and the person you looked at that way"—those are more Ari's version of being madly in love.

And with Tamar?

With Tamar it's more having the same plans.

He comes up with a scheme and she makes it as watertight as possible, and they go on like that. His plans are her plans. But when she comes up with something—well, her plans had better be his plans too, or he'll be in a world of shit. And why? Because she sees him as her equal. If only she could be more arrogant and try to do all the loving deeds by herself, just love him without respect, on the assumption that he doesn't have the ability or the depth of feeling to match her. Instead, whenever he does anything to damage the equality between them, she . . . well, hopefully we won't be around to see it. Well, you look well and truly horrified, daughter. But that's the story of Ari and Tamar.

Harriet wiped cold sweat from her forehead and muttered: **Does it even make sense to describe any of that as love . . .**

KENZILEA KERCHEVAL RANKED FIFTH. Kenzilea lived for work, at-home facials, and cinema dates with her son, who encouraged all onlookers to continue misidentifying her as his sister. Though Kenzilea didn't live with the other Kerchevals, she often requested that Rémy bring

Harriet along when he was visiting her. Harriet had been her patient too, and Kenzilea had decided to let the girl in on all the skincare secrets she would have passed on to her own daughter. Harriet spent whole Sunday afternoons receiving instruction on the best way to wash her face. In between treatments Rémy and Harriet were unofficial home clinic receptionists, greeting an irregular stream of girls and women who'd been given Kenzilea's address. Some were Traveler girls, many were not, but all had heard this doctor was good for non-surgical procedures that didn't come with pointless questions or attempts to contact your family. Somebody would come in with a scared look, a split lip, some uncertainty as to whether her arm was sprained or dislocated, and she'd find herself sat in an easy chair with a pair of cucumber slices over her eyes as she waited for Kenzilea's next opening. Kenzilea's son proved diverting too. He'd try to make small talk (**Isn't skin just a bit TOO absorbent, though? I mean, all that hand cream you just rubbed on three minutes ago . . . where has it gone?**) and the oracular phrasing of his speech induced communal freak-outs.

The occasional lull between patients gave Kenzilea time to follow Ari's directive and have Ambrose-related heart-to-hearts with Rémy: **You shouldn't talk to your dad the way you do; his whole life's gone wrong.**

When appealing to Rémy's better nature, Kenzilea addressed her son by his middle name, which was Nearboy. This only gave Rémy a pretext to ask about the grandfather he'd never met, but one day Harriet jumped in before Kenzilea could begin retelling one of her father's escapades and asked what had gone wrong with Ambrose.

I'll tell you, Harriet. Rémy says it's nonsense, but I'll tell you. We weren't allowed, him and me. He was just too brand-new as far as I was concerned, and vice versa. The way we felt about each other . . .

(Bye, Rémy said, walking out.)

OK, BYE—Yeah, the way we felt about each other made it seem like there was more to me than I knew, or more to him than he knew. We liked that feeling, but most of the people who thought they knew me well, or thought they knew him well, they didn't like it at all, thought we were pretending, or building up what was basically a physical thing into some spiritual link. I mean, there's Ambrose with these ultra-vintage supermodel looks. I was at this palace in Lisbon last summer and there's a portrait there,

of a black courtier . . . this friend of a friend of a very good friend of a friend of Luis I type sort of guy . . . but he's Ambrose Kercheval to the life, right down to the frock coat. Ambrose was just about allowed, and me, this scrappy girl who sprang out of a caravan and used her own head as a battering ram until those medical-school gates buckled, I was just about allowed. But the two together . . . My friends were polite with him, but after he'd gone, they'd tell me, That one's a no no—he's the opposite of lively, and his friends were kind . . . well, patronizing, really, and they'd ask him, What do you two talk about? Our vocab was so different we needed dictionaries or UN translators or something. Even now . . . you just go and tell Ambrose the title of any book or film or TV show I like and he'll tell you, in detail, just why it makes his eyeballs bleed. Dad didn't mind him, though. Loyal bugger, idn' he, that's what Dad used to say. Once he's on your side, he don't care what anybody else thinks. Oh, Ambrose was shocked, really, really shocked, the first time I took him to McDonald's. He took me to his favorite Michelin-starred joint, and I was like what the fuck is this and how come there's hardly any of it?

They'd met the summer before Kenzilea

graduated from medical school; Ambrose was her friend's piano teacher. Kenzilea, usually late for everything, somehow managed to be wondrously punctual when it came to meeting her friend for lunch on piano-lesson days, often arriving before the lesson ended and complimenting Ambrose on the ethereal music she'd heard drifting out of the window. Occasionally what Kenzilea had heard was a composition of Ambrose Kercheval's, performed by Ambrose himself, but most of the time it was a recording of a better pianist that Ambrose wanted his student to hear. Kenzilea's inability to tell the difference was something that Ambrose would've found impossible to overlook if he hadn't been smitten at first sight. He saw her. It was like looking through her personal timeline, past and future, and going, **Wow, yup, gosh, wow, WOW, wow, I want to be there too.** Kenzilea saw him right back, and they went on like that until the evening an ex-boyfriend of Kenzilea's saw them together. Kenzilea thinks of that evening as the turning point between things maybe being all right and definitively going wrong. What if she'd acknowledged that ex of hers, stopped and said, **Hi, how's it going**, just been her "old" self instead of sweeping past him without a second glance and not answering when asked if she knew him? Ambrose would never have ignored somebody he'd been close to. That ex-boyfriend of hers was going along on the other side of the road, on his own, and she was on her way home from a kunqu opera performance she'd watched with Ambrose and a few of his friends—it wasn't a good time for an ex to pop up, not while Kenzilea was cloud-walking like one of the singers she'd just seen onstage (heel-toe-heel-toe, smooth soles, dainty slippers of air). As she did so, she listened to the others talking about the performance, and she put phrases together in her mind, thinking, **OK, so this is the term for that**, but then the ex-boyfriend shouted, **Oi, Little! Kenzilea Little . . .**

The ex-boyfriend was carrying a six-pack of cider and was already drinking one of the cans, and Kenzilea was ashamed of absolutely everything about this person. She couldn't believe she'd ever thought she was in love with him. Him beside Ambrose—no, no, the disparity was horrendous.

After Kenzilea blanked that ex and her other friends got to know about it, a crusade began. Worried friends and insulted exes. **What's the matter? Am I too common? Would you blank me as well, Kenzilea?** They gathered at her flat and laughed when she played them music they hadn't heard before. **Pathetic—you don't even know what you're listening to. You only think you like this because he does.**

Nobody knows you like we do—that was the message. This fling with a piano-playing fop was a betrayal of her old self and her old friends, and they weren't going to stand for it. Kenzilea was disloyal—she admits it, but that wasn't learned from Ambrose; it was just how she was, and the trait had never really made itself clear to her and to her friends before. Or it hadn't really mattered before. Gretel might have made an observation from the professional perspective of a changeling that sometimes people are so determined for their lives to stay the same that they end up changing everything. Three of Kenzilea's friends—well, two exes and a friend—went to see Ambrose. They'd been drinking, and when he opened his front door, he greeted them jovially with the words **Hello, Darren, Darren, and Darren** . . . despite significant differences in physical characteristics, each one of the three men looked as if his name was Darren, and Ambrose felt he couldn't avoid alluding to that fact.

"Darren, Darren, and Darren" shouldered their way into Ambrose's flat and trapped his fingers under the lid of his piano again and again.

They broke his hands. He couldn't play or teach anymore, and the teaching had been more essential than the playing. These were the doings of Kenzilea's old friends. After their visit to Ambrose, she couldn't see him the way she had before, or if she did perceive that backward-and-forward timeline, all she saw in it was eternal deference to the cocky younger brother whose successes he could assist but not emulate. Ambrose lied to Kenzilea all the time, about inconsequential things, and he hid things, she didn't even know what, and Kenzilea stayed on and stayed on, trying to repair her fickleness until her own son (and his) said, **What are you still doing here? If you're staying for my sake, don't bother.**

Gabriel came in at number six on Harriet's list. He was willing to answer every question she asked him and to find answers if he didn't already have them, but his queries regarding Druhástrana's political system were beyond her, and that made her feel guilty . . . for not being able to satisfy that aspect of his curiosity and for not sharing it . . .

There were things Gabriel and Harriet had in common, though. One was a wish to be of use somehow. Gabriel was the most likely candidate for Head Boy come the school elections, and there'd never been a new pupil at their school who was made a prefect as quickly as Harriet was. Enthusiastic participation in extracurricular clubs and charity drives, the polite and personable enforcement of the school's code of conduct, our Gingerbread Girl could do it all. She made many friendly acquaintances among the "illustrious sons and daughters of the illustrious," as Margot dubbed them, but strange to say (and she doesn't know why this should be the case when she remembers all her fellow Gingerbread Girls), she wouldn't be immediately able to put names to the faces of anyone she met at that school if she ran into them again on the street today. Perhaps they wouldn't recognize her either: Tamar had asked Harriet to dye her hair black while she lived with them, so that's what she did.

Ari bought Harriet a bike, and Gabriel took her cycling around Whitby. The two of them climbed the 199 steps up from the town to the abbey, and they read the words of Caedmon's hymn together. **Sing it, please**, Harriet asked, but, just like Caedmon, Gabriel said he didn't know how. Standing among those much abandoned, much rebuilt ruins, Gabriel and Harriet tilted their heads as far back as they could go and regarded the roof of the heavens, seeking out the height at which lost music could be heard again.

Harriet had kept her wheat-sheaf ring on her engagement finger because that was the finger Gretel had chosen for it. Gabriel kept looking at the ring and thinking there was some romantic Druhástranian attachment he had no right to intrude on, and Harriet let that continue without amendment. **Yeah, people get married really young over there . . .**

Gabriel was a mix of honey and vinegar, a son Ari Kercheval ought to have been demonstratively proud of but wasn't. His qualities weren't consistent with those lauded during the course of Aristide Kercheval's lectures on "being his own man," so he viewed his natural inclinations with increasing antipathy. Gabriel Kercheval's goodness to Harriet put her in the unusual position of loving him and very much preferring non-reciprocity. Tamar would jokingly complain of feeling unloved by her son, and rather than laugh or reassure her, Harriet would just say: **Well . . .** Whatever Gabriel cared for, he cared for at the cost of his father's approval, or so he thought. Harriet could hardly say, **Blessed are those unloved by the Angel Gabriel**, but intuition told her that being loved by him would be terrible.

Ambrose Kercheval was seventh on the list. Ambrose and his white silk shirts with the splash of red dyed all around the back of his collar so that seeing him from behind always conjured up morbid thoughts. These shirts were the early works of a well-known designer, a good friend of Ari's from university. **The bloodstained look was one that none of the stylish men of the day really wanted to get behind**—this was years before his breakout piece, the unisex octopus jacket that took everybody by surprise with its eight-sleeved allure. Failing to show support for a friend was unthinkable, so Ari contemplated that fledgling collection and ordered two of the red-collared shirts, these being the least garish option. Having ordered two shirts, he received two hundred, all of which he had to pay for . . . some error in the order log. But Ambrose was fine with it. Ambrose Kercheval was mostly fine with whatever.

He heard that Rémy had submitted a paternity test, and he was fine with that; he empathized as Rémy made peace with the result. The kid must have been hoping and praying that he was somebody else's son. **Sorry, Rémy, you're mine. Sorry.** There were certain gestures he made as he said those words—tiny movements—but they must have really bothered Rémy because he later replicated them when describing the scene to Harriet. Ambrose had lightly patted the crown of his own head and gathered air in his fingers just above the region of the fontanelle, as if attempting to restore unity to the pieces of some sort of helmet—a flimsy one, only paper, perhaps—but it had lasted until that moment. **Like his skull was leaking and he was just trying to sort it out without saying anything . . .** Rémy stopped talking, his words fixed in some gummy web in disgust, and when Harriet asked him why he didn't continue, Rémy said: **That's all.**

Ambrose could be in the same room as his nephew Gabriel for a long time before offered a gently avuncular greeting. The younger Kercheval blinked a few times before saying: **All right, Uncs?** and the blinking was a tactful admission that up until then he hadn't really registered that he had company. Ambrose was fine with that too. And he gave every impression of being fine with Kenzilea's leaving him. According to Kenzilea, she'd moved out without hearing a murmur from her husband's direction. But in his wing of the house there was a room only Ambrose and Ms. Danilenko the house-keeper had known the contents of until the tabs Margot kept on Ms. Danilenko's dusting schedule paid off and Harriet's mother was able to lead her by the hand into a cavern of shrouded forms. The room was wall-to-wall presents, wrapped and unwrapped, large and small, everything still in its packaging or accompanied by purchase receipts so the recipient could return them if she wanted to. Birthday presents, Christmas presents, anniversary presents, joke presents, "just because" presents, curios spotted while traveling, all selected with Kenzilea Kercheval in mind, all brought to that room and kept there because at the last moment Ambrose had reconsidered. **He's mental**, Ms. Danilenko blurted out. **Just mental!** She had been keeping count, and month by month the number of unsuitable gifts increased. **He's going to need a house of his own to hide it all in.**

Rémy was number eight. Last on Harriet's list, and less and less readable as she turned fifteen, then sixteen. He was the only Kercheval Harriet ever heard saying, **Fuck this family**, though she was sure he wasn't the only one who ever felt that way. If Rémy's saying so had ever ruined the mood, it didn't anymore. The words held more animosity than the tone in which they were said, and according to Ari, it wasn't a real family gathering until they'd heard this from Rémy at least once. Perhaps the others thought he said it too often to actually mean it.

Harriet liked and didn't like the way Rémy

watched her mouth very closely, with a focus her words didn't merit. He'd look into her eyes, and then his glance trailed back down, comparing statements. She kept her reaction under control by reminding herself that Rémy didn't do this to make her or anybody uncomfortable; he was doing it because his hearing was impaired and he relied quite heavily on lip-reading. Rémy was making sure he didn't miss anything; she knew that. That look of contemplation wasn't intrinsically lustful—except when it was. For instance: a couple of years after Rémy had left the school he, Harriet, and Gabriel attended, there was still a corner of the common room that was referred to as Rémy K's corner. That was where Rémy used to sit reading with a shawl thrown over his legs, the very picture of an Andalusian old maid. Other boys occasionally commented on **the gheyness** of this pastime (you'd have to disrupt his reading to do this; you'd have to go over to him and make him look up at you), and Rémy would either say **Yup yup** and go back to his book, or he'd cast his blanket aside and begin a heterosexuality-threatening game of kiss chase, which he so rarely lost that by the time his schooldays came to an end, the only boys who continued to use **ghey** as a derogatory term in his earshot were the ones who wanted to see if he was up for a snog and had never learned how to ask nicely.

Gabriel tutored Harriet on weekends to make sure she kept up with the rest of her class. And Harriet liked it, and she didn't like it when just minutes after she'd got her room spick-and-span in preparation for a lesson, Rémy wandered in, asked to borrow a book (Rémy liked Zola too!), and turned everything upside down again in the course of his search for said book. It was strange . . . Rémy couldn't have known that just an hour earlier this skirt had been scrunched up behind the door and that mug could have been set on the window-sill, but his untidying was so exact it was like he'd cranked a dial on a time machine. Gabriel never said anything about her shambolic living conditions. He'd just clear a space and take a seat, and everything he saw when he looked around added to the marks against her. They weren't marks he'd ever reveal if he could help it, but they were there.

RÉMY STARTED WORKING FOR ARI'S company soon after he left school. This wasn't what he wanted, but Ari was quite clear on not wanting

Rémy working for anybody else, so all the boy's other prospects fell through. **Sorry, but your uncle's a big man . . .**

Rémy took his wages and moved into his own flat so as to be out from under Tamar's feet. Harriet, Margot, and possibly Ms. Danilenko missed him, but that was all. As mentioned, Ambrose was fine with whatever, and Gabriel—he and Rémy weren't friends. They didn't go to the same places or know very many of the same people, and their cordiality was careful, in that anything they said to and about each other had been very well considered beforehand. They might have been thinking that given all the other problems between parents, aunt, and uncle they couldn't afford cousin problems too.

Gabriel may have given Harriet her first extra-nice notebook, but it was Rémy who scorned Tamar's less scenic route to the dovecote in order to walk between the house's close-set windowsills and fetch stray messages. One night Harriet was looking at the day's list of new words and thinking, **My head's too full; these will never go in**, when a long shadow crossed her windowpane. She thought . . . or rather, deliberately not thinking, she went to the window and looked out over the rock garden. It was Ambrose's rock garden, since he was the one who cared most for it. She watched as shadows swept along grassy slopes and swirled down the stream: none were human-shaped. Harriet knelt on her tabletop, opened the window, and stuck her head out. She looked left and right, and Rémy was on the next windowsill with his back pressed against the front of the house. He was studying the rocks below with a look that wasn't anywhere near as life-affirming as she would have liked, and she said his name very gently, in case he got startled. He did, a little, but quickly recovered.

You all right? he asked.

What are you doing out there? You don't even live here anymore.

Rude. I'm out here talking to a pretty-ish girl on what could be the last night of my life . . . that's what I'm doing.

Rémy. Come and talk to me in here for a minute.

Aren't you going to get insulted about "pretty-ish"?

I . . . will do that once you come in. Just come in, please.

She'd already been leaning quite far out of the window as they talked, and now she began to climb out onto the ledge. When he saw that, Rémy spread an arm along the wall (certainly more of a spreading motion than a stretching one, as if he were a man of moss) and pressed the center of her forehead with two fingers. Quite gently, yet she lost her balance and rolled off her tabletop and onto the floor, **thump, thump**. She looked up . . . he was directly outside her window now. Somehow, very slowly, Rémy turned around on that tightrope of stone, and he bent to look in at her. His arms were above his head; in daylight she tried to see what he'd used to steady himself and couldn't find anything.

If I fell from here I'd be just about OK, he said. **My dad jumped off at this height years ago. Probably trying to kill himself. He says he wasn't, says he just slipped, but wouldn't you say that too if it turned out you weren't even able to get suicide right? He just ended up with egg on his face—and that limp of his.**

Harriet covered her face and was silent, not wanting Rémy to come in, not wanting him to fall. He seemed to get it and came no closer, just threw a folded square of paper in through the window.

You shouldn't listen to me . . . it's just that you're so earnest I couldn't resist. Anyway, I was up in the dovecote and found that. Read it and unwind a bit. Goodnight!

He left her and rapped at the next window, Ms. Danilenko's, or Mr. Bianchi's, depending on whose room had moved up or down a floor of late. The window opened, and Rémy went in legs first, stepping into the building as if it was a pair of overstarched trousers.

The letter was written in tiny cursive script across three thin sheets, and it was Gretel through and through:

Harriet, I'm sorry to call you away from the present moment. I promised myself I wouldn't do this to you, but you were in a dream I just had, so I think it must be all right to intrude for a few seconds. The dream: We were in times to come. You'd grown up, and as discussed, I had not. But we were a pair of prisoners up before some sort of tribunal, and our judges knew that I was older than you, even though I didn't look it. They were all little girls, every conceivable color and none of them above the age of nine. They were wearing those wigs barristers wear, so they all looked like deranged lambs, and they kept waving assorted objects in our faces—an extra-large bar of chocolate, a mortgage application, a Nobel Peace Prize medal, an assortment of old-fashioned porn, newspaper headlines, a baby's dummy, scientific research articles, a yoga mat, reams and reams of statistics, what else did they bring out . . . the list of things they didn't

bring out would be much shorter. And the shout-ing as each exhibit was presented: What do you make of this, then? How about this and this?

Eventually the leader stood up, unrolled a wheel of parchment, and read it all the way down to the floor and all the way along to the back of the hall—this was a list of all the laws we had broken—and when she got to the end of them, she said, Well, quite, but the main problem is that you're in breach of contract, ladies, so it's not looking good for either of you, I'm afraid.

And you said, Wait, what, what contract! What is it you wanted us to say to all this?

The leader said: Anything. I suppose you thought you could just hum and haw and meddle and take notes without anybody ever finding out what it is you stand for and what you oppose. Guidelines, all you had to do was lay out guidelines . . . now look at us—WE'VE GONE ASTRAY—

And the entire tribunal came running at us. They were screaming that they meant to get their support and inspiration by hook or by crook. Some of them grabbed me around the neck and near well pulled my head off . . . I saw that others had got hold of your shoulders and were trying to pull you away from me, but we held on tight and started using each other's bodies sort of like truncheons, and we sent those kids flying left, right, and center . . .

I expected their guardians to roll in and send us flying ourselves, but those little idiots didn't have anybody else. They all lay down flat on the ground, bawling, SAVE US, SAVE US . . . This was addressed to us, to me and you, but it wasn't clear exactly what they had in mind. I mean, if they meant "save me" as in rescue me, that falls under my remit as a changeling, but if they meant "save me" as in preserve me, surely that's more up your gingerbread street. I do think that if they meant both things they were in luck, because really we don't go anywhere without each other.

It was the last note the Druhástranian pigeons brought back before they retired. After she read it, Harriet got out an atlas and flipped through it, looking for the locations Gretel had pinned, wishing she'd paid more attention instead of leaving it all to Gretel. One place in England, one in the Czech Republic, and the third she couldn't remember at all. They hadn't even set dates, so even if they were both at the right place, the times to meet might well come and go unremarked, making Harriet just like those winners of the numbers game who'd lost their tickets and never found out that they'd won. Harriet and Gretel had form, though. They had luck.

Her thoughts continued past luck, as night thoughts do. And as Harriet thought and thought and thought some more, it seemed to her that there was something particularly Druhástranian about this dream of Gretel's. It wasn't an easy conclusion to arrive at, and initially she balked at it, being only barely aware of having inherited discourse that the only characteristic Druhástranians really share is a rejection of commonality, of some worldview only intelligible to a Druhástranian. **Quite right, it's all I can do not to tune out whenever anyone starts talking like that, but nevertheless, nevertheless,** Harriet argued with herself, **Gretel dreamed quite a Druhástranian dream. I mean, the absence of inclination to pass commentary, a reluctance to subscribe to any ideology in case the compromise proves catastrophic; those aren't the only clues as to the Druhástranian nature of this dream. What about the fear that not having a point of view is in some way a crime? If this dream had been dreamed by a non-Druhástranian perhaps it would have had moral or spiritual overtones, or** nationalist ones, or Gretel would have dreamed we were in a psychiatric hospital being treated for this chronic lack of a point of view.

Nonsense, nonsense, Harriet argued back, if we really must call the dream something, let's just call it Gretelian.

But listen, listen . . . a mind-set that's caught up in, even imprisoned by legality and correctness of form . . . what is that way of thinking if not Druhástranian? To be Druhástranian is to be dissatisfied with one's condition until one can find some official personage to sign off on it. And if someone says that what you're doing is all right today, won't you need to get that approval reconfirmed later, get another stamp at some other desk a year from now? Of course this is a mind-set that a nation can be stunned into. All you need is a century or two of freedoms and strictures that appear and disappear between one year and the next, words and deeds that were frowned upon just yesterday receiving vehement acclaim today . . .

Oh, then Gretel's dream wasn't specifically Druhástranian after all.

Just think of all the mayhem a mind-set like this is proving to be the basis of elsewhere, everywhere; there's nothing unique about this . . .

There was a smidgen of sadness that came with washing her hands of the night thoughts in this way—also . . . sneakiness? She felt as if she'd just told herself a good lie. A lie sandwiched so beautifully between a couple of truths that its form couldn't be delineated.

(Harriet's daughter squirms, and the dolls named Prim and Lollipop share a couple of night thoughts of their own:

"This is the kind of thing you thought about in bed when you were sixteen?"

"You should've played with dolls more when you were growing up. Luckily it's never too late to start . . ."

Harriet reminds them of Dr. Ilesanmi's express stipulation that talking to Perdita is part of the girl's therapy, that what she says is less important than letting Perdita hear her voice and letting Perdita hear words arranged and pronounced in similar ways to those in which Perdita herself spoke before the gingerbread. Perdita and the dolls quiet down, and Perdita gives Harriet an eye-smile of stunning purity: Tyra Banks would be proud.)

Anyway, Harriet did her bit of thinking in bed, and then she slept, but not so deeply that she didn't feel and hear levers and pulleys at work as her room went up two floors, down three floors so that it rested atop the basement, and then back up to her preferred height. Gabriel must be back. He and Ari were the only ones who didn't hesitate to keep pressing buttons like that.

(Harriet has fetched the letter from Gretel. Perdita and the dolls pass it around and confirm that it's written in what they believe to be Druhástranian.

"And when Rémy gave this to you, he said what again?" Bonnie asks.

"**Read this and unwind a bit**, something like that."

"Sounds like he'd read it first. He knows Druhástranian? How?"

Harriet tells them that that question has taken time to settle. Two Kerchevals wanted to forget they used to share a hobby, and a third wanted to cover up all traces of having gone against Ari's wishes. So after much fruitless sleuthing, all Harriet Lee had to do was put a couple of direct questions to Ambrose Kercheval in Druhástranian. He jumped. Right out of his skin, as they say; quite athletic, really. He high-jumped and then started chattering away. He'd taught his son and nephew Druhástranian when they were little. He'd been teaching himself, and they wanted to learn too—Rémy because he found the language easy to pick up and Gabriel because he found it almost impossible. It all started with some lullabies Ambrose came across in a job lot of recordings he bought when his friend's music shop was closing down. He played them to Ari and revived the rumor about their great-grandfather the Druhástranian hot-air balloon pilot. Ari did like a bit of heritage but wouldn't hold with lullabies. Namby-pamby drivel that doesn't prepare you for adulthood . . . he told Ambrose he'd better not hear him singing lullabies to their boys.

So Ambrose just made sure Ari never heard it. But after a few months of the language lessons, his pupils stopped believing that the "Druhástranian" they'd learned could be understood by anyone outside of the trio. Gabriel made a tactful accusation—if there can be such a thing as a tactful accusation, Gabriel would be the one to make it—that Ambrose was basically inventing the language and trying to use it as a relationship bandage. A father–son bandage, a cousin bandage, that sort of thing. And when Ambrose thought it over, it began to seem that really had been his subconscious project. Especially after he'd made contact with citizens of various countries who said they were Druhástranians. They all turned out to be people whose Druhástranianism was a nonviolent product of their alienation from every society currently known to them. He had some good chats with those ones, but not in actual Druhástranian. Harriet couldn't keep from mentioning her conviction that at least a handful of these contacts really could speak Druhástranian, but she didn't feel like being of assistance to the kindly man with scarlet spilled all over his shirt collar. There are plenty of reasons why a Druhástranian abroad would claim not to know a word of Druhástranian, but sheer bloody-mindedness is probably top of the list.

Perdita says that must have been amazing for Rémy, unfolding Gretel's letter and being unable to read it, then picking out words here and there and slowly realizing that he knew what they meant. The experience Perdita describes is very similar to that which Harriet and the dolls undergo as they listen to the half-words she's stringing together.

"I don't think it can have been that amazing if he was thinking about jumping off the side of the building afterward," says Harriet. "I mean, when there's that kind of change in the way words work, it can make you think you're no longer in your right mind."

Lollipop says: "You appeared before those two cousins like . . . like a fairy." Harriet doesn't know why saying this should earn anyone a nudge and a death stare, but this is what Lollipop gets from Perdita.

"Like a fairy?" Harriet repeats.

Lollipop isn't scared of Perdita. "I mean, they invoked you, and there you were in front of them, saying: **Hello, would you like some gingerbread? Furthermore, that chap over there . . . the one with the tasteless shirt and the peppermint cane . . . did you know that what you'd come to think of as his abject poverty of spirit is actually MAD SWAG?**"

"Well—ha-ha—OK. But Margot came too."

And Bonnie wonders aloud whether it's still nighttime or not.)

RÉMY'S LEAVING THE KERCHEVAL household coincided with Ari's being away from home more than ever before, traveling the country with his nephew and introducing him to clients and contacts. Gabriel sometimes studied in Ari's vacant office, but more often than not he was off-premises too, at some library or other, or staying over at a friend's house. The members of the 3:00 A.M. kitchen crew changed: Harriet would bake gingerbread while Margot, Mr. Bianchi, and Ms. Danilenko played a card game called "Marriage" and turned up the radio to obscure the sound of Tamar's ear-splitting telephone rows with Kenzilea. Harriet scanned the internet for indications of what it was Ari did for a living. Nothing came up when she searched his name—for some reason the search engines eschewed their usual practice of referring to people with the same first name or people with the same surname when it couldn't find anything on a person with that exact combination of first name and surname. Searching Ari's name got Harriet literally zero search results—still does. It was the same with all the male Kerchevals, though traces of Tamar and Kenzilea abound. When Rémy started work for Ari's company, it occurred to Harriet that she hadn't searched the company name. She did so, and read her way through a lot of positive buzz. Clients fully recommended the company's services without being at all clear about what it was the company had done or was doing for them. Well, who were the clients then? Those Harriet found any mention of were mainly notable for living off income inherited back in Victorian times. Members of online forums with usernames that matched some of those on Ari's client list wrote about a two-way selection process: you solicited Ari's services, but he only took you on if you met certain criteria of his. Margot was doubtful. Would people like this openly use their real names as usernames? They'd recently discovered that a Facebook friend of Harriet's they'd both thought was a famous actress was in truth an anti-fan of that actress who dedicated about an hour of each day to posting unflattering paparazzi photos and insipid status updates based on her estimation of the famous actress's inner life.

Harriet went to bed. Margot went to bed. Ms. Danilenko and Mr. Bianchi went to bed. Tamar reeled from closed door to closed door, crying and asking if Gabriel had come home. **Gabriel . . . Gabriel . . . hello? Is anybody awake?** Her hard-hearted housemates waited for her to realize she had work in the morning, and after one more journey around the house, she said, **Five A.M.!** and went to bed herself. Once she was certain the coast was clear, Harriet opened her bedroom door to go to Margot and found Margot already there on the landing. On the count of three they stated their interpretation of the search results on Ari's company.

One—two—three—is Ari . . . a hit man?
If they'd known they'd be helping someone

spend blood money, they would've just stayed in Druhá City.

A couple of days later, Ari came home, and Margot burst in on him while he was lunching at his office desk. She asked about his profession, and he laughed through a mouthful of salad and told her not to worry her pretty little head about it, in those actual words. Then he shuffled some papers and added that unless she had any other questions or concerns, he had to be getting on.

Margot and Harriet had already discussed what they would do in this eventuality, so Margot proceeded to go all nineteenth century on Ari. She spoke of largesse, unquiet conscience, and umbrellas of protection that must be retracted for the good of all. Ari's appointment book was open on his desk, and Margot took advantage of her partial view to note that his next meeting was with Gabriel. His own son making appointments to see him . . .

How about speaking plainly, woman?

If you think you can keep me and my daughter around forever just because you want reminders of your own generosity—!

Suppose that's exactly what I think— what then?

Well, it won't do. We're moving out.

Wonder who'll be next, Ari said sadly. **Maybe Tamar.**

Margot told him she believed his big brother would always back him up.

That right? To be honest, I'd never really thought about it. But yes, good old Ambrose. Well . . . best of luck with it all. Call if you need anything.

And Margot did call. Not to make any requests, just to tell Ari things she thought he might like to hear about. He warned her that she should spend her time more constructively, but if a week went by and he hadn't spoken to her, he'd phone and grumble about people who expected other people to wait around for their calls.

11

THE LEES DIDN'T LEAVE WHITBY. THEY stayed in town, but . . . well, I'll put it this way: For a year and a half, the view from Harriet's bedroom window had been a cue to start her morning. She'd wake up, go to the window, and, unless the weather was very bad, she'd see Ambrose Kercheval pottering around his rock garden, tapping his rainbow-striped cane with an air of being about to launch into a Gene Kelly–style showstopper.

She had not been unappreciative at the time, but she only really discovered just how splendid that view had been when she and Margot began living within their own means and the tiny window of their studio flat looked out onto a brick wall. The Lees' new digs were the best they came across after asking an estate agent to show them all properties with "as little natural sunlight as possible." Stating a budget was anathema to Margot Lee—she'd do anything, anything to avoid revealing that her funds were insufficient. It was like Ambrose and decision-making, only the contortions were more bizarre. Would Ambrose pretend to find sunlight deplorable so as to get out of having to make a decision? Come to think of it, maybe he would.

Given the parameters they'd searched within, the view from the studio flat was as to be expected. And as far as Harriet was concerned, the interior more than made up for it. She and Margot had said goodbye to their rental deposit, borrowed principles from the art of Kintsugi, and used metallic paint to augment the vein-like fissures that ran all along the walls of the flat. At one point during the painting process Harriet noticed that her mother was quietly sucking in a great deal of air through her mouth and letting an even greater amount of water out of her eyes. What to do? Harriet cleared her throat a few times, and Margot continued crying; then Harriet scratched her head with the handle of her paintbrush, a miserable scratch that only made her head itchier, and Harriet asked: **Are you OK?**

Yes, of course. Nothing's really wrong. It's just that here we are in this ugly room trying to make it nicer to live in, but we're probably only making it even uglier. It'd be good if I could manage not to make such a mess of things, for once. Maybe next time. Anyway, what about you? Are you OK?

Harriet mumbled that the paint had been a good idea and she thought it looked really nice, and she and Margot went on trying. Rays of platinum crossed beams of dingy plaster; the dimensions of their room deepened. As they painted, Harriet made an attempt to ask a question via telepathy. She would've loved to know why Margot went on dragging her daughter all over the place in the name of some better way of life that probably didn't even exist, doing this in the full knowledge that said daughter had no special needs aside from that of being wherever her mother was. And just when Harriet's telepathic message to Margot was almost ready to send, the woman flattened a hand across the girl's forehead and said: **Don't**

wrinkle your forehead like that; let's minimize frown lines while we can, OK?

With no benefactor standing between her and the jobs she'd daydreamed about, Margot tried a few of them, cheating a bit, since Tamar was her character reference. She lasted two weeks as a personal shopper and one week each on jobs as an assistant stylist for magazine photo shoots and an assistant curator of a museum (**I can definitely handle this, Harriet . . . it's a teeny tiny museum . . . all in one room!**). She voluntarily left each post. At least, she said it was voluntary. Having conceded that she couldn't opt out of building actual experience, Margot's new plan was to live off a Minimum FrankenWage, the cobbling together of wages from the three jobs she eventually found. Two of her jobs were paid in cash, so in official terms, she stayed below the tax threshold. The Minimum FrankenWage put them a few pence above it, and parting with 20 percent of that . . . the mind boggled. She knew people did it, it seemed like some of the people she ran into at the Job Center did it, but how? The Lees were on one meal a day as it was. Admittedly a big meal. Could it be cut down to medium size? Margot and Harriet got lean again. Not anywhere as lean as they'd been on the farmstead, but lean enough to prevent regular menstruation. Ambrose Kercheval came to see Harriet after school one day, and when he clocked her, she got some idea of the shocked expression he must have exhibited the first time he went to McDonald's with Kenzilea.

My dear girl. Wouldn't you like to have some—Ambrose checked his watch—**late lunch? On me. Please!** Harriet didn't want to eat a meal Margot had had to skip, but she didn't want to be unsociable either, so she and Ambrose sat on a park bench and shared her emergency gingerbread slab. According to Ambrose, he'd been about to put a job on offer through his "usual channels," but then he'd thought Harriet might be interested. She shook her head. He told her how much he'd pay, and she shook her head with a little less conviction.

I can't work for you . . .

It's just a delivery job.

There's no use asking; we're not taking any money from you . . . because of what you do . . .

What I do?

The company. You and Ari.

Come, come, we're not that bad.

They weren't hit men, though Ari's "whatever it takes" mentality often left Ambrose ruminating that they might as well be. Their company managed dynastic wealth, swept a searchlight across all the tributaries of an inheritance, and guaranteed that no matter how much of the original capital had been spent, there would always be more. Much more. If you were wealthy now and you put the Kerchevals in charge of your assets, your grandchildren would be four to five times as rich. This was the profession of both Ari and Ambrose's parents and that of their father's father and great-uncle. There were many close associates at work behind the scenes, but client liaison was straightforward. The business had two faces to it. One encouraged the client to spend when it was deemed necessary to spend, while the other encouraged saving when it was deemed necessary to save.

Father was Save and Mother was Spend. Now I'm Save and Aristide is Spend. Come back in twenty years or so and it'll be the same company, only with Rémy saying Spend and Gabriel saying Save. Spend's always the more creative one . . . there's a lot of troubleshooting on that side of things . . .

So if you're Save, all you have to do is sit on top of a pot of gold rubbing your chin?

Ambrose coughed a couple of times. That was how he chuckled.

Didn't think so. About the job . . .

Ambrose wanted Harriet to collect one package a day—a package she'd find waiting in the front hall of Kercheval House each morning.

How many mornings?

One thousand and eighty, with bank holidays off. Maybe more. We'll have to see how it goes.

Harriet was to deliver the packages to Kenzilea Kercheval, see that she unwrapped them, and tell him in detail what her initial reactions had been.

You can't outsource this one, Mr. Kercheval. It's OK . . . this isn't your decision. You have to deliver one package to Kenzilea Kercheval every day, and if she isn't in that day, then you deliver two the next day and so on until all the presents—

All the presents? Ambrose asked.

Oh, nothing. I don't know why I said that. Anyway, you have to. And that—that's an order . . .

He smiled at her and said: **I see.**

Kenzilea was irritated; it was too late for gifts, she had no room for them, she'd return them. Only she couldn't. She looked at the receipts, and the dates fell so far beyond the standard twenty-eight-day returns policy . . . she dug up her daybook for the year in which the gift had been purchased and phoned Ambrose to read him that day's doings: hospital, home clinic, dinner with Rémykins (or see what excuse he makes for not coming to dinner), a good gossip with Ms. X, Dr. Y, or Mr. Z before bed. This was supposed to impress upon him how irrelevant the purchase was to her current life, but it was awkward because when she thought about the day that was almost at an end, hadn't the substance of it been more or less the same as the one she was depicting as ancient history? Right down to setting aside of blocks of time for uninterrupted gossip . . .

Hmph. Since I'm stuck in my ways, shall we go for a milk shake, ex-husband?

Ambrose thought a milk shake would be just the thing. **Malted**, he added, since McDonald's doesn't sell those.

Margot and Harriet searched the Kercheval company name again and reread the results in a new light, though, as Ambrose had said, terms like "cutthroat tenacity" were only slightly less sinister in the context of hoarding wealth.

They're not hit men, though . . . damn and blast it. I did ask Tamar, and she was so cagey. What did Ari tell you? Well, daughter, what do you think I'm going to say now?

Let's go crawling back? Only joking. Onward, onward . . .

The Lees grew out their hair dye and went about gray-headed, sold the clothes the Kerchevals had bought them, swapped the bright silks and swishy skirts for secondhand jeans of the type that are usually sold to men and white T-shirts or the cream-colored jumpers that were consistently the cheapest available in charity shops. When Margot goes through a romantic drought nowadays she asks Harriet if she should go back to dressing like that. They both remember how often Margot got asked out during that period. By people she enjoyed too—it was something to do with charges they didn't emit and others that they did. Twice Margot brought a lover home and Harriet thought they might be considering something long term. Twice Harriet had the simultaneously intriguing and excruciating experience of watching two people having sex without touching, or even moving, apart from a few uncontrollable and quickly suppressed gasps. Intriguing would've outweighed excruciating if one of the people involved hadn't been her own mother . . . and wasn't this a sort of inversion of the non-physical cage fights Margot and Simon had dragged each other into right in front of their daughter? Both potentially long-term involvements stalled; Harriet never found out from which end, but she cherished the boozy picnic each visitor brought along with them. Flaky bread, the creamiest of cheeses, roasted pheasant breast, and tall bottles of wine that waxed flamingo-necked the drunker Harriet got.

But those were the two brief holidays her mother was able to find the time and inclination for. The rest of the time Margot was on her way to work, at work, on her way back from work or asleep. It wasn't her clothes that drew in the amorous response to her person—Margot Lee had an eidolic beauty in those days, her gaze downcast as she tended to what flickered within, the drowsy, drowsy beating of a heart that knows how few its needs are. One of Margot's jobs required her to think on her feet—a coalition of independent café owners paid her a monthly wage to stand outside selected Starbucks locations and "discreetly discourage potential customers from going in" (methods not specified). Of Margot's other four jobs, the most notable was probably the agency-facilitated one. Applicants were put through a few shrewdly anonymous checks for trustworthiness before they were approved for employment. (Margot submitted her CV and was told, three weeks later, that she'd passed both interview stages. **Who interviewed me, and when?! Answer came there none.**)

The job itself was waiting for deliveries at people's houses. You arrived as the customer was leaving, and there was no popping in and out of the house before the parcel(s) had been signed for, as you weren't left with any house keys. And Margot Lee didn't just sit around watching TV while she was waiting; she did any washing up that was lying around and rearranged furniture so that the rooms looked better. To say that is to simplify what Margot does; her talents lie in the psychotherapeutic realm. Nowadays she gets magazine write-ups describing her as an "architect of the emotion of living spaces," and though she wishes there was a less off-putting way to say it, she does own up to a structural approach to what she does. Once, as she paced around waiting for a package in a living room that made her dizzy whenever she approached the center of its floor, she fell to thinking of a way to either close off that whirlwind center or reset its level. Window-shopping had been good that week. She'd seen a folding screen . . . filigreed clouds hurried along across its cutwork sky, and it stood on little legs . . . Margot picked up her credit card. The shop she had in mind didn't have a website, so she phoned them and placed an order for delivery. Since the shop was just down the street, the screen arrived before the package she was waiting for. She positioned the screen, left the package in front of it (or behind it, depending on your vantage point), and moved on to her next waiting session. That evening the Waiting Agency called her to say that the customer was VERY EXCITED, wanted to know exactly what Margot had done to make the room so comfortable she felt as if she'd been born in it, and so on. She wanted to know how much she owed Margot. Margot quoted the price she'd paid for the screen and the customer phoned her back directly to ask her to take away the screen.

That's silly money. But maybe . . . if you have time . . . do you think you find some less expensive things that have . . . how to say it . . . similar force?

And with that Margot was on her way toward what she most wanted to do. Being able to work for herself was part for it, but she would have worked for anyone who allowed her free rein over the construction of images that dwelled in your own image, entering through the eye and enveloping all your other senses. A jazz lover Margot was seeing for a while lent her Dorothy Ashby's entire discography and said she wanted to live inside Dorothy Ashby's harp; in between her other jobs she clothed the jazz lover's home in shades of blue, each shade exalted in its temperature and texture.

The Margot Lee effect is one of visceral familiarity. Harriet thinks of the time a farmstead girl put on every piece of clothing and every accessory she'd been told to and walked along the corridors of a ritzy hotel as if she knew everybody in it and they knew her. Translated to physical space this means that any element in a room that seems to turn to you and say: **Oh, it's you . . . welcome home** is probably an element that Margot's dug up. You might not be immediately bowled over by the effect—even now there are suspicions that she's overrated—but if Harriet's mother has really worked a place over, then you know it when you try to make a definitive exit but keep going back for things you've left in there. Upon collecting a glove from a window seat and realizing that that was her final excuse to go back to that particular room, Harriet found herself gripping the door lintel before she went out. There were tears in her eyes—she was leaving a place of joy, a place that was confiding and confidential, and for what? Some cold, dark forest full of dead ends. She asked her mother if she'd always been able to do this.

Margot said: **Oh no—I learned while you**

**were gone and it seemed more and more likely
that instead of you coming back we were both
going to go even farther away.**

She'd wanted to be able to fix things up nicely
for the two of them wherever they went, so the
tinkering began . . . sending away for catalogs and
pairing this with that in her head as if money were
no object . . . then going down a level to the next
best pairings, and the next . . . and she practiced.

Unexpected complications arose once Margot
was finally able to work for herself. The power
to make things cozy attracted dubious admirers
and repelled those she most wished to support.
She worked on her tact; she had to when turning
away fiery types who could sink her business if
they threw enough of a tantrum, but some conversations were unavoidable. One fellow's refusal to
take no for an answer was adversely affecting the
rest of her work—calls were missed and delayed
while she tried to get this non-client off the
phone, and eventually he got the explanation he'd
asked for. Margot told him it wasn't the budget
(he'd said he could increase it) or the fee she'd be
paid (he'd said he could increase that too) or the
timing (he'd said he could wait until her schedule cleared up). Harriet listened in on the final
phone call, recording it just in case the man made

a threat, but Margot's voice was more audible than her caller's was. Pushed beyond tact, Margot told her caller what the real problem was. She told him she couldn't think of anything more sad or less interesting than putting her heart and mind into making him feel secure. How on earth could she make someone who believed there are too many foreigners in his country feel secure? She told her caller that replicating the inside of a dustbin would be much more interesting and fulfilling for her than replicating the inside of an airtight safe. Her caller mostly spluttered, and then all of a sudden—**Hello? Hello? Oh, he's gone**—

Even as she burned bridges with some VIPs, Margot Lee struggled to get beyond preliminary phone calls with others—the directors of women's shelters, halfway houses, and other outreach organizations, people who could give her work that would improve her work. Namedropping the Kerchevals didn't wash with them at all, and even if she was offering to work for free, all materials included, and there was no time to consider such services as Margot seemed to be offering: **You'd like to come in and rearrange some cushions? We can do that ourselves.**

All that was up ahead. Before that there was the Minimum Franken Wage, and if Mr. Airtight

Safe had come to her during that time Margot would've just done his bidding. You've heard about Margot's two cash-in-hand jobs, but her third job, and the only one she received a pay slip for at that time, was as sales assistant in an antiques shop. More minding antiques than selling them, as plenty of people came in to have a look around, but only a few made a purchase. Harriet took the day off school and stood in for her mother when Margot's other working hours overlapped with her antiques-shop hours. A Lee standing in for a Lee who was busy standing in for somebody else.

Gabriel Kercheval came into the shop one afternoon. Harriet was leaning on the counter at the back of the shop reading **La Bête humaine** and thinking what a different beast this book was in English. Whilst reading she hoped that the group who'd just entered the shop and were going around picking things up and putting them down again weren't going to break anything and that their slightly sneering expressions were a haggler's method of disguising ardent attachment. Harriet had trotted around after them for a few minutes trying to tell them the stories of the objects they were handling, but a member of the group had warned her that they'd all leave if she didn't "calm down," so Harriet had returned to the counter, where she read and thought of her Professor Procházka. She also thought of making a sale, a good sale. She mustn't make a bad sale . . . if she lost this job she'd lose the perk her mother most prized: getting to arrange the shop window display.

(In fact Margot was already on the verge of letting the job and the window-dressing perk go. She didn't want Harriet missing any more school—**you, my one and only, first and last daughter, you who loves school the way others your age love clubbing or finding out each other's a/s/l in chat rooms** . . . This wasn't inaccurate, with the caveat that Margot made it sound as if Harriet was popular at school. She wasn't, but she enjoyed syllabi as ways of knowing what she had to learn. It was good to follow one alongside others who also needed to learn the same thing. This was far less daunting than that task Gretel had identified . . . the one that involved working out an asking price for her gingerbread. Even if she got her sums right and it turned out life owed her something, there was no way such a bill would ever be settled. Life isn't ill-natured; it's just dirt poor, like any other public resource.

Tamar and Ari had given her to understand that a state-school classroom is one in which it's impossible to see the blackboard through the thicket of fists flying in every direction. But either Harriet's new new school wasn't that rowdy or even the rowdiest inmates of after-school detention were disarmed by the slightly nervous approach of a gray-haired girl who was all of five feet and one inch tall and carried a large tin of homemade gingerbread with her. As a social experience Harriet didn't find school bad, but it could have been better. Harriet would join groups, groups of boys and groups of girls, groups of student librarians and groups of teen iconoclasts, and so on, and she'd exchange smiles with the people she found gathered there . . . all genuine smiles. Nobody had anything against Harriet, and she didn't have anything against anybody, but, bit by bit, in twos and threes, the group she'd just joined migrated and recongregated elsewhere, and she didn't have the heart to chase it. Once Harriet turned to the last girl left standing with her beside the snack vending machine and said, **Why don't we talk a bit . . . just talk?** To her credit, the girl Harriet questioned did take time to try to think of a proper reply. **You seem really nice**, she said, after a few seconds. This seemed to serve both as answer and consolation prize; very soon after saying that, the girl rejoined her group across the hall, and Harriet thought about how a lot of people are just looking for acquaintances. Which is understandable; a lot of the people one meets have already formed close attachments, and there's quite enough going on in those friendships already. In an environment like this, Harriet Lee must have seemed like a bit of a social chore, one of those girls who weren't satisfied with mere conversation . . . having a little chat about nothing with her today bound you to more little chats the next day and the day after . . .

But it wasn't true! Harriet seriously considered having little cards printed up for circulation purposes: **Harriet Lee—Friend or Acquaintance: It's Completely Up to You!** Margot found out and nixed this plan.)

Harriet's shop-floor uniform was a work of faded grandeur—its collar had once been covered with brambles of bronze. Such a collar . . . finely worked and richly threaded—sometimes Harriet smoothed and tapped that part of the robe for the sake of what had once been there . . . she'd seen it all in a photograph that was older than her. Margot said the photo was nice, but as things stood in the here and now, the robe was nothing more than an ankle-length rag. From a distance its color was a grainy gray, but the fabric draped well, and up close (but you had to come very, very close) you could see its true multicolor, tens of thousands of tiny rainbows tumbling and vaulting across the cloth. The wearer of this gown had the provenance and special features of every item in the shop ready for recital, but all anybody asked about was the price; she'd get flustered, give incorrect information, and have to amend the price just before the final sale. The object on the counter always cost more than she'd initially said it did, and then she'd replace the antique while the customer went off in a huff. Harriet often sent Ari psychic reprimands for giving her clothes and a bicycle instead of giving her tips on how to persuade a customer to make that investment in her as a salesperson and buy the things she wanted them to buy. One of the greatest blasts of despair Harriet sent Ari Kercheval's way followed a visit from a woman wearing a leather jacket and a tutu skirt who walked up to the shelf where the antique books were displayed, picked up a leather-bound Latin tome in both hands, and asked: **What is this about?** in a harried tone of voice, as if she wasn't the one who'd picked up the book but the book was harassing **her**, had cornered **her**, and was mumbling about how it had something to say. Apart from times like that, Harriet didn't mind spending a few school days at the shop; it made her like school even more when she went back.

(Perdita says, "Hopeless," and her enunciation is the clearest it's been in weeks.)

Also, seeing Gabriel was worth missing school for. He hadn't come in with the group Harriet hoped were hagglers, but she didn't see or hear his arrival. Rather, she became gradually aware of him moving around the shop too, picking things up and putting things down as the others were.

It had been about eight months since Harriet had last heard from Gabriel; she'd switched schools, but Tamar had called to tell her all about his having finished school covered in the glory of seven A's at A Level. Harriet presumed he was working for Ari now, like Rémy was. He looked good. A little on the thin side, but, as he said later, she could talk. The shop was poky and narrow and L-shaped, so sometimes Gabriel was snuffed out of her line of sight, only to rekindle in a different spot, looking at her over, under, and through the displays. Each time this happened he showed her an object he'd taken from one of the shelves, and he seemed to want to know whether or not she thought he should buy this thing. She laughed, thinking, at first, that this behavior was out of character, then conceding that the character she must have previously assigned to him—whatever it was that made her think "this is out of character"—could've been a misapprehension on her part. She nodded when he picked up a brass measuring wheel: **Yes, you may approach with your well-chosen purchase.**

What is it? Gabriel asked, as he handed over his card.

She told him everything. She told him where, when, and by which company the measuring wheel had been made, she told him the location of the seamstresses' workshop the measuring wheel had been used in and the dates between which that workshop had been in operation. Harriet told Gabriel staff numbers, key names from the history of the workshop, and the exciting honor of being selected to supply chiffon to one of Paris's grand fashion houses (now also long forgotten). She told him how the brass measuring wheel had found its way to the shop in a boxful of other objects that had already been sold. She laid out tracing paper and showed him how the seamstress would have used it to gauge how cloth would curve around a neckline or the opening of a sleeve, where buttonholes could go, from what distance a pattern should repeat itself. Gabriel stuffed the measuring wheel into his coat pocket and said he'd cherish it. He was looking at her wheat-sheaf ring. Harriet

stifled her laughter; he'd been all happy and play-
ful when he'd thought she was no longer wearing
it, but now that he saw she still was . . . she put
away the tracing paper and whispered the rest
of the story of the measuring wheel to herself as
she moved boxes around underneath the counter.
Gabriel was still there when she returned to the
surface.

Sorry I didn't call you back, he said.

Huh, call me back when?

Gabriel stood aside while someone asked how
much a gilded statuette of the goddess Athena
cost. Then he said: **I think it was last week?**

Last week? I didn't call you last week.

He smiled (more smirked, really—what was
the matter with him?) and said: **OK. Anyway,
sorry. And now I've got to go, but I wanted to
see you . . .**

That's . . . nice to hear.

He wanted to see her . . . , and he kept saying
he had to go and then just staying. She wrapped
and boxed the Athena statuette and a strand of
green malachite beads, then asked Gabriel if he
was going back to work. He said he was going back
to uni. She could see how this would have come
about—Gabriel preparing to join the company
and Ari telling him to go and train as a solicitor

first, perhaps sugarcoating the long delay: **We need a great lawyer, and you've got more of a head for this sort of stuff than Rémy . . .**

As he headed for the shop door, he said that even if Harriet wasn't the one who had called him, she should keep a better eye on her phone . . . thirty-eight missed calls were a bit much . . .

OK, stop right there . . . er, please. Gabriel had his phone in hand. Harriet took it and scrolled through his call history (Mum, Mum, Uncs, Mum, Dad, Uncs, who's Jocasta, who's Kaidi, who's Polly, lots of calls from them, Uncs . . .) and eventually she found her own name, in red, with the number 38 in brackets beside it. She was taken aback by the fact that she really did seem to have done this, and she was dismayed by his having seen all the calls and still not calling her back.

Same thing last month, but the record doesn't go that far back, Gabriel said, taking his phone.

I . . .

Should I go first? Gabriel asked. **OK, I missed that window of time. You know, the one that lets you respond without it being blatant that you thought too much about how to respond . . . or too little. And then I thought it's not as if we talk much on the phone anyway. We're always good in person. Aren't we? There was something**

you really wanted to talk about, so. Here I am in person.

Something I really wanted to talk about, eh? I wish I knew what it was!

Really? His voice, or perhaps just the closeness of it, made her realize they were the only ones left in the shop. He put one arm around her waist, then the other. Her hands rose as his lowered. She laid both hands against his chest, just to let them rest there, but he stepped back as if pushed away; he was saying **Sorry** and **I shouldn't have—**

That was no good. She put her arms around him this time, and his hands covered hers. They breathed, hand over hand. She looked up at him and thought:

I think he thinks I—

He's right. (Mostly? I think? Seventy-five percent? Sixty percent? More than fifty, anyway.)

Oh, he's going to—

She grabbed a large snow globe and a crossbow, held them up on either side to obstruct the views of both security cameras, and she and Gabriel kissed and kissed and kissed the way they'd wanted to for years, the way only a hormonally enflamed sixteen-year-old and a likewise enflamed eighteen-year-old can. He kept trying to talk but she kept kissing him, and she tried to talk but he kept kissing her, but eventually they were able to hold off just long enough for her to put down the snow globe and the crossbow and rest her arms, though she and Gabriel kept very close together in case of urgent kiss deficiency. During this pause he was able to tell her, **I was seeing someone, but we broke up . . . we broke up because you called me thirty-eight times in a row . . .**

HARRIET STAYS OFF ALCOHOL because it brings out deviousness in her—a self-directed deviousness. Drunken Harriet creates puzzles that sober Harriet is then expected to solve. Take those two dates on which Harriet bombarded Gabriel's phone with calls (and left voicemail . . . it took him months to tell her about all the voicemail she left)—both were boozy picnic days. Drunken Harriet had retreated to the corner of the studio with her phone and decided to work on her own love life. She felt exempt, marvelously exempt from all those rules that usually seemed to be in place to keep her from full and honest expression of her thoughts . . . perhaps this was what it was like to be her mother. Now she could inquire whether Rémy would risk it for a chocolate biscuit. Or she could call Gabriel. Gabriel or Rémy, Rémy or Gabriel. Wouldn't chasing Rémy be like running after a tiny kitten that turned around, morphed into a cheetah, and hunted you down because you'd stepped on its tail? Whereas Gabriel would be the kitty that got a bit cross, then just lapped up some milk and went back to sleep.

I know, thought Drunken Harriet. **I'll phone Gabriel and ask if I can ever be anything more to him than a good deed his family did. Oh, he's not answering. I'll leave him the question in a voicemail. That was a mistake; I'll call and tell him to delete that voicemail without listening to it. Still not answering . . . now I'll scream WHO CARES, YOU'RE JUST SOME BOY, JUST SOME BOY . . . I WOULD BE A GREAT GIRLFRIEND, YOU WISH YOU DESERVED A GIRLFRIEND LIKE ME. What to do now? Apologize, apologize, and apologize. No more calls. Wait, just one more. This is the voicemail I should have left in the first place. When he hears this he'll come to me. I'll tell him he is Paradise and that I want him really badly, and then I'll laugh and cry and snuffle like a little piglet. He will find this endearing. No, he won't. Why did I make a mess of all those voicemails . . . I know, I'll delete the call records from my recent**

calls and turn my phone off. Sober Harriet won't remember a thing, Gabriel will be too scared/repulsed to mention it, and it'll be just as if this never happened.

Both times Drunken Harriet had done this, Gabriel had been with his girlfriend—

Polly, Kaidi, or Jocasta?

He wouldn't say. But Polly-Kaidi-Jocasta had been amused and then suspicious, had held on to his phone saying, **Let's see how many times she calls**, and thus become the villain of both evenings. Then the voicemails themselves... Gabriel let Harriet listen to the voicemail she'd left, and afterward all she could say was: **Clever, clever drunken me.**

I just thought you... must like me a lot, Gabriel said.

And you liked me a lot, Harriet told him.

Play the messages that demonstrate this?

Don't need to. You listened to all that voice-mail, and you still came to find me.

Gabriel's room at his Oxford college was just like his room at Kercheval House—so clean and neat and bare it was like a crime scene. The unsightly deed had been tidied away, but its magnitude filled the room invisibly, scraping away at each molecule of air, scraping away. The other girl was still there, incredulously observing Harriet's struggle with the simple act of undressing. **See that?** Polly-Kaidi-Jocasta jeered. **That's a button—don't you know how to undo those? And that's a zip.** But naked she and Gabriel lost all circumspection; skin to skin, Harriet didn't care about anything else. Gabriel laid her down on those sheets so pristine that something dreadful must have happened there, and his look was so soothing, his touch was so soothing, it was about to happen again, the same thing that had happened to the other girl; Harriet was in the crime scene now, and she didn't care. Ultimately the sex was like the kissing in that they didn't seem able to stop it at all—nor did they want to, of course— their rampant repositioning and eagerness to do absolutely everything to and with each other was sometimes comic and sometimes Romantic (not lowercase romantic—hardly that at all) in a flesh-bound-quest-to-supersede-flesh sort of way . . . the coupling of a succubus and an incubus. You can say "it's always the studious ones" or whatever else you want to say, but really who knows what it was. Gabriel was in love. Harriet . . . loved him, but.

She didn't love Gabriel's friends and the "pranks" they played on him—

(Someone's at the porters' lodge for you—

looks like your dad . . . sorry, did I say at the plodge? I meant outside the chapel.

What are you talking about, he's waiting in the bar! Oh, there was no one there? He must've had to dash . . .)

She never would like their raising and dashing of his hopes, no matter how much he laughed it off. University was demanding much more of his intellect than school ever had, and the boy who'd liked Druhástranian all the more for its difficulty was dead and gone. Gabriel had lost interest in learning. The grades he used to receive as rewards for his dedication were now necessary to maintain . . . what? He never told her, but she did know that he put more time and effort into turning out essay-length pieces of plagiarism than he would have just thinking through his arguments and writing his own essays. He copied paragraphs out of myriad books and glued his artful collages together with thesaurus substitutions. And even after all that his marks were middling. Gabriel told Harriet to enjoy all those A's of hers while they lasted. He didn't know that she knew what he did at his desk, and she didn't confront him because she had no cure for the malady his essays were symptomatic of. Originality wasn't a strength of hers either, so there was a possibility of her going up to Oxford too and finding herself doing exactly the same thing. Another reason for not confronting him was that she thought she might have stolen some of his brainpower. The notion of fucking Gabriel's brains out as a physiological actuality—of course you may sneer at this, but it didn't seem like an impossibility to Harriet, who'd experience the sexual equivalent of phantom-limb syndrome for a few minutes after their bodies had disconnected. It could really have been love after all, but. And when Harriet thought about the "but," she divided down the middle into Drunken Harriet and Sober Harriet. Sober Harriet couldn't tell whether Drunken Harriet had tried to help her by revealing that she was in love or had been trying to make her life more difficult by obligating her to hide that she wasn't in love so that they could keep fucking without either side holding back. Gabriel was probably better off with his ex-girlfriend, who loved him without a but. Harriet saw it in the photos they'd taken together and read it in the affectionate notes Jocasta tucked into the snack boxes she left for him at their porters' lodge. **You know you forget to eat when you're essaying.** Tamar must have told her Gabriel would come back once he'd had time to think. Jocasta was sunny-natured, had the kind of first-rate brain that was equally well applied to both academics and activism, and on top of all that, she was the kind of leggy beauty model scouts chase down Oxford Street. Tamar took Gabriel and Jocasta out to lunch whenever she was in Oxford, offered to send them away on holiday together. It was funny . . . they were so young. But Tamar wanted to get a mother-in-law lock on Jocasta. In the fullness of time, the daughter-in-law would be made prime minister, and Gabriel would hand his role at the Kerchevals' company over to their son or daughter and focus on scrubbing up well as the Prime Ministerial Spouse. The UK's first black prime minister would need a full-time husband/consultant and a steady home base. Gabriel and Jocasta were a win-win. Jocasta seemed game, but Gabriel just picked at his lunch and left. Something was badly wrong . . . Tamar phoned Margot and told her she felt that someone was corrupting her son . . .

Corrupting how? Margot asked, putting the call on loudspeaker so Harriet could hear the answer.

Hmm . . . it's just—he's just—maybe it's nothing. Tamar said that in a tone that strongly suggested it had better be nothing.

Before she went back to sleep, Margot said: **It's**

not you, is it? Oh shit, it is, isn't it? Listen, if you wanted to make a splash, why not just seduce Ari . . . when Tamar finds out she's going to act as if you did just that.

Shhh, she's not going to find out.

One afternoon Harriet and Gabriel ran into Jocasta at Oxford train station, and Jocasta said: Oh, is this is your friend, the one—the one you told me about? It's so nice to meet you at last. Now that Harriet was standing before her, Jocasta saw that it had been silly of her to worry about all those phone calls and she became solicitous, kept her tone gentle, signaling, I am willing to adopt you, just like my boyfriend did.

Gabriel put his arm around Harriet, and the embrace was . . . stilted . . . he held her as if he was holding a parcel, so it might have looked and felt better if he'd used both arms. Jocasta took in this scene and far from seeming jealous, she looked touched.

On another afternoon Harriet ran into Tamar at Oxford train station and froze. But Tamar hugged her, was pleased to see her, fired a round of questions at her, and somehow managed to answer them all herself before Harriet could get a word in edgeways. Harriet watched Tamar Kercheval get onto the train satisfied that the Gingerbread Girl had no designs on her son and had just come up for an Open Day. She sat down in First Class, and Harriet could practically read the think bubble above her head: **Hope she gets a place . . . how wonderful to think that thanks to us she's been able to make something of herself . . . so glad to have been able to introduce her to opportunities beyond gingerbread . . .**

Tamar waved at Harriet. Harriet waved back. Tamar didn't do half-hugs—she hugged tight, and she'd left traces of her jasmine perfume on Harriet's jumper. Harriet walked to Gabriel's room in a sumptuous haze of scent, and as she walked she thought it would be best if she and Gabriel reached their limit before Tamar was able to confirm that anything had changed.

GABRIEL . . .

Harriet was in Gabriel's bed writing about Martin Luther at the Diet of Worms, and Gabriel was at his desk going over notes from a lecture. From time to time he murmured fussy titbits of vocabulary and surnames involved in landmark cases, and his back was to her; they were better at keeping their hands off each other when there was no eye contact.

Gabriel.

Mmmmm?

She asked if he thought doing well at his degree would matter to Ari and Tamar.

Tamar yes, Ari no.

She asked if he thought failing his degree would matter to them.

Tamar no, but she'd be surprised. Ari . . . huh, actually, Ari might be both surprised and interested.

She asked if he was thinking about failing in order to surprise and interest Ari. (If so, then Harriet was off the hook: She didn't deserve Tamar's wrath for holding on to an ill-loved son in this way; she was just a necessary step in Gabriel's plan to produce paternal surprise and interest.)

He came to her and said yes, or no, he came to her and she didn't care what he said.

12

DEAR PERDITA, DEAR DOLLS, IT'S ALMOST morning. You've already been told that Harriet and Gabriel were thin in those days, and now you must hear it again: even after Harriet and Margot left the Minimum FrankenWage zone, Harriet and Gabriel were thin. They were too nervous to eat properly, too precariously happy (**If I stay close, can't I just stay close to him/her?**), too worried that they'd be made to stop what they were doing. You know that they were both thin and that

Harriet's thinness meant she couldn't track her periods with any regularity. And you know that she and Gabriel were . . . you know that Gabriel Kercheval was spending more time inside Harriet Lee than he was anywhere else. As they lay in bed watching TV one morning, he ran his hand over the curve of her stomach and frowned. She moved away without quite knowing why, but he brought his hand back to the very same spot and pressed down, hard. She slapped his hand.

Get off.

They were watching **The Jerry Springer Show,** and usually they talked over it . . . OK, not talked . . . usually they fucked their way through all the shrill mudslinging and the shock testimony of the secret mistress, philandering father, dowdy-looking housewife who was also a pimp who defended her girls and boys with such violence that customers took care not to even so much as raise as their voices to them. That day Harriet and Gabriel just watched the show. And when the credits rolled, Gabriel handed Harriet her clothes and got dressed himself. They bought a pregnancy test at Boots, and some food. **From now on we're eating more.**

She wondered about his saying "we," especially after the test said she was pregnant.

Dunno how accurate this thing is . . .

They waited two days, and Harriet took another pregnancy test—a different brand. That test said she was pregnant too. He didn't even bother saying "we were so careful"—she was a fecund farm girl, and he was a stud and they hadn't been careful. It was simple; Harriet didn't want to go to the Kerchevals' family doctor, so she booked an appointment at a clinic in Bradford. Harriet didn't want a kid. She was seventeen, and she wanted to go to Oxford and study and not have to look after a kid. Keeping an eye on her mother was preoccupation enough—Harriet felt she'd been doing that since she was born. And it wasn't just that Harriet didn't want a kid; she didn't want to have one with Gabriel Kercheval. Gabriel Kercheval didn't want a kid either. His not wanting a kid was initially quite understated, but when Harriet missed her appointment, he made her sit down at his computer and book another one. She missed that appointment too, and the next. They didn't stop having sex—they couldn't somehow, but they left scratches and bite marks on each other that were deeper than before, and the bruises reminded Harriet of the pinching session at the Gingerbread House, the semiautomated spite of it.

Harriet. Harriet, I can't have a kid. I can't, OK?

OK. I don't want to either. She had a few reasons for saying so, but the primary one was that he was holding her by the throat at the time—a pleasurable sensation for the moment, but one that could become rapidly less so if she said something he didn't like.

Don't say it like that. It's not about wanting to; it's that I can't. We can't. It's not the right time. I—we've got to . . .

That's true, that's true. We've both got a lot of things to do first. You're right, it's not about wanting to, you can't, we can't.

He kept saying he didn't want to hurt her, but he couldn't have a kid.

When he said that, Gretel spoke up. Not at the back of Harriet's mind, more speaking directly in her ear: **Change alert. Hurting you has occurred to him as an option.**

You may have noticed the absence of informational boundaries between Harriet and Margot, but it was at around this time that one went up. Harriet tried to tell Margot that she was worried about certain actions Gabriel might take in order to see to it that he didn't end up with a kid, but Margot didn't believe her.

An uncommon occurrence, so Perdita and the

dolls have to wonder in what manner Harriet's concern was conveyed and whether Harriet really wanted Margot to believe her. The line of thought could have gone something like this: **If Margot doesn't believe it then it can't be true.** Even though Margot saw no dark potential in Gabriel (**Shall I tell you who's a complete wrong 'un? That girl you went around with for a bit at the farmstead . . . Gretel . . .**), that didn't keep her from making a fuss of her daughter and the possible Third Musketeer she carried, getting in supplements and keeping a "Days Since Last Bout of Morning Sickness" count going. Margot also took an average of the number of times Harriet had told her she wanted the kid as compared to the number of times Harriet had told her she wanted to just keep being a kid.

(**I do still count as one, don't I? Sort of? Upper end of kidhood?**)

It was exactly fifty-fifty.

I don't want to rush you, Margot said. **But: tick tock.**

Can I ask you something, Margot Lee?

Go for it.

Would you say you're a good mother? Hand over heart, would you say that?

Would I say I'm a good mother . . . but why

would I need to be one of those when I've got a daughter like you?

Mum. If you get any worse than this I might not be able to take it anymore . . .

Oh, poor Harriet. So persecuted. But you shouldn't glare at your mother like that . . . you should be good to your mother while she's still alive to be good to. Listen . . . just listen a second . . . when I was younger, my dad was always shouting that things wouldn't go well for me. Just make sure you have a child of your own! Have a child just like you, and you'll know how I feel. He loved dishing out curses like that. And obviously that curse was a flop, because you—well, I think it's one of the hardest things in the world to somehow make sure that the ones you love receive your care for them as physical information, as definite as—raindrops hitting your palm. Like when you hold out your hand to check if it's raining and it is. But with you, it's that definite every time I hold out my hand to check. So just . . . maybe it won't be this child, but at some point, if you do want to give it a go, you should . . . have one just like you and you'll know how lucky I feel.

Harriet's stomach felt full of what she could only describe as glitterfizz; it seemed the baby had decided to have some fun and convert its amniotic fluid into prosecco.

Perdita and the dolls are shaking their heads, and Prim speaks up: "Are you saying this to make Perdita feel like a filial slacker? Perdita's a loving daughter too, OK?"

But Perdita raises her hand and draws a line across the air, separating her opinion from Prim's. She's either sticking up for Harriet or saying she could do without this talk of loving daughters. Then, as if realizing she hasn't made her position clear enough, Perdita Lee leans on her mother's shoulder, gives her three brisk nods of encouragement, and even suffers her forehead to be kissed. To Perdita, and only to Perdita—the dolls can stay out of this—Harriet says: "Yes, I loved it when my 'take you for granted until the very end' mother suddenly seemed to have had a true heart for me all along and told me I should have a child just like me. But that really is a curse no matter who you say it to, so I'm thankful it flopped again. Do you think that could be our family legend . . . that curses just bounce off us? But what I really want to say is—why should you be loving anyway? Yes, you're a daughter—that's just how things have worked out. But it's like I was saying about me and my own mum—because of Margot, I'm a daughter too, and if you love or even like the person who put you in such a situation, then that loving or liking is happening inexplicably."

Perdita shrugs . . . you pour your heart out to Perdita Lee and she shrugs. The girl drops back onto the mattress so she's fully horizontal and tucks handfuls of her hair behind her head so her neck is well supported. She closes her eyes, opens them again, taps Harriet's knee with her foot.

"So I go on," Harriet says, looking around at the dolls, who immediately begin talking among themselves and making it clear that if some listeners are going to keep being left out like this, there doesn't have to be a joint bedtime story at all, that there can be one for the dolls and one just for Perdita and her mother, no problem.

"But, dolls! Dolls and Perdita! Are you really going to be like this? What about the scare Gabriel gave me . . . "

The dolls took a vote. Three to one in favor of hearing about the scare, which was given around the beginning of the fourth month of Harriet's pregnancy. She no longer went up to see Gabriel at university, but they talked on the phone—argued, really. He had end-of-year exams to take, and what was she trying to do to him, and so on. She booked two appointments at that same clinic in Bradford, the site of all her other no-shows—she used her middle name and his surname this time, so Araminta Kercheval, and she sent him a notification for the first of the two appointments necessary for a medical abortion and hoped the arguments would stop for a while. Her appointment was at a date and time that meant Gabriel couldn't go with her. She told him she'd go with her mum (**Your mum knows???**) and he should just take his exam and there was nothing to worry about.

And the scare went like this:

Gabriel called her just after she'd got home from school that afternoon—if she'd gone to the appointment, it would have been about an hour after she'd taken the first round of medication and begun the procedure. **How did it go? Are you OK?** "How did it go" seemed a bit of a casual way to ask what he was asking, and she told him so.

She looked at the clock and thought, **But his exam won't be over for another half hour,** and just as she was thinking that Gabriel said, **I'm asking how the other thing went . . . the thing you skipped the appointment for.** And he asked if he could come and see her. **Gabriel. Are you telling me you missed the first exam of your Law**

Mods to make sure I was at the appointment? He continued to ask if he could come and see her, and she asked where he was.

Still at the clinic, Gabriel said. **Can I come and see you? Don't you think we should talk?**

Yeah, we should, and I do want to. But you sound a bit . . . I don't know. Let's talk tomorrow?

No, today. It'll be OK, Harriet. We're good in person, remember? Where are you? At home?

No, she said. **I'm at the shop. Got to go—bye.**

After they hung up she went out of the flat, took the lift down to the ground-floor entrance to the building, and looked out of a window that faced the street. Gabriel was there, and when he saw Harriet, he came up to the security door and pounded on the glass until another tenant stuck her head out of her front door and asked, in very reluctant tones, whether Harriet wanted her to call the police. It didn't look like the kind of lovers' tiff that ended with the couple kissing and making up—the man's face exhibited no emotion whatsoever . . . he had none left. Or he was no Romeo, but a debt collector.

Thanks but there's no need, Harriet said. She couldn't wait for the lift to come, so she ran up the stairs, and when she got back inside the flat, she bolted and chained the door. As per prior arrangement, Margot wouldn't believe this, so Harriet sent Rémy a very long text message.

RÉMY ARRIVED ON A MOTORCYCLE. He'd bulked up a lot since she'd last seen him out on the window ledge at Kercheval House, so when Harriet looked through the peephole, she saw a rugged young man in a leather jacket carrying a bouquet of sweet peas. Under any other circumstances she'd have been tickled to receive such a tribute, but when she let him in, she asked him what the flowers were for.

Oh, is this a bad time to woo you? He laughed at her expression. **Harriet, a man can never get tired of winding you up. They're not "for" anything—I just wanted to give you some flowers.**

Oh. Thank you. How are you?

I'm well, thanks. Learning the ropes at work. Oh, I've got a pet tortoise, and I'm learning a lot from her.

What are you learning?

How to eat lettuce as if it's caviar. Tell me

about your text message . . . what's all this about wanting me to ask Gabriel where your body is if you go missing?

For once she was reassured by his concentration in reading her lips and hearing all that she said and didn't say. She confessed that it seemed to her that almost all of this had arisen from her not knowing how she felt. Willful ignorance, in fact. He touched her face—that light touch that almost toppled her—and he uttered a single, regretful **Hmph.** Then he became business-like. **OK, we're taking this out of his hands. The longer it's a secret, the more difficult it will be for that cousin of mine to get a grip. By the way, after this you're never to ask me for anything again.**

That's fair, Harriet said.

I mean really, never, ever.

Yes, I understand.

Of course any de-escalation plan devised by Rémy "fuck this family" Kercheval involved preliminary escalation. It involved calling a family meeting, during which everybody's face was a masterwork of unsuccessfully concealed emotion except for Ari's. Ari couldn't have been more surprised and interested and looked like he was on his first trip to Disneyland. Rémy leaned on her for a moment, his head on her shoulder; she raised her hand and didn't let it fall; it was less than a moment, really, but he laid his cheek against the cloth of her ragged antiques-shop robe before he took her hand and spoke to them all. **Harriet's pregnant, and we didn't want to hide that from you anymore. Mum, Dad, Margot, Uncle Ari, Aunt Tamar, I know we've already had so much help from you, but we're going to need even more . . .**

Nobody knew how to begin asking what they wanted to ask—what, when, how . . . Tamar's eyes were on Gabriel, though, and the shallow breaths he drew, as if the air had turned foul. Then he spoke as if he, Rémy, and Harriet were the only three in the room:

You sure it's yours, Rémy? Really sure?

Margot said, **Oi**, and Ari told Gabriel to pipe low. Ambrose and Kenzilea exchanged glances, trying to see each other as grandparents and not disliking the view. Tamar took four different pills from four different pillboxes, washed them down with some green juice but didn't seem much calmer afterward.

Harriet was aware of Rémy's personal mission to wind up the whole wide world, so her heart didn't skip a single beat when he told his family that he'd felt love at first sight. He walked

291

Harriet and Margot down to the driveway, and Tamar Kercheval followed them. She held the taxi door before Rémy could close it, and she bent down to look into Harriet's eyes. As for Tamar's own eyes—they bulged. A swollen vein fluttered across her temple, and her words came out in fits and starts—what she was saying was far less disquieting than the overall impression she gave of being about to spew intestinal tissue: **So what now—what is this—can't wait a little longer for a passport so you're having a passport baby? Or is it that you think you'll get more from us if you join the family? Thought—we were taking you in—but we—were the ones—completely taken in by—you—little tramp—after all we've given you—how—how dare you try to get more!**

Rémy began to reply, Margot began to reply (with nuclear asperity), but Harriet had her own answer. She said, **I'm sorry you were tricked, Tamar. You probably feel poorer now. Not money-wise—I know you didn't mind about that. It's because you believed in something that turned out not to be real. That's what happened, but I wasn't the one who tricked you. Trickery occurs all the time, all the time . . . people exchange fake money for things of genuine value, people spend their life savings on lies. Let each** person involved in those exchanges consider their losses and gains, the benefits and drawbacks of trusting others and gaining the trust of others, but as for you, Tamar, don't you dare say it's trust that's made you poorer today . . . first of all, what was the source of that trust? Wasn't it the value you placed on my obedience? Isn't that what you thought you'd bought . . . affectionate obedience? Somebody who wouldn't feel any more or any less than you wanted her to feel, someone who'd love but not dare to—whatever it turns out I've dared to do. But really you shouldn't be surprised this happened; this is what you get for placing people in your debt in such a way that they can never repay it!

Of course she didn't say that. This is a protest Harriet only has the words to make seventeen years later—at the time nobody but her friend Gretel could have seen to the bottom of her gingerbread heart and expressed these things verbally. Harriet's actual answer at the time wasn't so bad when you take into consideration her age and her not being a changeling and her being face-to-face with the wrath of Tamar. Harriet mumbled something about how she and Margot had invested faith in the Kerchevals too, a barely audible reminder that the Lees had believed without seeing and come to live with Ari without knowing what he would really be like, what any member of that family would really be like. Harriet might have spoken a bit louder if she hadn't had the guilty awareness of not having tried her best to be worthy of the generosity shown her. She'd tried, but not her best, and had been hoping to settle the balance with gratitude, but there hadn't been enough gratitude either . . .

Tamar said nothing, but took a couple of steps back. Margot, correctly guessing that this was no retreat, that Tamar was in fact preparing to dive into the back of the taxi with them and make them fight for their lives, reached across Harriet and pulled the door shut as soon as its handle was released.

Harriet hasn't seen or spoken to Tamar Kercheval since that day, nor has she seen or spoken to Ambrose, Kenzilea, or Gabriel. A minor correction: Harriet does see Gabriel in nightmares—the first came after Ari's offhand mention that Gabriel had been sent down from Oxford; Ari seemed rather pleased by this, as this made his son a member of a club even more exclusive than the one comprised of students who'd been admitted to the university. Ari mentions Gabriel from time to time and then Harriet has a nightmare, but they don't really alarm her anymore—Gabriel Kercheval runs her a bubble bath and makes her lie in the bubble bath forever, that sort of thing. She only thinks of these as nightmares because she'd rather not have such dreams, or see him in them, or something.

Harriet and Margot made their way to London town, where a super-duper lucrative project of Margot's was already in the works, and where Harriet had her kid, the kid she kept by her side when at home because that kid definitely didn't want anybody seeing or hearing what she was up to and worked out how to turn the baby monitor off as soon as her mother left the room. On school trips Perdita Lee was the first to remove and discard any hat or sticker that linked her to the other kids before scampering off into the depths of the zoo/park/museum . . . and the manner in which the girl scampered was analogous to the CEO strut depicted on cinematic screens. Cue the gravelly voice-over: **Rushing headlong into obscurity was her forte . . . in that field she had no rivals . . .**

This same kid took and placidly donned Harriet's bachelor's and master's degree hats without so much as a "congratulations" at both ceremonies, though she did consider turning thirty a notable achievement and wrote in that year's birthday card: **Good news—past the age of thirty there's a dramatic decrease to your chances of being murdered by a serial killer.** This was the child named Perdita, who didn't grow up as a Kercheval, so she never discovered whether hers was a face that said "Save" or a face that said "Spend." Where the Kerchevals are differentiated by "Save" and "Spend," the Lees are "Rent vs. Buy." Margot prefers to live in property that she owns, but whenever Harriet reads or hears anything about mortgages, she can't help but hear it all said in the voice of Clio Kercheval, and she dares not exchange something as weird as money for something as crucial as permanent shelter— that's a wicked prank she won't fall for. So she just makes sure there's always a spare bedroom Margot can have whenever the truth about her mortgage comes out, or in the event of somebody showing up with a contract that predates Margot's and seems to prove that the bearer of the contract paid even more for the place than Margot has; perhaps a second antagonist might also appear with a claim to the land upon which the house is built . . .

Ari Kercheval says he will buy a hat shop and eat it if any of that happens. To this day he's refused to leave Harriet's life, and she's stopped trying to shake him off. "You're our good deed," he tells her. "You're our good deed, and I'm your benefactor, and nothing changes that." He may be right, though talking to him can be bad for her nerves, and for Margot's. So many lies of omission, however cheerful the conversation.

And as for Rémy—

Rémy came to the antiques shop in Whitby too, all those years ago, before London and Perdita. Harriet was standing in for Margot again that afternoon, and Rémy didn't make a game of this visit; he came straight to the shop counter and asked her when she was leaving. She told him, knowing he would be glad not to have to keep watching over her.

Come with me for a sec, he said.

I've got to stay until six.

The clinic closes at five.

The . . . clinic?

Harriet. Be a bit wiser than you have been so far, OK? Choose freedom.

Freedom to do what you want. By the way, why are you "advising" me to—?

It's hard to describe what's going on at home right now, but just think of it this way: The wrath of my dear Aunt T passeth all understanding—she neither gives nor hears any explanation, no matter what we do or say. As for a way that she

might leave you alone if you have this kid . . . there is none. But I'm not only thinking of you. I'm saying: Why reproduce? Personally I'd be a lot easier in my mind if this branch of the Kerchevals just gets cut off altogether.

Even though we've already announced the next generation?

Yeah, that announcement sets the scene for further announcements. Once you're gone, I'll tell them something that lets them call up any image they please. You miscarried and we had a breakup so bad I don't ever want to talk about it again. Done.

Hang on—

That's what I'm telling them, Harriet, no matter what you do.

She made a sort of hiccupping sound, and he sighed. That was when he asked Harriet if she thought she was someone who had a future, and that was when she'd gone with "yes" although she hadn't a clue. Rémy gave her that look of curious sympathy and then he went back to work.

13

PERDITA'S FOUND IT INVIGORATING TO HEAR about the people allied against her birth. She says she could get big-headed if she dwells on it, so she'll just allow herself a moment of smugness for existing and then move on. It was strange too, to hear about Kercheval House as Harriet knew it—Perdita paid the Kerchevals a visit there, she invented that school trip to Canterbury just so she could go to Kercheval House, and it's still the same Brutalist building site, never to be completed, its walls whirring as units of space yawn and are filled with room-sized cubes that are just passing through, just passing through . . .

When Perdita visited, there was no way for her to know that none of this was intended to have a menacing effect. She was yet to spend time with Ari Kercheval and gain some understanding of his idea of fun. All she did know was that no matter how many staircases she fled down or in which direction she hurried, the person she was trying to get away from was able to stride toward her as soon as she arrived on a new floor.

"Who was that person? Gabriel? Tamar?"

Perdita says she met a man and a woman at that weird white building, and that the names they told her to call them by weren't their real names. They seemed really confident as they said the fake names too, confident that she would never be able to find out their real names unless they wanted her to. The man told her his name was Hansel and the woman said her name was . . . Gretel. The woman who said her name was Gretel was the person Perdita had gone to see and the reason she left so quickly.

"Perdita—honestly—you. Don't you have any common sense? Going to a place like that without even knowing who you were really dealing with . . ."

Perdita says she thought they were being like that because of money—they asked her to wait a moment while they had a quick chat, and retired to the next room for a massive quarrel. Gretel was a little at a disadvantage; it seemed she wasn't at all used to Hansel pushing back against her. And Hansel had plenty to say . . . he was in fact a fount of long-suppressed vexation. Gretel would flare up and get doused down to the faintest flicker—each point Gretel made got hit with three of Hansel's ice-cold and crystal-clear rebuttals. The name Ari was repeatedly mentioned, in varying tones—as if speaking of someone omniscient, as if speaking of someone brainless, someone adored, scorned, feared, in need of protection, a habitual turncoat, a bully, a disappointment. Hansel and Gretel saw all that and more in this Ari, whose name they kept invoking—Perdita thought he must be the one with the most money. And he wasn't there at the house. Perdita should be long gone before Ari returned (this was the law Gretel wanted laid down). Perdita should stay and meet him (this was Hansel's insistence). **This girl's family; this girl's no family of mine.** Perdita heard all this as she waited in a drafty antechamber lined ceiling to floor with family photos. She picked him out immediately, the "Ari" they were talking about, and even though you can't really tell from pictures, she thought he seemed like someone she could have a few laughs with.

Whose child is she?

. . . not a penny more from us . . .

Perdita half listened to all this as she ran a finger down each row of photos, keeping on the vertical so it felt like a physical analog of scrolling through Tumblr. Sport, parties, picnics, fashion, silliness, and solemnity, and when she looked at the photos in which six faces squeezed together in a frame she thought it did look a bit crowded, she could see why at least one of those pictured felt six should be the limit.

. . . my grandchild . . .

. . . your damn grandchild . . .

Perdita considered putting in her earphones. She was happy for Hansel and Gretel to just keep their Gothic drama to themselves. She might have been a bit more vigilant if she'd had some prior knowledge of the cast, but even if "Gretel" had said, **Hi, I'm Tamar,** and "Hansel" had flourished his rainbow-striped cane, straightened his red-spattered collar, and said, **My name's Ambrose,**

Perdita wouldn't have turned a hair. Her mother had never mentioned either of them.

"Listen, you," says Harriet. "Our social circles are a bit different, so the probability of your ever running into them and needing to know who they were was fairly slim, don't you agree? How did you even come into contact with them?"

Harriet had brought this on herself

("Charming," says Harriet)

with all her wistful talk of Gretel and how it had been twenty years since they'd last seen each other. Perdita had been doing all she could toward reuniting them for Harriet's thirty-fifth birthday—"It is morning now, happy birthday, Mother-of-Perdita," the dolls say—and to that end she'd researched private investigators . . . not expensive ones, obviously, more in the "Tesco Value" range.

Harriet is laughing, but she is also angry at any investigator who'd take on a case for a Tesco Value fee whilst promising—well, Fortnum-type results. Perdita says she could only just about believe her luck when she came upon a guy who said that, depending on the difficulty of the case, he could find anybody in the world for a very low fee. Perdita was able to speak to people this guy had helped out, and they were on the level—plus the guy said that since it was a Druhástranian she was looking for, he'd do it for free.

This guy, Perdita explains, is the sort of gentleman detective you used to find all over England in the olden days—he doesn't need money, so finding people is his hobby. He told Perdita his name, but it wasn't his real name either. And he was so much more handsome than anybody really needs to be that Perdita giggled idiotically whenever he looked at her. Neither Perdita nor Harriet have photographs to compare, so the gentleman detective could be Rémy Kercheval or he could be Gabriel Kercheval or some other excessively handsome black man.

Wait—Perdita thinks for a moment. There were a few occasions on which the gentleman detective had seemed to completely ignore something she'd said, and if what she'd said definitely required a response she'd touch his arm, he'd look at her, she'd repeat herself. Then the gentleman detective would respond as if hearing her for the first time. This could just be how a person behaves when somebody else isn't letting them get away with being rude, but Perdita's decided the gentleman detective was lip-reading and that he is Rémy Kercheval.

When Perdita met Rémy—and, indeed, when Perdita met "Gretel" and when she met "Hansel"— the reaction of each fell along the same spectrum. Dread and fascination combined—they were like witnesses to a most unnatural wonder.

"Behold, the child that should not have been born sort of thing?"

No. Perdita's been giving it a lot of thought, and she thinks they mistook her for Harriet. She is, after all, about the age that Harriet was when they last saw her, and they are as much alike in build and facial features as one would expect a mother and daughter to be. One wouldn't call them twins, but seeing Perdita for the first time must have been like seeing Harriet after an interval, after a few details had been forgotten. The gray-haired seventeen-year-old comes in and she's like a gingerbread ghost, her chronological age bearing very little relation to her exterior. Then Perdita spoke, and Halloween was canceled.

"So it was Rémy you met first—and then he told you he'd found Gretel and . . ." Harriet's grabbing her coat; now that she knows who to go and hit, they can finish talking later. But the doll named Lollipop says: "Mother-of-Perdita, I really wasn't going to mention this, but . . . if the arrangement with Gretel was that she'd be in touch once you'd grown up, might it not be the case that she hasn't been in touch because you still haven't . . . ?"

And Perdita tells Harriet she needs to sit down and hear her out, just as Perdita has heard Harriet out all bloody night.

Harriet sits down and hears that Rémy met up with Perdita at a train station café, took down all the details Perdita was able to give, and then contacted her a few days later, saying he couldn't take the case after all. He told her it was for personal reasons and took the time to send her a list of alternative birthday presents, each of which actually came in under Perdita's budget . . . she'd been impressed not just by this but by the presents actually being the sort of thing Harriet would like—so when Harriet had begun talking about Rémy, Perdita had sort of hoped he was her dad. Perdita says she knows the gentleman detective has his boyfriend and his pet tortoise to think of.

("Rémy Kercheval fell for someone? Rémy Nearboy Kercheval fell for someone?"

Perdita says yes, provided the gentleman detective is Rémy Nearboy Kercheval . . .

Whoever the boyfriend is, Harriet is ready to take his master class on enchanting the hard-hearted. Or are the hard-hearted only conquered when their deeds are outdone?)

At any rate, Perdita stopped herself from asking the gentleman detective for more time than he gave her of his own accord. But even after he dropped Perdita's case, he stayed in touch, sent her links to YouTube playlists and online essays and articles, all with accompanying jokes of the dad variety. Perdita responded in kind—they emailed more or less daily until he told her there was a family situation ("family situation," "personal reasons," . . .) and he'd have to be out of contact for a while. The situation seemed to have been a result of tracking down Gretel Kercheval . . . and the woman who said that was her name, the woman Perdita thinks must be Tamar, she was the next to contact Perdita.

"Oh," says Harriet. "And have you heard from your Tesco Value investigator since?"

Perdita hasn't. She misses him. Perdita thinks only two people knew she was visiting Kercheval House that day, and that the two people were "Hansel" and "Gretel." Ambrose and Tamar.

"Go back to Tamar emailing you under Gretel's name."

There they were in Perdita's inbox, a handful of emails, sender's name Gretel Kercheval. To Perdita these messages seemed legit, partly because of the fond reminiscences of Harriet's baking prowess

307

and an unmistakable familiarity with the unedited history of the Lee family gingerbread. Tamar's fifth email invited Perdita to her family home, out in Whitby, and sent an address. Perdita ran that address by her gentlemen detective to see what he thought. **Could this person really be Mum's friend Gretel?**

"But he didn't reply."

He didn't, but someone replied from his account saying Perdita should go.

"How are you so sure it wasn't him?"

He'd blatantly been hacked, that was all. If Harriet still doesn't know what Perdita means, then she should imagine getting a message from Perdita that's so utterly inconsistent with the tone, style, and even punctuation of all Perdita's other messages that she, Harriet, is tempted to send the imposter some helpful tips on how to make the ruse less transparent next time.

"Still, you went to visit . . ."

Still, Perdita went to visit. It all seemed like such a caper. Until she got to the house and saw Hansel—well, she'll call him Ambrose now—and met Gretel—all right, Tamar. It was all such a caper until Perdita sat down with those two and a certain mind-bending pressure that came in with them, a blend of the things Ambrose hoped and wanted Perdita to be and the things Tamar was very much afraid Perdita was. Welcome and get lost.

What Perdita now thinks Tamar wanted from this meeting: never to be scammed again. To keep six family members as the functional limit, and not to sit idly by while some newcomer pops up and pushes Gabriel down to an even lower position on his father's list of priorities.

What Perdita now thinks Ambrose wanted from this meeting: acknowledgment of Rémy's daughter (Ambrose must have been sure Perdita was his granddaughter—only a child of Rémy's could be this bloody-minded) and assurance of said daughter's safety.

What Perdita wanted and still wants: to do something nice for her mum for a change. And she told them so, Tamar and Ambrose—she told them so repeatedly!

What went on that afternoon and evening: Tamar poured Perdita purple tea, which Perdita didn't drink. Ambrose blundered into the room (to "Gretel"'s intense displeasure) and there was some talk of Druhástrana, things both Tamar and Ambrose remembered the Lees mentioning, much of it new to Perdita, so possibly misremembered. Still, Perdita kept trying to steer the conversation back around to the real Gretel Kercheval and how she might be found or contacted, how to bring about the reunion Perdita was seeking . . . and how she stressed that help reuniting Harriet and Gretel was all she was seeking from them! All that was of no use, the conversation got on to Druhástranian lore gathered from other sources, and Tamar, as if struck by sudden recollection, opened a little drawer on the table beside her and took out a sachet filled with powder. Perdita watched Ambrose, who didn't seem to have seen this powder before but didn't seem happy about it, and Perdita listened to the story of the sachet: it had come to Tamar from a reliable source, someone who had once given her husband three carrier pigeons that had turned out to be truly Druhástranian.

The contents of this sachet—Tamar leaned forward, placed the sachet in Perdita's palm, and closed her fingers around it. **This is how your mother and grandmother left Druhástrana . . . Margot made gingerbread with it.**

That's only half the truth, Ambrose said. Perdita turned to him: So—half a lie?

No—it's just that the truth goes on beyond what she said, and no transit records were kept, so if you're inclined to believe her, I can't show you anything that'd change your mind—

Tamar shook the sachet and continued as if Ambrose hadn't even spoken.

This is how they left, and this is how you can go there and look for Gretel Kercheval.

Tamar told Perdita that this was the last of eight sachets, and that thanks to these sachets, she, Tamar, had been to Druhá City and back several times now.

Half-truths again . . . that was what Ambrose muttered.

What's Druhá City like? Perdita asked.

Tamar frowned. **Pricier than you'd think.**

Ambrose looked scared witless, so it was more for him than for herself that Perdita said: **Hey, fake Gretel, you're not trying to kill me, are you?**

Tamar blinked. **I'm not trying to kill you. Your desire to go abroad coincides with my very dear wish for you not to be here, that's all.**

So you gave me one sachet. That way it'll be hard for me to come back.

Not really, Ambrose said, studying Tamar's face. **Not if you're going to the same place the stuff in the sachet came from. Shouldn't be long before you're back—and then there are a few people to introduce you to.**

Tamar said they'd see about that. But in the meantime, she swore on her son's head that the sachet would get Perdita to Druhástrana in one piece. After this, Perdita drank some of the purple tea and enjoyed it.

Perdita Lee may have refused to be dragged into an inheritance drama, but Ambrose Kercheval must have been more mindful of how difficult it is to stay out of such a story, especially when somebody else is hell-bent on that being the way things play out. By the time things passed a point of no return (that is to say by the time Tamar had chased Perdita all the way out of the house, shouting, **Just take that powder and go back . . . I'm sending you back**), Ambrose had switched the sachet several times. Several times because Perdita had cottoned on and kept switching it back. They tried to do this as if it was all just another part of the evening's circus act, but Perdita wasn't going home with a sachet of mere powdered sugar. She was taking the sachet Tamar had given her. It was that or nothing.

Ah, but Ambrose Kercheval. Ambrose, who would live such a peaceful life if it weren't for his brother and his sister-in-law . . . looking back on the rest of that evening reinforces Perdita's intention to give the man a monster hug next time she sees him. The evening was one long interview— funny overall, Perdita thinks, but speckled with woe—Perdita being interviewed for the position of granddaughter and Ambrose being interviewed for the position of grandfather. Perdita was ready to go ahead, and Ambrose seemed keen too, but they had to think of all the people they'd have to check with before the bond could be made official.

Harriet is embarrassed that she's left her daughter so starved of fatherly and grandfatherly affection that the girl's just going around pledging herself to any male Kercheval who crosses her path.

"Well, good," says the doll named Lollipop. "You should be embarrassed about that."

After dinner, Ambrose put Perdita up at a hotel for the night. He took the room next to hers, just in case Tamar had further plans of some sort. Harriet's guessing Ambrose didn't sleep a wink and trembled all night.

The next day, Ambrose saw Perdita home and left once he'd made sure that she used the sachet he gave her in the gingerbread she made. She really did use the powdered sugar—in the first of the two batches. And yes, the dolls saw this themselves, Ambrose did lie down with the girl he wanted for a granddaughter and sang to her—she asked him to.

What is it with you Lees and the way you appear before us Kerchevals like . . .

"Fairies," Harriet says, but the doll named Bonnie corrects her: "Like a fairy, he said. Singular, not plural."

Ambrose sang every Druhástranian lullaby he knew. He cried over her—she didn't know why, and she didn't ask. Her stomach was hurting; she feigned sleep, and Ambrose went home. When Harriet presses Perdita to talk about meeting Gretel, the real Gretel, Perdita's mind wanders, as does her gaze. She says a strange thing about the wheat-sheaf ring being "in" her hand . . . **I put my hand in my hand and there it was**, something like that.

The trust with which Perdita took the powder that had been given her—Harriet can't think of any form of trust more insanely severe, more probing of the other party's intentions.

Perdita's trust was so severe that at the very last minute, possibly unsettled by the girl's refusal to blink first, reality took her side. And now Harriet's daughter shrugs and yawns hugely before asking her what she wants to do for her birthday.

14

Hmmm . . . still here?

Huh, then it seems you wouldn't mind hearing about the three houses. I mean the three places where Gretel and Harriet agreed to meet again. And you can't hear about those without hearing about how all three Lees returned to Kercheval House one rainy day about six months after Harriet's long night with Perdita and the dolls. Perdita and her therapist had been working hard, and six months, more or less, was the time it took to confirm that her speech was fully intelligible again. The therapist admitted a niggling feeling that Perdita had recovered even sooner than this and that the date would've been easier to pinpoint if she hadn't been working with somebody whose mind seemed so comfortable operating on that border between inability to form speech and preference for withholding it. Basically by the final month or so Perdita Lee's therapist was almost sure her patient was malingering but couldn't definitively prove it.

As soon as she saw that her daughter was all better, Harriet Lee began thinking of revenge. That's what the return to Kercheval House was about, and that's how Harriet encountered Tamar standing outside the gates. Tamar, dressed entirely in red and holding a purple umbrella, was talking on her phone—interesting that there was no room inside that sprawling property that she deemed appropriate for whatever conversation she was having—she was talking on her phone and dragging a high-heeled foot back and forth over the patch of earth she stood in, as if triple- and quadruple-sealing a minuscule gravesite. Harriet saw Tamar from a long way away and knew who it was even before the face came into focus. Tamar saw Harriet too. She ended her phone call and stood there waiting as Harriet, dressed entirely in black and also carrying a purple umbrella, walked faster and faster and then, no longer able to put up with the delay imposed by this long stretch of grass and lampposts and shaggy-leaved shrubbery, broke into a run. Margot grabbed the hood of Harriet's jacket to try to hold her back, but the hood just ripped off as Harriet put on more speed and outran her, outran Perdita too; Harriet hurtled toward Tamar with her teeth bared, her umbrella raised high, and the soles of her trainers catapulting mud. And as she ran she was thinking, **This is mental! Tamar's Mum's age; how can I hit her, even though she has put us through all this . . . please let her be scared that I'm running at her like this, please let her be gone by the time I get there.** But Tamar stayed where she was, only lifting her arm to deflect Harriet's blow with her own umbrella before bashing her attacker right back. There followed a tumultuous clashing of spokes and springs and ferrules and purple nylon . . . the rain fell so hard that both women were blinded by it; they heard Margot and Perdita shouting, but nobody tried to pull them apart, and to Harriet the fight was like being in a self-inflating, self-deflating canopy. When she felt the rain coming in through her shredded clothes, coming in to wash all the new cuts, Harriet knew Tamar had won. Did the weather bow before money too? It maddened her that there didn't seem to be a day on which she could win a fight with Tamar Kercheval, even when she deserved to.

The funny thing (funny-ish) is that Tamar thought Harriet had won. She thought this not because of any wound she felt but because Harriet was still standing. Once she'd ascertained that that wasn't going to change, she dropped into a crouch and croaked, **Go inside, then**, in the tones of a guardian spirit that had been bested in battle. Margot and Perdita stepped over this fallen lady in red and pressed the buzzer beside the gate and told Rémy: **Yes, it's us. We're here.** The gate opened, and Margot and Perdita went through; Harriet stayed with Tamar, who held her crouch and mumbled that she could lose to Harriet this once, that it wasn't really a loss, anyway, really she was letting Harriet off, because—

"Because?"

Harriet tried to make eye contact with Tamar, but it wasn't easy; Tamar seemed to see a chessboard where her face was, a series of threatening moves. "By rights you could have gone after Gabriel," Tamar said.

"Eh?"

"You know, my child for yours—but you didn't, you were better than that, so I should lose to you this time."

It was hard to keep a straight face, but Harriet didn't laugh. Everybody around her was living out a different story in which events had different causes and motivations according to how they were perceived. Laughing at this didn't create too much of a problem when the differences seemed slighter, but Tamar's take was so markedly different . . . well. Harriet didn't wish to see someone this passionate become a walking Druhástrana, cut off from the rest of the world. Harriet told Tamar to get up. She said, "I'd hold out my hand to you but I don't think you'd take it. I don't know how much attention you're going to pay to this but I'm not plotting against you or your son. Me, Margot, Perdita—we did march up to your gates like an unholy triumvirate, but we're not plotting; we just can't let you keep on being like this to us. You just fucking can't, Tamar. You said you lost this once, but, Tamar, even in the middle of all this hating us, don't you ever get a feeling that if you don't stop this, you're going to end up losing every fight?"

Harriet also said she wished Tamar would go

back to liking the Lees again because she was so much better at that than she was at hating them. Harriet wasn't sure she actually believed that, but some flattery seemed called for.

Tamar still didn't move. "Hold out your hand to me, then," she said.

Harriet did, and Tamar took it, and stood up. "But if you ever cross me . . . ," Tamar said, a statement Harriet tested by laughing whilst looking to see if Tamar was laughing too. She was, but what if it was fake laughter . . . no, Harriet, no. Thinking like that is part of the problem.

A FEW OTHER THINGS happened that visit:

The first was that Harriet spoke to Gabriel Kercheval again. The reunion was entirely impromptu and probably would have gone badly if it hadn't been. Upon entering the house and catching a glimpse of her scratched and rain-soaked self in a mirror, Harriet's first instinct was to hide so that Rémy (ugh, it had always been Rémy for her, hadn't it) wouldn't see her like this. Tamar pointed out a bathroom she could use, but either there was still malevolence drifting around or the doorway was misidentified or Harriet simply misunderstood which one . . . the door Harriet opened led into the kitchen where both iterations of the 3:00 A.M. crew had whiled away the small hours years before. Mr. Bianchi and Ms. Danilenko had moved on to other posts years ago—Ari had told Margot: **It's just me and Tamar now. The boys visit when they have time, and they hardly ever have time.** Harriet went into the kitchen to see any trace of it remained, the huddle she and Margot and Rémy and Gabriel drew one another into whenever they thought the angry cook or the angrier housekeeper might be about to burst into the room. She traversed the tiled countertop widdershins, took a wooden spoon in hand, and struck a couple of the brass pans that hung above the kitchen range; they still caroled like bells. She thought of the time there was a power cut and for five, ten, fifteen minutes, the 3:00 A.M. crew were convinced that Mr. Bianchi had gone down to the fuse box and turned off the electricity so as to ruin the gingerbread that was baking in the oven. **Bianchi can never stop us**, Rémy had whispered into the huddle. **We're as indivisible as gingerbread dough. Shhh, don't ask me what that means!** And of course just a few months later, Mr. Bianchi had taken Rémy's place in the huddle and Ms. Danilenko had taken Gabriel's, as they all kept an ear out for Tamar. Yes, it was the same kitchen, the same 3:00 A.M. crew clubhouse. And now? Tamar could be in the huddle too, if she liked; but what would the gingerbread conspiracy be in aid of now?

There was a laptop open on the kitchen counter, and beside that an open spectacle case and a glass of juice. Harriet walked past the laptop, making one last round of the counter before leaving the room, and she caught a blur of movement across the laptop screen. A voice, also from the screen, said: "Hello?! Stop. Come back!"

It was Gabriel, half-frowning at her out of a Skype window, broad-chested and bearded now—the shepherd boy had ascended Mount Olympus. After greeting Harriet politely, he asked her to charge the laptop: "I have a feeling it's going to conk out any minute." He was right—the battery was down to 5 percent—she did as he asked.

"Where are you?" Somewhere relentlessly vertical—behind him, through gauzy curtains, she saw rooftops, golden, pink, and white, rising up out of an avenue of trees. Off-screen somebody spoke to him in Cantonese, and it was good to see the way his face changed as he switched languages to answer, slightly tongue-tied, as is inevitable with new words and new lovers. It seemed possible that he didn't need things to be easy anymore. In English, he said to her: "Hong Kong. And you're . . . there."

"Were you talking to Ari?"

"Yup. He said he'd be back in a minute."

"Ah. And how long ago was that?"

He shrugged.

"I'll get him."

Before she went, Gabriel said he had to tell her something. He said he would honestly never have hurt her. The inclusion of the "honestly" jarred for some reason, but she said OK.

"I don't know what it was, but I immediately felt like you were better than me, in some way you were truer, or something like that . . . you just kept trying to be truer. It was just really strange having to act like some kind of sponsor when really I was the one who'd have to work at being your equal. And I did want to do, I did, but there was other stuff that meant I didn't have time, and trying to do it all was . . . scratch that, this is coming out wrong . . . Harriet. Harriet! Are you seriously just walking off? Wait. Please. You might not remember this, but I didn't used to like gingerbread. At all. Then you came and you wanted to give me gingerbread, and I took it because you were the one offering it to me. I could eat it, but I still didn't like it."

"Ha ha—I actually don't remember this at all."

"Hated the stuff, actually. **Hated** it. One day when you gave me another box of the stuff I think I actually said 'Urgh' aloud—or I made a face, or something, and you looked at me and said I should just keep it for later. **You might like it later**, you said."

"I said that?"

"Yes. You just don't remember. Anyway, you said that, and you looked so hopeful that I think you must have done something to me, because . . ."

"Later you started to like it?" Harriet wasn't sure what Gabriel is saying; obviously he was saying what he was saying and she didn't think he meant anything bad by it, but this recollection of his reinforced a feeling she had (a feeling that she'd always had?) that this is the impression she made, that of being a person who can be saved up for later.

"Yes, I started to like the gingerbread, Harriet. Really, really, and a lot."

"OK."

Gabriel unhelpfully told her she looks the way he felt the day Ari told him, **Stop following me around with those clipboard eyes; it's as if** you're taking notes on everything I say and do so as to quote it all back to me . . . and worst of all, sometimes you do bring out the quotations! Gabriel said this in a low voice, in case Ari suddenly interrupted them, shouting, QUOTING AGAIN! This wasn't a review of Harriet's facial expression but the state she and her clothes were in after the umbrella fight she'd just been in with his mum. To all this Harriet could only say OK again, and ah, frail ego, why should Ari say things that made Gabriel feel the way Harriet looked just then—and why should some attempt at kindness on Gabriel's part also make her feel the way she looked just then . . . Harriet was about to cry, and then she was crying, but she also kept saying OK, OK, and strangely Gabriel cried too; they sniffled until the friend he was with came up to Gabriel's laptop camera, raised a fist at Harriet, and said something along the lines of, **What do you mean, OK, OK? What's OK about this?**

WHEN HARRIET FINALLY went to fetch Ari, she found him in one of the living rooms. Music was blasting throughout the house, and she simply went to the room where it was loudest, the room where Ari and Perdita were dancing together like a pair of vagabond wizards—jerking shoulders, grinding heels, twirling fingers as a question thunders through the loudspeakers: **Where do you know me from . . . WHERE DO YOU KNOW ME FROM?** Kercheval House wasn't ready for this; the windows of the room were sagging a little below the window frames—the room was thinking about sending itself down to the basement to recuperate. It couldn't do that without dislodging Rémy and Tamar, though. They were perched on the windowsill looking on. Harriet joined them; the windowsill seemed to be the place where the grown-ups went. Rémy said something she couldn't quite catch, so she asked him to repeat it.

"I said: How was it?"

"How was what?"

"That future you were so sure you were going to have."

After a moment of hesitation, of trying to think what a good deception would be, Harriet shuffled over to Tamar and whispered in her ear that Gabriel was waiting to speak to her in the kitchen.

"Me? He asked for me?"

Once Tamar had gone, Harriet turned to Rémy,

covered her mouth with her hands, and, gazing very sweetly into his eyes, proceeded to bestow a cornucopia of curses upon him, swearing repeatedly and at length, for the duration of the very loud song that was playing. She left it to Rémy to guess what she was saying, and judging from the look on his face, he was guessing fairly well.

Meanwhile Ari screamed at Perdita: "What's the name of the young man whose music we're dancing to?"

"Stormzy, Grandpa—this is Stormzy . . ."

Aristide Kercheval switched the music off and, head tilted, listened to the last few syllables of Harriet's swearing marathon before giving Perdita the gimlet eye. His response to being annoyed was slowing down a bit as he aged and reliance on lip-reading increased.

"**Grandpa?**" he said.

Perdita linked arms with him. "Can't I call you that?"

"You can call me that," Ari decided. It was the snappiest of his snap decisions.

("Putty in her hands," Rémy remarked. He'll get along famously with the dolls named Prim and Lollipop when they meet.)

After a decent interval, Ari Kercheval returned to the subject of Stormzy—did Perdita happen to know if anybody was currently managing this young man's wealth? Rémy had ample opportunity to say, "Fuck this family," but he didn't. Not even once. Plans were afoot that morning, and they were to do with the Kerchevals' good deed for the year.

"I got mugged a couple of months ago," Ari said gruffly. "In an underground car park. Nothing too violent—some boy just pushed me over and took all my stuff. Phone, cards, keys, money, all of it. And for that hour or so that I didn't have anything, I kept asking myself if I have any relationships that wouldn't be adversely affected by my losing everything for real. Everything in my bank accounts, for instance. And I thought of you two, Margot and Harriet—" He looked at Perdita. "I didn't know about you yet."

There was a jumble of spoken responses— what, the Lees had been the first to come to Ari's mind as people who'd stand by him in times of dire need? Tamar had walked in just in time to hear her husband say this, and she was very far from thrilled. Rémy said Ari might as well mention his "health scare" while he was busy creating an awkward atmosphere. "Me and Gabriel were actually with him at the hospital around the time I noticed someone had, er, hacked what you call my 'gentleman detective email' account," Rémy told Perdita. Margot wanted to know what Ari had been hospitalized for. Ari waved a hand.

"It was stupid."

"If you call a heart attack stupid—!" Tamar said. "We thought you were going to die."

"Die?" Margot told Ari he wasn't allowed to do that. Ari said he'd do as he pleased, and Perdita said Ari was right not to make a big deal out of it since the heart only makes up 1.5 percent of body mass at most. One-point-five percent, eh? And with what grim composure Harriet's daughter stated that quantity . . . her tone implied firsthand knowledge, the kind that comes with having done all the dissection, weighing, and measuring yourself . . . What else? Harriet watched Ari blow kisses at his granddaughter and listened to Tamar telling Perdita, "You can't call me Grandma, though," and heard Perdita answer Tamar in tones hundreds of degrees colder than the tones in which she spoke to Ari: "That's absolutely fine with me, Tamar" (Tamar hung her head; her penance would be long), and Harriet Lee was happy. No? Joyously giddy? What if I just say she experienced some emotion of extremely high hedonic value—like a diamond, only a feeling—and she experienced it so strongly that it . . . echoed. No?

Oh, because it's a sound word and no particular sound was singled out for Harriet's attention? You give me a word for it, then. You tell me what it is when some sensation leaves you for the space of one heartbeat and returns at double strength. It seemed to Harriet Lee that her father must be happy too. They'd agreed that they were alike, she and her father, whether happy, cross, or sad. **I'm alive, so he is too, isn't he? Isn't he?** There's no end to the serrated edge of this illogic; might as well press on and read the fulfillment of so many other hopes into it . . . this thing that I'm apparently not allowed to call an echo meant that Zu was happy too, ditto Dottie and Rosolio and Cinnabar and all the Gingerbread Girls, everyone at the farmstead, and . . .

. . . Gretel . . .

But Ari was unfolding his plan, and Harriet had to listen if she wanted to help.

"You came to us willing to join our family, and you did it, you're family. What we want to do now is start three new families. This was originally Tamar's plan, actually."

This was to be this year's Kercheval Good Deed: Ari proposed to begin with three houses, each house to be occupied by a group of people not necessarily related by blood who were prepared to live together as a family unit. Not some sham family, politely avoiding having to care about one another, but people who would share a surname and the task of weaving a collective meaning into that name. People who would support and protect and staunchly cherish one another.

Margot gave Ari a sour look. "Sorry, what? Did you say this was Tamar's idea?"

Tamar answered before Ari could: "That's right, and it's better than any you've ever had!"

Margot got up, stood over the seated Tamar, and pointed at her. Tamar bared her teeth and pushed Margot's hand away, but Margot kept pointing. "Did you come up with this plan before or after the outcome of your dealings with our granddaughter?"

"After," Tamar muttered.

Margot sat down. "That's all I wanted to know! I've been looking for clues all this time, searching for this woman's sense of guilt."

"Tamar's guilt is my guilt," Ari said. From the look on Tamar's face when he said that, Harriet could see that this was how Ari got through to his wife, with words matched to deeds in exactly this way. "And her plans are my plans. I'm the one who thought of asking you Lees to advise, though."

"Now we, we Kerchevals and Lees, Kercheval-Lees, Lee-Kerchevals, we've had, er, we've had our tiffs, we've had our little disagreement, and I'm sure there's more where they came from, but all of us here know what family's about. Gabriel off in Beijing knows what family's about—"

"Hong Kong," says Tamar. "**Hong Kong** . . . our son is in Hong Kong."

"Yes, exactly, Hong Kong . . . and Ambrose and Kenzilea off in St. Kitts know too, and if I don't praise some of the rest of you for also knowing what family's about, that's because I don't like praising people for doing exactly what they should be doing. Anyway, I'm not asking you Lees to help pick the people who'll live in the houses—I'm asking you to help pick the actual houses. There are three in particular that I've been offered as a job lot, and at a price so low that I'm almost sure mischief is afoot . . ."

"The estate agency is a reputable one, though," Tamar put in. "We've been dealing with them for years. Miss Maszkeradi said that the thing to bear in mind about two of the houses is that they're absolutely, definitely not haunted—"

"Meaning she thinks they're as haunted as fuck and wants to mention it in advance because one of the pre-sale stipulations is that a potential buyer has to spend a night in each of the houses," Rémy said.

Perdita liked the sound of this.

"But apparently there's something else to bear in mind about the third house—"

"Yes, what is it Miss Maszkeradi said about the third house again?" Ari asked.

"She said we can have it if we can get in," said Tamar.

Margot managed to establish that Miss Maszkeradi was the estate agent who'd come to them with the three-house deal, and that though the Kerchevals' estate agency of choice did indeed have a venerable history, Miss Maszkeradi herself was new to the job. All three Kerchevals present had met Miss Maszkeradi in person, and all three disagreed on basic aspects of her physique.

Margot's opinion: "She sounds . . . well, I've never heard estate agents talk about houses they're supposed to be trying to sell in this way . . ."

"Doesn't mean she's not on the level," Perdita said.

"Well, let's see . . . we'll set up viewings . . . first house weekend after next . . . Harriet and I have to do a bit of work. And, Perdita, you should get back to school. I think I'll call my tattoo artist friend too."

"Your tattoo artist friend?" Tamar asked.

"Yes—he has some very good patterns that ward off spirit possession."

"Make it an appointment for four," said Tamar.

Ari wanted the Lees to stay the night, wanted them to move back in, actually. Not a chance. For the Lees, home was somewhere else—they'd visit again very soon, though. Yes, there'd be lots of visits, and he must visit them too . . . and they caught the last train back to London with Tamar in tow.

15

THE TATTOO MADE HARRIET'S HEART ACHE for days. She liked it, but it was drawn on to a sensitive place, the place between her breasts where it seemed to her that the skin was thinner. Thinner and itchier, but also more easily soothed with a fingertip dipped in lotion. As for the device Margot's friend chose, it was seven crisscrossed swords—or seven arrows—the sharp points curlicued as though twisted at gale force. Perdita didn't end up getting tattooed. "Any spirit that wants to have a go at possessing me is welcome to try," said she, and out came the jack-o'-lantern grin, along with a few exclamations from both her grandmothers, who'd never seen it before. For Tamar, Margot, and Harriet, though, the tattoo was a reassuring precaution to take. Especially once they'd read up on the house they were going to view. The Baker House. Its bad reputation wasn't due to its being a very old house, though it was very old. Nor was the bad reputation due to reports of ghostly apparitions or supernatural occurrences. A sad, strange, and nefarious scheme had been conceived of and carried out in the rooms of this house a decade ago. There was no ghost, not a ghost, but there was something there. So people reasoned that the house must be haunted by all the goings-on. It was a shame, because most people who spent a little time in the house agreed that it was a nice house and could not help gathering the infamous Baker family's dreams and memories and belongings up in its bricks and mortar; the house was only doing what it had been built to do. So it did that, and remained empty. This was Harriet's assessment when she looked through photos and documents pertaining to the house, the facade of which she felt some low-key rapport with. She'd walked past this house many a time, she didn't remember doing so, but she must have done. She was often in Camden.

As for what had happened: high-achieving Jackie Baker and her similarly high-achieving youngest daughter, Tara, had got together and evaluated the other members of their family and found their flaws too detestable and their endearing qualities too insignificant to be borne. Tara and Jackie Baker had no choice but to reject all association with these scroungers and finalized this rejection by engineering accidents for them all: mostly electrical accidents, taking care to factor in a few shocks and spills for themselves too. Family friends thought at first that the Bakers were simply . . . clumsy? Unlucky? Tara Baker and her mother didn't manage to kill anybody, but mentally, emotionally, and atmospherically speaking, the house became a madhouse. So many accidents, and nobody who could openly be blamed for them . . . all this had been systematically brought to light by the best friend of one of the targeted siblings, who turned Sherlock not even in the pursuit of justice, necessarily, but out of sheer disbelief that his mate kept denying that he'd been subject to at least three instances of attempted murder. Confessions having been secured, one thing Ma Baker said in a newspaper interview stuck in

Harriet's mind: **They didn't even love us.** Harriet imagined that this was said casually, with equally casual subtext: **So we couldn't let them live.**

The Bakers dispersed—some to lead lives that sounded ordinary enough, others to full-time care facilities. Perdita thought there might yet be a ghost in their house. In one of her printouts of the newspaper interviews there are three parts Perdita's underlined in red—Jackie Baker's three answers to the same question: How many children do you have, Mrs. Baker?

Jackie Baker's first answer is that she gave birth to five children, but only one is really her child—the rest are leeches.

Jackie Baker's second answer is that she gave birth to six children, but only one is really her child—the rest are leeches.

The third time the question is put to her, Ma Baker counts on her fingers, counts again, adds, subtracts, counts again: **Why do you keep asking me this!** It's the only part of the published transcript in which Jackie Baker loses composure.

The Lees and Tamar agreed that it seemed as if the interviewer had had some sort of tip-off that seemed credible to her but, being unable to secure factual evidence, had hit upon the child inventory as a way of trying to shake a little more of the full

Baker family story loose. Harriet had intended to ask the estate agent Miss Maszkeradi what she thought of this the afternoon the five of them met outside the Baker House, but there was too much unease, so she forgot. The primary source of the unease was realizing that the rapport she felt for the Baker House only came from looking at photographs of it. Standing outside it, there was no memory of having been there before. The connection she felt to this house was due to a photo she'd seen, a photo that differed from the estate-agency portfolio photo in only one respect—the inclusion of two blurry figures approaching it, the old woman and the young woman Harriet and Gretel had joked were them. And now, was Harriet to go into this house and find that her friend Gretel was in some way the basis of this house's bad reputation? She preferred to wait outside while the others had a look around and decided whether they felt able to stay the night—but she hadn't factored in the wishes of Miss Maszkeradi. Miss Maszkeradi, it has to be said, was a secondary source of Harriet's unease, with her beehive-shaped turban and her sunglasses worn over an eyepatch and the creased cuffs of her sleeves that didn't look quite right. You looked a little closer and saw that they were bandages in the process of slowly unraveling.

Miss Maszkeradi was a woman somewhere around Harriet's age and somewhere around her height, and her skin tone and coloring were somewhere in the Kartvelian region, but for all this somewhere nearness, when you looked away from her the accessories she donned were the only things that felt likely to still be there when you looked again.

"You're Drahomíra Maszkeradi?" Margot asked, with some skepticism, but Tamar said, "Yes, of course it's her," and the lady herself said, "That's right . . . and isn't it a lovely day for viewing a definitely-not-haunted house?"

Harriet said she didn't feel like going in after all. "Don't be silly; you're going to love it—" The trill in Miss Maszkeradi's voice was loud and clear, and Harriet followed them all into the house for fear that the estate agent would add FA LA LA. A loud burst of song at that moment would've been all it took to finish Harriet off.

Aside from having at one time been a madhouse, the Baker House was a heritage house, the interior of which couldn't be altered without permission from and consultation with various cultural bodies that ensured any changes made were historically accurate restorations. It pleased Miss Maszkeradi to point out to them some features that immortalized the thriftiness of the house's first owners, the Dalhousies. "As you see, here's a hearth but no chimney—that was removed to dodge the Hearth Tax of 1662. And kindly note the sparing natural light . . . a number of windows were bricked up in order to avoid paying the Window Tax of 1696. And see here, beneath this staircase, ladies, what do you think this handsome hollow may have once housed?"

"Handsome hollow may once have housed," Perdita murmured under her breath; never mind answering, the words had to be processed first.

"Grandfather clock," Margot volunteered. Miss Maszkeradi beamed. "Correct! Of course the clock was removed and sold in 1797 so as to avoid paying the Clock Owner Tax of 1797 . . ."

Even after all this, the Baker House hadn't given up on the dream of being a pleasant home someday. Margot touched the walls and made comforting little clucking sounds; she told the Baker House what she planned to do for it if the council would let her, and Tamar opined that the council would allow about a quarter of the plans to go through if they were really pushed, which they certainly would be. Perdita said she thought a quarter would be enough. Harriet stood in the gentle gloom of one of the bedrooms and fought the mesmerizing effect of ugly wallpaper, the patterns that recur, not as one would wish a pleasurable visual event to be repeated, but recurrence for the sake of filling space. Blob blob blob . . . Harriet only broke free of the wallpaper—with a synaptic snap that was almost painful—when she heard Miss Maszkeradi's voice in the hallway: "See you in the morning, girls!" She slammed the front door, and they all heard her lock it, the grinding of mechanisms, like a great maw chewing iron. The crafty woman had locked the back door too; they hadn't seen when she'd done that.

"Well, we did agree to spend the night. And we can climb out of a window if we need to," Margot said, heading to the kitchen to put the kettle on while Tamar tried to get hold of Miss Maszkeradi on the phone.

DARKNESS FELL—ALMOST AN HOUR earlier than it would have in a house with more windows. That was going to be one of Margot's greatest obstacles when it came to reclaiming this place as a family home. And the wiring of the Baker House had been so extensively tampered with that the overhead lights in some rooms didn't function at all—in others they blazed like an accompaniment to sirens, in yet others the lights flickered until it felt as if knuckles had been roughly pressed to your eyelids, and in a couple of rooms there were light switches that nobody wanted to try pressing; none of them was sure why. There was just a "one last booby trap" feel, a snickering suspicion that hopped across the tendons of the hand before sliding down the palm and pooling into sweat. Harriet couldn't elude a fear that the seven swords nestled between her breasts had disappeared, and not considering what she would do if she found they really had abandoned her, kept looking down the front of her top. They were there every time, and sentencing her companions to death remained an unappealing idea no matter which way she looked at it. The group spread out, Tamar and Margot choosing bedrooms on opposite sides of the second floor, and Harriet and Perdita choosing neighboring and wallpaper-free rooms on the third floor. Once everyone had settled into their rooms, Harriet did an extensive Gretel-check, soft-footing around the house and finding it happily/sadly changeling-free. She occasionally crossed paths with her mother, who was armed with measuring tape and a camera and would then make Harriet read off a number for her or hold something steady while Margot had a think about it. Tamar had stationed herself in a corner of one of the rooms with the bricked-up window frames, and she appeared to be meditating. The lights in the room Perdita had chosen didn't work, so she'd lit a candle and was doing her homework by it. The lights in the room Harriet had chosen were working, so she went to bed and tried to read the latest batch of essays her students had submitted. When the house felt too quiet, they all called out.

"Feeling haunted yet, Margot?"

"No. You, Perdita?"

"Nothing. What you saying, Mum?"

"I'm fine. Hang on, who started the 'Are-you-OK' chain?"

"No need to stress yourself out, Mum . . . it was Tamar."

"Me? I hadn't said anything yet. Only joking . . . it was me, it was me. And I'm fine too. Goodnight."

"Goodnight!"

"Night."

"G'night."

"Goodnight . . ."

And Perdita Lee, who had been counting the "goodnights," smiled in the darkness.

GRETEL WAS IN THE FRONT HALL of the Baker House, arms folded as she surveyed a silver-birchwood grandfather clock from head to foot. The grandfather clock was brand-new; she'd brought it along for that crestfallen hollow beneath the stairs. No, the appointment had not been forgotten, today was the day, nothing had prevented Gretel from coming, she was there, but couldn't stay long, as a changeling's work is never done. The knowledge that Gretel was there didn't seem to be enough to get Harriet out of bed, so Perdita stepped in.

Get up, Mum . . . get up, get up . . . if you don't get up right now you'll miss her.

Why couldn't Harriet get up? She wanted to, so very much, but it just wasn't happening.

Can't even raise an arm, let alone a leg . . . it looks like this'll have to wait until the second house . . .

Don't you realize you'll be even older then?

I know, but . . .

She says she's not going to bother coming

to the second house if you don't show your face downstairs right now!

Perdita really was shaking Harriet, but she wasn't talking about Gretel. Perdita was saying, **Mum, come next door, my candle keeps going out . . .**

"Surely just a draft," Harriet mumbled. "Jump in here with me if you're worried about it, though."

Virtually mouthing the words, the way you do to minimize the possibility of being overheard, Perdita mouthed, "I'm not worried. Somebody keeps blowing out my candle. I light it again and then . . . don't start shouting . . . I must nod off, because I don't know how it's happened, but a few minutes later my eyes sort of switch on again and the candle's out. It's cute—I think it's someone worried about health and safety—unattended flames and all that. I just want to catch them doing it and it might take two people to do that."

Harriet went next door and got into the bed there, feeling considerably less sleepy than before as she eyed the candle flame and the shadows and every place where the doors, walls, ceiling, and floors joined. **How many children do you have, Ma Baker, and in your count have you made sure to include the one who most considerately blows out candles to protect this heritage house from**

fire? Perdita sat at a desk placed behind the bed, watching some show that was making her laugh . . . usually Perdita did this with her earphones in, but tonight she had the volume up, and every now and again Harriet sat up in the bed and looked back at Perdita—the long, tapered dimensions of that room might have been what made it echoey, but to her ear there were two people laughing.

Not an echo. There was a second laugher. It was the cupboard door that made Harriet dead certain of this. Behind the bed, behind the desk Perdita sat at, there was a cupboard set into the back wall, cupboard or wardrobe, some cross between the two. Anyway, the door opened softly, softly, wider and wider, because they had a gawker, someone capable of staying out of sight for months and years but seeing these two together, Harriet and Perdita, proved too much for him.

He was southern Mediterranean in appearance, like the rest of his family, and he was about twenty years old. He was tall and slender and his eyes were really beautiful—I mean that they conferred beauty—you felt that when he looked at you. Perdita said that he had the eyes of a bear; there was that mixture of strength and a strange humility (was it just that he didn't know or care about his strength?) in his gaze. He gave them a lot of aliases at first, trying out names with the shy excitement of one who doesn't often get a chance to introduce himself, but after Tamar and Margot had given him a lot of **Look here, young man**s they learned that his name was Jonathan Baker, and that he was the sanest member of his family by dint of having escaped his mother and younger sister's notice altogether. When he was still quite small, one of his brothers had told him he mustn't answer if either Tara or their mother spoke to him and to simply flee if either one of them approached. A few years of this persuaded Tara and her mother that Jonathan was some by-product of the repugnance they felt for the rest of their unacceptable family. So the sibling who'd given Jonathan the good advice helped him keep on the move between cupboard fortresses and box-room fortresses, and the same sibling made sure Jonathan always had something to eat and drink and some educational material, as well as entertainment every now and then. "I still visit him every week, and he's still a bit shifty with me . . . I've had to promise him I won't tell anybody that he was the one who helped me out."

"Oh, so your brother thinks you're imaginary too?"

"It's hard to be certain, but I'm leaning toward yes, that is what he thinks . . ."

Tamar and Margot were roused from sleep, and the five of them gathered in the sitting room. Harriet and Perdita wanted to know everything about Jonathan Baker and how he had been making a living—he had been making one, and had been able to prove to himself that he wasn't imaginary through certain scaled-down, though determined, interactions with the world. Recently there had been more good days than bad days. Tamar cut through the chitchat with a question: "So the house isn't even for sale? I don't think I can settle for less than seeing this Miss Maszkeradi behind bars."

"You'd better not harm a hair on Miss Maszkeradi's head," shouted Jonathan. Drahomíra Maszkeradi was a friend of his. She'd told him about the Kercheval-Lee housing plan, and things had played out this way because he needed room to back out if anything about it felt wrong. But now he felt almost sure that his home was ready for another family, as long as the new family didn't mind him being a non-imaginary member of it this time.

"I think that'll work, Jonathan," Harriet said.

Margot said. "Do you really? I'm not impressed

by the way this young man hung around inside a cupboard without saying a word while my granddaughter was presumably changing into her night things and whatnot—"

"He didn't look," Perdita said, and Jonathan shook his head, silently condemning these low thoughts of Margot's.

That was the first house, and the first of the missed meetings between Harriet and Gretel. It was also around that time that the doll named Sago and the doll named Bonnie moved in with Jonathan Baker. Perdita thought their personalities would complement each other, and Sago and Bonnie thought it was nice for Perdita to have an excuse to visit Jonathan. Apparently for the first three weeks Jonathan and the dolls didn't converse, but they comfortably observed each other from beneath tables and through banisters—this is going to happen all over again when other people move in with these three. As far as being alarmed goes, weeks of wordless hide-and-seek won't come anywhere near some of the situations the newcomers will have already outlived. But ideally the newcomers will also enjoy the settling-in experience just as much as Jonathan and Sago and Bonnie.

16

THE SECOND UNHAUNTED HOUSE WAS IN western Bohemia, a low-lying structure easily missed amid fountain sprays of autumnal greenery, reddery, orangery, brownery, &c. It seemed to have been assembled in adoration of the castle that stood higher up on the riverbank—the length and width of each window was filled with the view of the castle. Not the soaring semicircular arches—you had to leave the house and look up if you wanted to see the castle's spire and turrets—but you could probably signal to certain windows that peeped out of the castle walls, if you and your counterpart in the other room had flashlights or lanterns. The bad reputation of this converted lodge, like the bad reputation of the Baker House, had been incurred in modern times. And just as with the Baker House, the estate-agency portfolio photo of this Bohemian house was very close to the version Harriet had seen in Gretel's atlas. Miss Maszkeradi met them outside this house too, with the notes she'd prepared, but Tamar knocked off the estate agent's turban with her umbrella and Margot pulled off the wig the estate agent was wearing beneath the turban. There was another wig beneath the first wig, and Tamar or Margot would have pulled that off too, but Miss Maszkeradi saw which way things were going and fled into the woods, sending Tamar an email a few hours later to say that she was back in London and understood their feelings toward her but would nevertheless be sending an invoice for a replacement turban and wig.

The requisite night in the Bohemian house passed, and Harriet's meeting with Gretel was missed. The next morning, at breakfast, Margot rolled up her bad-cop sleeves and Tamar rolled up her good-cop sleeves and together they attempted to persuade this house's secret dwellers (a couple brought together by their discovery of their spouses' joint plot to kill them for insurance money) that it was better for ten guilty people to go free than for one innocent to face punishment. "I congratulate you on the success of your counterplot, I really do—convincing each that the other was the one who really killed you both and getting them to point the finger at each other for all these years, I like it, but all four of you have lived with this long enough now, so what about letting all that water pass under the bridge and taking on a new project? Well, what we have in mind is this . . ."

Harriet rose from the breakfast table and said she was off to see about this river that kept running by . . . it looked as if rowing boats and stepping-stones were readily available and she thought they should be made the most of. "Yeah, why not," Perdita said, and, in accordance with Harriet's hopes, she was the only one who came along.

They picked a pea-green boat and rowed past the castle complex, slowing down to wave as they passed the house where Margot and Tamar were not yet prevailing over the desire for revenge. They rowed in perfect rhythm and at a temperate pace that bordered on the desultory; stone houses and other boats drifted by.

"Perdita, I want to ask you something," Harriet said. She'd been thinking—the night thoughts Perdita's dolls disapproved of, but also day thoughts . . . she'd been thinking about Perdita saying she'd put her hand inside her own hand and brought forth Gretel's ring . . . that had been all Perdita seemed able to say about having gone to/been in Druhástrana.

"Mum, if you drag this out I'm going to jump overboard," said Ari Kercheval's granddaughter. (Funny to think that she's also Simon Lee's.)

"Do you remember my saying Gretel Kercheval was a changeling?"

Perdita nodded. They were face-to-face and couldn't turn away from each other without messing up the rowing—**ha-ha, Perdita, you just try evading your mother now.**

"And you remember me saying that she talked as if she could change too . . . bodily, I mean . . . be born as different people?"

"Yeah. So?"

"I've been thinking I wouldn't put it past her to treat two whole families as clients of hers—the Lees and the Kerchevals—I wouldn't put it past her to try to change their relationship by switching sides . . . I mean getting born on one side and then getting born on the other . . ."

They'd veered off center—Perdita put a leg over the side of the boat; it tilted against the bank, and wet grass brushed them all along their left sides. "Mother! Ask your question! What is it?"

"All right, keep your hair on! I was just thinking. About the two houses," Harriet said. "Those houses where we were going to meet, Gretel and me. She wasn't there, but I was, and you . . . so were you . . ."

"And?"

"And . . . when you were little . . . with the gingerbread . . . I mean, before you, I only knew of one other person who would probably die for gingerbread. Wasn't that some sort of announcement . . . ?"

Perdita leaned forward.

"Are you asking me if I'm Gretel?"

"Fine. Yes, that's what I'm asking."

Without blinking, Perdita asked: "Why? I mean—is that an important thing?"

This, for Harriet, was more perturbing than a straight "yes" or "no." Water-sky roulette, water-sky roulette . . .

"Mum?"

Perdita's being (or not being) Gretel was of importance to Harriet because Harriet needed to know that Gretel was well, that she had a friend, that . . .

Actually, Perdita's being (or not being) Gretel was of importance to Harriet because Gretel was the cause of Harriet's inability to be a proper friend to anybody else. Consider all the friendships that have gone unmade by and with Harriet Lee because she was saving herself for great amity that was on pause, that had not properly begun. Why, if Gretel Kercheval was here right now, she'd get told off. How dare she make a friend of Harriet and then just leave the rest for later . . .

"I see," Perdita said. "Can I just check that I've understood? You think that because of Gretel Kercheval you haven't been a good friend to anybody?"

When Harriet nodded, Perdita said she didn't buy it. "Is this really the line you want to take— that you never met anyone you liked as much as that girl, and that you never met anybody who seemed to care for you as much as she did? Also . . . ALSO . . . if you really have been letting this keep you from making other friends all this time, if you really think Gretel Kercheval would quietly take the blame for that, then there's nothing to be done about you . . ."

"Interesting. That's a very Gretelian thing to say . . ."

"Listen, Mum. If I was or had at any time been a changeling, and I'm not saying that's the case, but **if** it was, this is what I'd say: First off, Tamar's given me some idea of what you're going to be like once you go into retirement yourself. Honestly . . . in your own way, getting all **interpretative** like this makes you just as much of a loose cannon as she is . . . I just think you should know that. The other thing I'd say is this: Here you are rowing on this river with a nice bit of mountain behind us and a nice bit of forest ahead, and maybe some commuting salmon on either side of us. Here you are with your daughter, who thinks worlds of you . . . not just a world but all of 'em, every last one. And—"

Harriet interrupted her: "Yes, here I am with this Perdita I love so much and truly . . . hair's already gone gray so what more can your behavior do to it . . . all this plus fine weather . . . yes, I'm sure you're right. Why insist on pinpointing who was who and what is what and when was when?" That's what Harriet Lee said aloud, but her inner resolve said something else: **Gretel Kercheval, I am warning you. The third house is our last chance. Our last last last last chance.**

17

MISS MASZKERADI WOULDN'T TELL TAMAR and the Lees which country the third house was in, but she did say that the house was located on an island, the most beautiful island in the world. "Though when I say 'most beautiful,' I don't mean 'least scarred' . . ." The portfolio photograph was 95 percent beach, and perhaps 5 percent house . . . though at that distance the "house" could have just been a cardboard box.

"More soon, ladies—we've got a tracking team

on the ground out there, and if they're able to catch up with the house, you four will need to prepare for a minimum flight time of fourteen hours . . ."

"Catch up with the house?" Margot said. "You talk as if it stands on chicken legs and keeps running away."

With more than the usual edge of hysteria to her voice, Miss Maszkeradi said: "Oh, the merry dance this house has led me. This house! It really isn't a house one can speak of unless one knows. If I manage to sell the damned place before I die it'll be my greatest triumph . . . I'll be an icon among estate agents."

Margot had only one question left. In Druhástranian, she asked: "Drahomíra, my dear . . . are you by any chance Druhástranian?"

She was answered in English, and Harriet held her phone away from her ear to protect it from the Maszkeradi trill: "Of course I am . . . I mean, aren't we all?"

Tamar and Margot turned their full attention back to organizing new homes for newly assembled families. There were other houses to be viewed, and far more professional agents to deal with at the same otherwise august estate agency, even if those agents did show a puzzling deference to Miss Maszkeradi, describing her as the agency's "ace." Perdita was on hand to advise, but she had school too, and as she herself put it, "I've got this **social life** now . . ."

GCSE exam time was drawing near, and Harriet had example flashcards to prepare, buzzwords to imprint, flagging attention spans to boost, and like any conscientious teacher, she overprepared to the extent that if her students slipped even half of these terms into their answers, they'd do all right. There was a surprise email from Alesha Matsumoto of the Parental Power Association too; Alesha asked about Perdita and hoped Harriet wouldn't miss very many more meetings. So Harriet turned up at the next PPA meeting. Both Perdita and Margot tried to make Harriet promise she wouldn't bring gingerbread this time, but she appeared in Gioia Fischer's sitting room with a defiant look and a repeat tin of gingerbread for each PPA member. And she was welcomed with open arms and without exceptions. Eh? She'd expected to have a chance to say something snippy to Emil Szep; Emil Szep, who'd "very much hoped" she wasn't saying his kids were bullies; Emil Szep, who'd said that to her even as Perdita lay in a hospital bed. But this same Emil Szep was overjoyed at Harriet's return, was the soul of solicitousness, was the first to tuck into the gingerbread, and said so many worshipful things that she had to be gracious. In a quiet moment Harriet went up to Hyorin Nam and whispered: "Did something happen to Emil? He's making me think of that man whose personality completely changed after a brain injury . . ."

Hyorin said: "I'll tell you later. In the meantime . . . what about us, Harriet Lee?"

"Us?"

"I thought we were friends."

"Eh?"

"Well, it looks like one thousand paper cranes and one recipe do not a friendship make. Fair enough, but that brilliant news about Perdita getting well—why did I have to hear it from Alesha and not from you?"

"Oh—" **Paper cranes and a recipe do not a friendship make . . .** what was it Harriet had been half thinking at the time . . . that the cranes and the **danpatjuk** were two signs, but she should wait for the third. It hadn't occurred to Harriet that she herself could bring about the third sign.

"I," said Harriet.

"Yeah, you," said Hyorin.

"I think I owe you a coffee."

"And?"

"Cake?"

"And?"

"A turnip that's actually a convincing marzipan replica of a turnip?"

"And—"

"What more do I owe you, Hyorin Nam?!"

"I just wanted to see if you'd keep adding things."

Over coffee Hyorin revealed that Emil Szep's personality change was political: he was plotting to replace Gioia Fischer as head of the PPA. Rather than abstain from voting, Harriet asked if there wasn't a third way.

"Couldn't you just take over, Hyorin?"

"What, you want me to get in Gioia's way at the same time as causing a problem for Emil? This is like asking someone to stand between two axes aswing, all for the sake of a paper crown."

Harriet saw she had some work to do. There was a third way, and the third way was PPA member recruitment. Her gingerbread came in handy there.

As for the third house and the last last last last chance to meet Gretel, Harriet didn't forget about that. She remembered all right, but in the midst of revision sessions and PPA meetings, in the midst of film nights and arts and craft classes (Harriet, Hyorin, and Alesha were learning how to paint on glass), Harriet Lee occasionally put a question to herself: Would I drop all of this and go if Miss Maszkeradi phoned right now and said this island house had been secured?

Most likely yes, Harriet would go. This was Gretel-related, after all. But she'd go at walking pace instead of at a mad dash.

One day, on her way to work, Harriet Lee saw that a shop had opened on a side street she normally crossed as a shortcut. She was running late for a staff meeting, and the display in this shop window extended her delay: it teemed with detail, like a Bosch painting, or the ascetically decadent gates that lined the streets of Druhá City. The scene was a valley-wide picnic. A river rushed around a series of bends, whispering like starlit silk, and hills shot up and dropped flat in its wake. The picnickers were teddy bears, and they were feasting on latticed jam tarts—ah, that must be what was on sale, that's what all this made Harriet want to go in and see about—what kind of jam tart could inspire such unions and divisions among these valley-dwellers, such feats of physical strength, such breakthroughs—for instance, the intellectual one that Tesla look-alike over there seemed on the brink of?

She checked her phone—she'd come back.

Or maybe looking just once was enough; all her experience as a baker combined with years of experience as an eater told her there was no way these jam tarts could taste as good as they looked.

Someone came to the shop door as Harriet turned away: "Excuse me—excuse me!" Harriet turned back and saw the shop's proprietor; they both smiled. Ever since Gabriel and Rémy had first graced her bedside, Harriet had looked upon beauty as an amusing thing for nature to do. The perfect coordination of different shades of sun-blushed brown seen here, for instance—skin, eye color, short hair that waves as if air is water. This person wanted to know why Harriet hadn't come in. She tapped the window as if reminding the teddy bears to be on their best behavior.

"I mean—is the overall effect too twee? Do I add more bears? Subtract some of the food? I was thinking of doing that any way, because of mice. I don't know . . . I like it as it is, but . . . you didn't come in. What am I doing wrong?" The woman was a native speaker of a Romance language; Harriet couldn't narrow down the accent any further than that—and another thing: there was a sudden click of precognition, on then off, the near future as a memory, there was romance with a lowercase "r" too, this woman would nip Harriet's lower lip just before they kissed for the first time. And Harriet would like it. Really, really, and a lot. It was a slightly awkward thing to know about someone before knowing their name. So Harriet introduced herself and learned that the woman's name was Salomea. She told Salomea she loved the window display and that she'd be back later.

(**Later, when I'm not in workwear, later, when I'm wearing a more appropriate shade of lipstick and am ready to praise your baked goods no matter what, later when I've had time to daydream about this a little bit more, later when I'm not running late anymore . . .**)

"When? What time?"

"Salomea," Harriet said, then went quiet. She didn't know what to say next. Salomea opened the shop door and waved Harriet in: "After you."

Inside, the shop was more laboratory than toy shop; tubes and vials . . . **vials of jam** . . . and sparkling glass cloches through which you could see mannequin heads wearing jam tarts with a certain insouciance, as if the pastries were berets. Harriet sat down at a round table in the center of the room and Salomea assembled a selection of bite-sized tarts; as she did so, she told Harriet that bite-sized was best, that as an infant she'd waited until she had two good strong teeth and then, hello, world; she bit her way through it. "If I have a gut feeling that something will taste good I just bite it. It's really worked out well; you'd be surprised . . . but I suppose the problem with instinctual biters is that they usually can't be bothered to take another bite; they just leave the rest . . ."

Oh. Still, remembering how delicious seeming biteable to Salomea would turn out to be, Harriet still found the courage to attempt flirtation. "Which two were your first teeth?"

Salomea laughed and showed her, laughing still more when all Harriet could think of to say was: "They look sturdy; you can tell they're pioneers."

Harriet tried not to look at her phone when it rang—it would only be someone from the university—but it was Miss Maszkeradi. To Salomea, she said: "Sorry—just a second—" and to Miss Maszkeradi, she said: "Hello?"

"Hello, Harriet, are you busy? Is this a good time to talk?"

"Well . . ."

"It's about the third definitely not haunted house . . . I don't think you can count on viewing it any time soon . . . we've just confirmed it went out to sea last night . . ."

"**Went out to sea?**"

"Harriet, this house, seriously, this house . . ." There was a spray-mist sound as Miss Maszkeradi drew on the solace of some bottled serenity or other. "May I speak with you confidentially?"

"Yes, of course," Harriet said, accepting Salomea's pantomimed encouragement to put the call on speakerphone.

Miss Maszkeradi told them the legend of the third house, the island house. The legend began at the foot of a volcano's bed, the volcano having lain dormant amid fields of silver grass for hundreds of years—long enough to have acquired at least six different and equally accurate names, long enough to have watched over many lives and deaths, and many changes, of which the appearance of this third house was one . . . a minor change for a mountain, but a big headache for an estate agent—

"What year were you born, Harriet?"

Harriet told her.

"Right. That was the year that some disembodied voices were heard talking amid a few fronds of silver grass one night—"

Miss Maszkeradi thought Harriet would interrupt at that point, but she didn't. She and Salomea were on the same side of the table now, cuddled up and listening. And so Miss Maszkeradi went on to relate that the two friends who heard the voices talking were convinced at first that there were people talking out of sight—the voices were talking about building a house. **They'll be here soon, and we don't even have anything ready for them**, one of the voices said, and a second voice replied: **Whose fault is that? Mine?** And then the first voice said: **Don't start, I don't want to get into this, let's just make the preparations . . .**

Night sky, silver grass, and a scattering of yellow, green, and red dots, the cold light fireflies emit from their bellies—that was all the two witnesses saw as they overheard this conversation. Could it have been the fireflies talking? Quite a discovery, if so: not only do fireflies speak, but they speak Korean. The fireflies may not have been the ones speaking, but they do appear to have been the ones who built the house—

"This heartless woman, selling us on a house we can never buy," Salomea whispered.

It seemed to the two witnesses that there had been tens of fireflies at first, but once discussions regarding measurements and positioning had been concluded, thousands more fireflies flocked to that spot and—all this is sworn to—grouped themselves according to hue of phosphorescence. The yellow team tackled the foundations, and the green team sorted out the roof, and the red team did everything else. They worked all night, and the witnesses watched all night and couldn't identify the material the fireflies were working with. It dripped like honey but quickly set into glass-like panes, which the fireflies shaped before setting them into place. And the shaping of these panels was one of the loveliest things the witnesses had ever seen. The panels were cut with light, but not as cleanly as lasers cut. The fireflies would gather into one glowing body. There was a red team, a yellow team, and a green team— and when everybody was ready, they flickered as one and the panels were divided at the spot of the collective flickering; rough at the edges but the pieces looked very nice together once the house was standing in three dimensions. It looked like a house you could eat. By then it was morning, and the fireflies made themselves scarce. Naturally the two witnesses wanted to have a look inside this house. They approached but didn't reach it. They walked through the silver grass for a long time, even ran, to see if that would speed anything up, but the house never got any closer. A German hiker had slightly better luck a few weeks later; nobody knows why . . . the house seems to have moods.

Anyway, the German hiker recognized this as a gingerbread house, a classic gingerbread house at that, straight out of a story he'd been told as a child. A group of tourists from Kyoto who also managed to snap some photographs of the house don't think the house is made of gingerbread; they reckon it's made of thinner, crisper stuff . . . **That's yatsuhashi**, they said. Both the hiker and the tourists got close enough to see a signboard set up in front of the house, and neither party was able to read it, though Miss Maszkeradi's familiarity with Druhástranian meant she was able to tell them what the sign said:

Only those who have nothing can enter this place.

Until recently, when it went out to sea, it was said that the house didn't really move; it only seemed to move. After all, the only thing that's changed about it in the years since it first appeared is the overnight addition of a nutritional label that states the millions of calories the house contains. But in the year 2013, a woman whose name we don't know made it to the front door of this house. The woman made it to the front door but couldn't get in; the door was locked with a double lock the woman took her time inspecting. She states that only two strangely shaped rings can unlock the door of this gingerbread house. Yes, rings, the type you wear on your finger . . .

Harriet Lee, you're right about that house being a last last last last chance for you and Gretel. That it is and that it will be, and a long time from now, when you have nothing left, we'll meet at that house and pass through it. You can hardly hear me right now, and that's good. Better to listen to Salomea repeating that you've got to watch out with instinctual biters because they just take one bite and then leave the rest. Yes, Salomea is repeating this with the slightly anxious bravado of someone who is no longer sure that theory is going to hold up to practice this time.

Oh, you're definitely not listening to me anymore, Harriet Lee. So for now I'll just say that I, your scribe, your friend, hope I've also managed to be a friend to all your other friends. Let's talk when we get to the house, that third unhaunted house.

See you there.

(Just as I've seen you here.)

**October 17, 2016, Bupyeong-gu, South Korea—
April 4, 2017, Prague, Czechia**

ACKNOWLEDGMENTS

Thank you, Dr. Cieplak, thank you, Marina Endicott, thank you, Sehee Choi, thank you, Tracy Bohan, thank you, Jin Auh, thank you, Sophie Jonathan, thank you, Misun Seo, thank you, Yoonjoe Park, thank you, Sarah McGrath. And I'm grateful to Sora Yu and all at Seoul Art Space Yeonhui.